She had gotten him into this, now it was up to him to get them both out...alive.

Before Veronica could open her mouth to protest, as Pete was sure she was about to do, the door burst open. The flimsiness wasn't just his imagination. The door gave way beneath the heel of the large boot that smashed through the ancient wood, softened by age as well as humidity, time, and rot. The crash pulsated throughout the room louder than a strobe light set to autopilot.

He yanked her to the other side of the bed, away from the door, as shots tore through the vast expanse separating them from freedom. She opened her mouth, and he slapped his hand over it. He could see the anger in her eyes, but he didn't care. What he cared about was getting both of them to safety, and if that meant keeping her mouth shut—as her eyes glistened with hurt, confusion, and rage—that's exactly what he'd do. She could give him hell later, as he knew she would. But at least their chances for survival significantly increased. If she happened to spew forth anger like an open wound, at least it meant they were both still alive.

He pinned her against the wall, his arm covering the tops of her shoulders, his hand reaching for the weapon. She shook her head once. He nodded and implemented his stern look, and she finally relented with a soft sigh.

The bed exploded as more shots ensued. Stuffing, padding, and dilapidated pillows filled the air. He ducked lower and pulled her down with him.

To Veronica Baird, escaping from an underground dungeon and racing through the woods, is anything but convenient, even as her captor in rubber mask attire proves rather persistent in his continued pursuit. Despite her apparent independence, she considers a partnership, albeit reluctantly, with a former classmate who may still have feelings for her.

Pete Nealey still has flashbacks to Iraq and, with the bottle as his eternal companion, tends to fall off of barstools at the most inopportune moments or pass out face down in the tavern parking lot. But what he may lack in cheerfulness, he more than makes up for with his steadfast loyalty to the cause, even when he ends up handcuffed to an air conditioner in a shoddy motel.

But unless Veronica can learn to trust Pete for more than just intermittent intervals, the slipshod relationship, and her freedom, won't last...

KUDOS for *The Convenient Escape*

In *The Convenient Escape* by Robert Downs, Pete Nealey is a private detective with a drinking problem. One night as he is walking home from the bar, because he can't remember where he parked his car, he runs into an old flame, Veronica Baird, who has just escaped after being abducted. Since the bad guys are still after her, Pete is reluctantly drawn into her troubles—not that she wants him around. Now Pete has a contract out on him, too, so he may not survive long enough to help Veronica finally get away. The author has an unusual voice for a suspense/mystery in that the writing is quite laid back and unhurried. Still the plot is strong and filled with enough surprises that I found it hard to stop reading, wanting to see what would happen next. ~ *Taylor Jones, Reviewer*

The Convenient Escape by Robert Downs is the story of a woman who knows too much for someone's comfort. Veronica Baird has been abducted. Not being an heiress, and therefore a likely target to be ransomed, the only conclusion she can come to is that she knows too much about something. Escaping from her dungeon prison, she is now on the run. But the bad guys always seem to be one step ahead of her. Enter Pete Nealey, an old flame from high school turned private detective, who is usually too drunk to find his own home, let alone solve any cases. Veronica runs into Pete the night she escapes, and now she can't seem to get rid of him. She needs him to help her stay alive, but refuses to admit it, convinced she can take care of herself. *The Convenient Escape* is full of twists and turns, the characters intriguing, and the author's voice unique. I had a hard time putting it down. ~ *Regan Murphy, Reviewer*

ACKNOWLEDGEMENTS

There's a long cast of characters who made my fourth novel possible: I'd like to thank Black Opal Books for taking a chance on *The Convenient Escape* when no one else would. Lauri and Faith and the rest of the team have been wonderful, and I can't sing their praises loud enough. This novel is the best it can be because of you. I plan to stick around for as long as you'll have me, and I'll continue to push a steady stream of manuscripts your way. Consider yourselves warned.

I owe my dad a huge debt of gratitude. He has single-handedly built me a steady stream of readers in Fairmont, and he's called in so many favors to help me out I know he's lost count. My brother and his lovely wife for making a rather astute suggestion for my book cover. Consider yourselves promoted to my official cover consultants. My mom and all of my family for promoting my writing and my Facebook page. My readers who ensure I don't spend all of my time talking to myself, and my fellow writers for providing tips, trade secrets, and countless rounds of encouragement. And I'd like to thank God, who always makes the impossible possible. Any errors in judgment have, and always will be, my own.

ACKNOWLEDGMENTS

THE CONVENIENT ESCAPE

ROBERT DOWNS

A Black Opal Books Publication

GENRE: MYSTERY-DETECTIVE/PRIVATE DETECTIVES

THE CONVENIENT ESCAPE
Copyright © 2016 by Robert Downs
Cover Design by Jackson Cover Designs
All cover art copyright © DATE
All Rights Reserved
Print ISBN: 978-1-626945-60-9

First Publication: NOVEMBER 2016

Published by Black Opal Books **http://www.blackopalbooks.com**

DEDICATION

*For Elrod,
may you live forever*

CHAPTER 1

Her high heels dug into the soft earth beneath her. Her skirt and blouse, damp with sweat, clung to her body.

The trees whistled above her, the wind whipping through the branches.

Her heart raced, slamming against her chest. Her right side ached, shooting the pain up toward her chin. Her mind raced as fast as her legs moved—escape remained her only option. A grimace twisted her lips, as the stitch in her side grew stronger.

Footsteps lingered behind her. Not far. Close. Veronica glanced over her shoulder, tripping on a branch beneath her. The soft earth padded her knee and braced her fall. *Up.* She shot to her feet, as her adversary threatened to close the distance even more.

Glancing over her shoulder, she saw only blackness. Nothing more. She strained to hear his labored breathing, but she heard only her heartbeat instead.

A shot rang out, slamming against a tree branch off to her left. Her head whipped around, as bark sprayed in every direction. A piece caught her cheek, slicing it, and she swiped it away with her left hand. Brushing it aside like a dead fruit fly.

The blood on her fingers lingered.

Saltwater dripped into her eyes, obscuring her field of vision. With the same hand, she wiped away the remnants of sweat—and transferred the blood to her cheek—as a voice called out to her.

"You won't get far," the voice said. "Daddy's going to get you."

She shook her head, just one quick motion to clear the voice from her mind. Her arms pumped at her sides, like two pistons working together. She grimaced as the darkness found her and a hand touched her shoulder. The hand was stiff, and it lingered longer than it should have. When she turned her head, she discovered it was a tree. An owl hooted above her, as dark shadows crept over her and the surrounding forest. The moon guided her. It was more than enough light to offer her a sense of direction.

She picked up her knees and pushed herself forward. Her hands pumped at her sides faster and faster, as the darkness nearly swallowed her whole.

She stumbled again. This time a rock caught the toe of her left foot. A knee glanced off a root and shot pain up her thigh. The stitch in her side continued to throb and grow with each passing second.

Another shot rang out.

This time the bullet whistled above her head, and then more bark exploded like small projectiles. Darts of wood splattered and shattered around her head. She cursed under her breath, clamored to her feet, and didn't bother glancing over her shoulder this time.

She wouldn't give him the satisfaction.

He was close, though, and the slapping of the earth behind her pushed her onward.

She felt a hand grab her shoulder. Just for an instant. She shrugged it off and tossed an elbow in the direction of her adversary. As bone met flesh, she heard a grunt.

She smiled. And then her giddiness vanished along with her smile.

A distance opened up between them—her and her adversary. As her mind raced through an infinite number of possibilities, she discarded the ones that wouldn't work one by one, and she was left with only one option. Run. It was her only hope, even though she was tired, weak, and nearly half-starved.

But the thought of getting away gave her more hope than she'd allowed herself to feel for the past two days.

She cut hard to the right, losing one of her three-inch heels in the process. Her other one held on for dear life. She bent over, yanked it off, and tossed it behind her. She heard a crack, followed by a grunt, and a series of curses filled the night air.

This time she did not smile.

She feinted, broke hard to the left, and tore her skirt in the process. Even though she wanted to, she didn't look down. Instead, she kept her eyes forward. Her hair tumbled down, and she swiped it away. The pin that held it in place fell to the ground and glistened.

She tumbled into a bush. The leaves tickled her arms, legs, and face. A hand dove in behind her poking and prodding, and the man followed his hand. She tossed her elbow behind her and felt only air. Shoving herself forward, she moved away from the man with the errant hand. Her mind wrestled through more possibilities, one after another in quick succession.

Even though she had only been in the woods seven minutes or so, it felt more like two days. The running made her feel weak and vulnerable. Night tumbled on top of her. Her breath came in ragged, erratic bursts.

Her heart sped up, faster than a bullet and with twice as much power.

Another shot rang out. *Would the madman ever run out of ammunition?* Maybe he had reloaded on the run with the magazine jammed against his thigh.

She didn't recognize the gun. It was small and black, and every time a bullet exploded in her direction, it reminded her of a shotgun blast.

Leaves fell down on top of her, like bricks tossed from a third story window. Distractions that blocked her vision. Instead of black with spots of light, she saw red, yellow, and orange.

Numbers raced through her mind: The odds were still in her favor. Numbers didn't lie, even if people sometimes did.

"Why even bother to run?" the voice said.

It sounded harsher, strangled, like the vocal cords had been pinched with pliers. The night grew softer as the voice grew louder. The words—sharp, colorful, and filled with hate—weren't worth repeating to a therapist or a trusted friend.

She wrapped her arm around a large trunk, as her breath came in short, punctuated gasps. Her heart beat at a marathon pace. Her lips, once soft and supple, were chapped and dry. She licked them. Not that it helped much.

The footsteps behind her grew closer. She tried to quiet her breathing and slow down her rapid heart and thoughts. A steady series of explosions rocked her chest.

As a hand reached out for her shoulder, she ducked and pushed herself onward. Her head tilted down, and the motion of her arms widened. Her skirt flapped about her thighs, and her white blouse was now a dark shade of brown. Her hair was filled with random debris: leaves and bark, dirt, and grass.

The stitch in her side shot all the way up to her head. An explosion of color and white light assaulted her. She stopped, slapped her forehead, and continued on.

Her feet slapped the soft earth, sinking into the hollow ground. She uttered one four-letter word, then another, and then regretted it. Her adversary, never too far behind, grunted in response. Her mind processed another series of mental calculations, each one more negative than the last. But she found strength in her temporary freedom.

She cut hard to the left. Another tear in her skirt: this one even larger than the last. She'd almost slit the skirt to her waist with the upper part of her thigh exposed to the cool breeze. Wool brushed her leg and slapped her thigh, the tear flapping about like a bird with only one wing. The rubbing sensation caused her scattered thoughts to focus on her torn outfit.

She stopped. Listening to the night around her, she gathered the courage to make her next move. The woods remained foreign to her. She preferred indoors, with air conditioning, bug control, and walls that offered the proper humidity barrier. Thick mist enveloped her and made her breathing irregular. Ragged.

She reached the edge of a precipice. The water churned below her, swirling in a small, circular pool. It was nearly a hundred feet below. Maybe less.

The man called out to her once more. His words were swallowed up by the night.

She glanced up at the moon above her: The full globe that had guided her to this point. Veronica considered her options: either jump, and possibly die; or don't jump, and the possibility of death increased. She chose jump and leapt off the cliff, thrusting her body out before slapping her arms against her sides. The sensation of falling lasted for a second, and she hit the water with all the force her small body could muster. The water swallowed her, plunging her below its depths. Striking the bottom, she stubbed a toe and scrambled toward the surface, thrusting her arms high above her head as she did so. She popped up like a water-logged shoe, swam toward the shore—the water even colder than she imagined it would be—and looked up to the top of the cliff.

The man was gone.

CHAPTER 2

She'd escaped from a pit of nothing. A fortress really. A stronghold left over from the remnants of a war fought long ago. Long chains dangled from the ceiling, metal spikes protruded from the walls, and rats crawled on either side of her. A warped wooden floor was beneath her, while dirt-covered walls surrounded her. Had she not escaped, it might have consumed her last moments on Earth. Her mind had slowed to a dull ache, and the thought of giving up had consumed more than one of her fantasies.

As far she knew, she had one guard—the only one she'd seen—and she'd called out to the darkness around her, a darkness that shocked her and kept her on edge, along with the rats. She'd picked the rusted, old lock with a fork, not because she was an expert in lock picking, but because the lock had given away more easily than she'd expected. The rusted metal crumbled around her hand, and she allowed herself a small smile of triumph before her features had turned cold and hard once again.

Over the two days in the dungeon, she'd had a bowl of

rice and some soup with unidentifiable objects—all of which had nearly caused her gag reflex to work over-time—floating among the murky depths. He also gave her a piece of blackened chicken, for which she had needed the fork, and probably could have used a crowbar as well to tear through the surface.

She replayed the scenario over and over again in her mind, still unable to find the reason for her abduction. The scenario slipped and slid over the edge of a cliff, and left her mind exhausted with the dull ache pounding away at her brain. Being an accountant, and therefore focused on numbers, debits and credits, balance sheets, along with various spreadsheets, the crime couldn't be broken down to a simple mathematical formula. But it didn't stop her from trying to solve the equation.

She'd dated some real deadbeats when she was younger, but none in recent memory. None of whom were crazy enough to abduct her, hold her against her will, and feed her inedible meals in metal bowls. But then again, she'd known grudges to go on for years, and she'd been in some rather unpredictable relationships. None of the guys had turned violent, or even hinted at the possi-bility of kidnapping her, but anger proved to be a rather peculiar emotion, and she'd seen more than her share of red faces and flying objects, one of which had actually grazed her head before it shattered against the plaster wall behind her.

She was an accountant for Brogue Consulting. This kind of crap wasn't supposed to happen to her. She sat behind a desk all day, or what passed for a desk, crunched numbers on a computer, balanced the firm's budget, and populated quarterly statements. Excel, PowerPoint, and Quicken helped her get through the day. Being shot at should have never entered the equation. Or formula, for that matter.

Turning her attention to her body, Veronica assessed the damage: She was missing both shoes; the bottoms of her feet were tender and covered in dirt; her hair felt as though it jolted out in every direction; and she was cold, wet, and out of breath. Also she'd lost her purse, but she'd salvaged her wallet, although it was now as wet as she was; the throb in her side had slowed to a dull ache; she had a small cut on her left cheek and two on her right; and her big toe was red and twice its normal size. She'd ripped her skirt and torn her blouse. And she'd lost her tin of Altoids.

Her only comfort was the large, flat rock she sat on and the moon above her head.

Her feet ached, and she reached down to rub them, picking small specks of dirt from between her toes. She was rather disappointed about her heels. While they weren't her most expensive pair, or her favorites, she'd had them for a couple of years, picking them up at a Nordstrom's sale. They were black, with small, thin straps. Both of the straps would have broken eventually, since they weren't meant for running, with a lanky madman wearing a George Bush mask chasing after her. The mask scared her, even more than his gait and his deep, gravelly voice. She had never seen his face.

She pulled her hair away from her face, twisted it up on top of her head, and shook out the brutal images that had entered her brain. Every time she closed her eyes, she saw George Bush and his long, thick fingers. He'd reached out to grope her—or at least she assumed that was his intention, because she couldn't see his expression behind the mask—and she'd slapped his hand away. He'd reached out and slapped her across the face, catching a large ring on her left cheek and opening a cut that had caked with dried blood. That had occurred the first night. He never tried to touch her again until her jaunt through the woods.

Had she not been running for her life, focused on the dirt that had attached itself to her feet, dodged the shots that had filled the somewhat calm night, and lost both of her shoes along the way, she might have been paralyzed with fear. As it was, she had no such opportunity. Her mind had raced forward as quickly as her legs stomping through the soft earth. Anticipation and quick reflexes had saved her life on more than one occasion. Luck had also been on her side.

Despite the warmth in the air, she shivered. And then she did the only thing left to do. She picked herself up off the rock and started walking. Marching toward what she hoped would be her freedom. After her freedom, she wanted answers. But not before.

CHAPTER 3

Pete held a drink in his hand, the particulars of the drink didn't matter. He'd stopped focusing on the alcohol, the bar in front of him—the hard lines and dark wood—and the people that surrounded him after his third concoction. And now he was on his fifth, or possibly his sixth. He'd gotten up to pee every hour on the hour, and he knew he had a few more rounds to go: both in the bathroom and at the bar. He hadn't reached the point where the world blurred and turned into a cloudy haze, and he knew he needed to reach that point, otherwise he shouldn't even bother drinking at all. Blacking out helped, even if it wasn't always enough.

He'd come to his present situation about two hours ago, give or take about thirty minutes, and he figured he had a good two hours left, before he'd have to call it a night. Unless his money ran out sooner, he managed to overstay his welcome, or ended up in a fight—that had only happened once when the bartender presented the extra drink. A drink that wasn't his, even if he didn't know it at the time. He didn't even see the fist, until it had struck his chin, knocked him off his stool, and had him staring up at some evil bastard the size of a city block.

He'd visited this particular bar called The Wet Rhino every night for the past week, and possibly the week before that as well. He'd stopped keeping track of the days ever since Stuart Track, his best friend, had been killed in Iraq, his brains splattered all over his BDUs. A terrorist had killed Stuart, while he was on watch. The two bullets in quick succession had removed half of his head and placed them on his uniform. He, Pete not Stuart, still had nightmares, even though the event occurred three years ago. If he could have taken the next plane home, he would have. Instead, his acting commander had cleared him for duty, and he was back in the line of fire the next day—the army hadn't even bothered with a psych evaluation. When he returned to the states, he'd handed in his paperwork, right after he'd cussed out the commander, using a string of words so long and so convoluted that, even if he spent the rest of his life thinking about it, he wouldn't have been able to reproduce them in the exact same sequence. The acting commander might have punched him in the face, turned bright purple, or stood his ground in a calm, collected manner: He couldn't remember. He'd blacked out about halfway through, and he'd dropped to the floor, right before the paramedics had shown up. It was the second worst day of his life: the first being when Stuart had died.

He lifted the glass in front of him to his lips, took a long swallow, leaned back in the rickety wooden stool, right before both he and the stool tipped to the floor, where he fell spread-eagled amongst a vast ocean of peanut shells, spilled booze, and broken glass. Except for peanut shells attached to his clothes, he went unscathed, missing the largest and sharpest glass shards. And other than a high-heeled shoe that jammed his solar plexus, he went virtually unnoticed. The crowd that was available focused all their attention on the stage where a hard rock band jammed louder than a Nine Inch Nails concert.

"Are you all right?" a female voice asked.

He wondered if it was the same one who had introduced the high heel. "I think so. Can you help me up?"

A large hand grabbed his shoulder and yanked him to his feet. "You need to find more stable ground. You looked damn near incoherent for about thirty seconds."

He nodded, stepped back, stumbled, and almost tripped over his own two feet. He decided to take one more piss, before he went in search of a mode of transportation, possibly one where he could be in control, since there were a lot of idiots on the road, and he didn't need to end up in an accident.

After he relieved himself, he stumbled toward the door, smacking his head against the large wooden obstruction standing in his path. Cursing under his breath, he punched the wall and nearly broke his hand. Wandering around the parking lot, not quite sure where he had parked his car, he passed out face down on the pavement in a dark, somewhat secluded area of the lot. Sucking the scent of blacktop, stale beer, and the faint remnants of vomit into his lungs, he slept for nearly two hours.

The world hadn't always been like this. He had a steady girlfriend, his best friend in the whole world, Stuart, ever since they were stuck in a sandbox together for an entire afternoon in a public park, while their moms sat at opposing benches, neither looking in the other's direction. Matchbox cars banged back and forth on a collision course toward reality, two of the cars showed dents and dings that would have been present to this day, had the cars remained. But like Stuart, the unknown had taken over the known. The scars, on the other hand, had made themselves a part of his existence.

A loud voice jolted him back to reality.

"What the hell is with this guy?" the voice said. "Doesn't he know he can't sleep here?"

Pete grunted, turned over, and promptly emptied the contents of his stomach on the empty space next to him.

"Euwwww," a woman said. She added an extra euww for further emphasis.

A meaty hand jerked him to his feet. He staggered away, weaving in a semi-circular direction, before he promptly sat down, his feet splayed in either direction, as he wiped his mouth with the back of his hand.

"I need a ride," he said.

"Where are you going?" a voice asked. It might have been female.

"I have no idea."

"Then how are you going to get there?"

"I wish I knew."

"Good luck with that," the voice said.

Now he was no longer certain if he had been imagining his reality, or if the vision had only been in his mind. He had a bump on the back of his head, but he couldn't remember how long it had been there. He bent over one more time, swiped his mouth once more for luck, and stood up.

He'd lost track of the number of shots he devoured,

but his head had started to clear, or showed the first signs of it anyway. He'd had a little too much to drink, for what was at least the seventh night in a row, although he'd managed to lose count along the way, knowing the truth would not set him free, and alcohol probably wouldn't save his life. But he decided to stick with his present course of action anyway, since it was the only way he kept the demons at bay.

Through more effort than it should have taken, he managed to stumble out of the parking lot, hang a right, as he avoided a near collision with two teenagers talking on their cell phones and another one whose hands flew across the keypad in rapid succession. None of whom had bothered to look in his direction. One of them managed to yell at him to watch where he was going. If he knew where he was headed, it would have made his departure that much easier. As it was, he still had a lot of explaining to do, and not a damn soul who would listen.

CHAPTER 4

Two and a half hours later, he'd managed to walk nearly four miles, although he had no idea of the exact time. He'd pawned his watch six days ago for a night of drinking, and he didn't have the cash to buy it back. So it sat in a pawn shop on some street, in some area that he couldn't remember, along with the name of the pawn shop, and an oriental woman behind the counter with short hair and a tattoo on her bicep. His chances of finding his watch and actually buying it back hovered damn near close to zero. Possibly even less than zero.

His direction when he'd left The Wet Rhino was a mostly northern route, although he'd managed to veer both east and west when the occasion, or his sense of direction, warranted it. He'd stumbled in two places where the pavement was uneven, stepped off a curb at the wrong moment, and nearly twisted his ankle. He stood for a minute in front of RadioShack, staring at the vast darkness inside and the two fifty-inch LCD TVs on display, both of which looked promising, even though he was unable to afford them. He stubbed his toe on a fire hydrant that had been placed in the wrong location and almost gotten run over by some crazy, spaced out teenager in a Prius, probably texting while driving, when said teenager barreled through a red light at an otherwise deserted intersection. He hadn't even had time to utter a single curse word. And a woman with scraggly hair and a lisp followed him for three blocks before she figured out he had less money than she did.

He'd cut through a park with empty benches, two oak trees, three sycamores, and a small pond, where he'd stopped to quench his thirst. He saw three ducks which swam in a mostly uniform line, and he managed to stumble upon two more teenagers, who had managed to play tonsil hockey for nearly five minutes while he drank, neither of whom had seen him, and who, on occasion, managed to accentuate their tonsil hockey with rather vigorous sucking noises and the possible shedding of clothes, even though it was too dark for him to tell for certain. He averted his eyes at the first sign of what might have been bare skin, pale against the moonlight.

After his jaunt through the park, he sat for a minute at a white bench, at the opposite end of the park, ducked his head, and heaved, but nothing managed to come out. He tried again only to be met with the same resistance. For the moment, he had nothing left in his system. And he hoped it would stay that way.

Although he couldn't quite remember all of the specific details of how he reached this point, he stood at the edge of a large wooded area that looked vaguely familiar, and he scratched his right ear followed by his left before he scratched the skin around his belly button, his shirt rising as he did so. Out of the corner of his eye, he thought he saw movement, so he turned to his left. Nothing. He turned to his right. Still nothing. And then he whipped his head around to peer behind him. A small woman with what was once brown hair and possibly what was once a white shirt stared back at him with large brown eyes.

He reached out to touch her, right before she smacked his hand away and clocked him on the jaw.

"What the hell are you doing?" she asked.

He slurred some sort of unintelligible response. She slapped him on the cheek this time and reared back for another round. Before she could land her blow, he caught her hand in midair.

He shook the cobwebs out of his brain, squinting at her and turning his head to the side.

"Wait—I know you," she said.

"No," he said, "I don't think you do."

She squinted at his forehead, her stare nearly causing him to step backward. "You're Pete Nealey."

He scratched his jaw and burped. "Who the hell are you?"

She harrumphed. "You don't remember me?"

He shook his head again. Lights above her head danced, and the mist around her spiraled upward. He took a step backward to put his feet on solid ground.

"You always did have a problem with alcohol," she said, "and you couldn't remember shit in high school either. I'm surprised you even made it out."

"What?" he asked. *Had she actually spoken, or was it the mist?*

"The glassy look is a nice touch, too. I seem to recall

one time too many with your father's liquor cabinet. You never did know when to say when."

He rubbed his eyes and wiped the back of his hand across his mouth. "Do I know you?"

"Oh, that's rich," she said. "Veronica Baird. We went to high school together, you nimrod. All four years. But the bottle probably killed all of your brain cells, and then you probably reached back to finish off the ones that were left."

"I'll have you know I was sober—"

"I really don't give a shit." She looked at a point above his head. "You live around here?"

"Why?" he asked. "You going to accost me and steal my house keys?"

"Paranoid much?" She motioned toward her appearance, her hand moving up and down across her front. "As you can see, slick, I'm not in the best shape at the moment." Her hair stood out like a porcupine, and dirt and mud covered her clothes. She had eyes the color of mud pies. She wasn't wearing any shoes either. And one of her toes was bigger than the rest.

Like an interrupted signal, she faded in and out of focus. "I'm a little drunk."

Her hand tilted back, ready to strike faster than a cobra. "That's fairly obvious."

He smacked the side of his head. "No, it's captain."

"Okay, Captain Obvious, do you even know where the fuck you are?"

Veronica. That name did seem familiar. The mouth on her could have raised the *Titanic*. He'd also heard a story or two about her that might have involved bleachers, either on top or underneath, and a touchdown on the fifty-yard line. But that was a long time ago. Her mouth, though, still appeared able to go the distance.

"What are you doing out here in the middle of the night?" he asked.

She showed the first hint of her white teeth. "I asked you first."

"I told you," he said, "I'm walking home." He swung his arms to further emphasize the point. And, in the process, disorientation took over once again. Maybe it was his further reorientation with society that had caused him more than a few problems over the years. It couldn't have been the alcohol, or then again, maybe it was.

She glared at him. "Do you always drink and walk?"

"Sometimes," he said. "But it happens most often when I forget where I parked." He didn't know how he'd ended up at the bar, or how he'd ended up here, but he did remember the shots. He probably should have bothered to focus on his consumption level. But that would have required too much effort. It was much easier to just let go.

She balled her hand into a fist. "You'd drive in your condition?"

"Why not?" he said. "Everybody does it." He'd heard statistics on automobile fatalities, but he couldn't recall the specifics. Something about drinking and texting—probably not in that order.

"That's not an excuse." She shoved him hard, and he stumbled backward, nearly taking a seat on the grass. "That sounds like the act of justification."

"I'm a little lost." He'd already forgotten her name. He still held out hope that she wasn't real. Nope—it was Veronica. His stomach flipped, and he bent over at the waist. "What about you?"

"I'd rather not get into it at the moment."

He spun in a circle, flipping his head around as he did so. *Probably not the smartest idea.* He'd been filled with plenty of bad ideas this evening, and probably most of this week. "You came from the woods?" He didn't want to call her an apparition, just in case she wasn't one.

"You're smart," she said. "Maybe if we pump a few more in you, your IQ will shoot up forty points. Then you might actually reach positive territory. Just how many brain cells did you bury in that bottle, Pete?"

He walked ahead of her, leaving the apparition—with the torn skirt nearly to her waist; her brown hair caked with mud, leaves, and possibly even a few sticks; the mud-stained shirt; and the missing shoes—behind. Life was a lot simpler when all he needed to worry about was alcohol and the cold, hard pavement. Of course, a sense of direction often helped as well.

"Hey," she said, "where the hell do you think you're going?"

"For the second time, I'm headed home."

"Can I go with you?" she asked.

There was the slightest hint of vulnerability before she masked it with a grimace, and possibly a curse word that he missed. Her feet slapped at the ground behind him, just out of his reach.

He tried to walk in a reasonably straight manner: He wasn't sure he succeeded. He also tried to outrun her; he wasn't sure he succeeded at that either. "Why?"

"I'm in trouble."

"That's an understatement," Pete said. "Why are you walking around in the woods without shoes?"

"Because I lost them along the way. One of the straps broke, so I tossed the other one aside as well." She rushed to catch up with him, her feet slapping against the soft earth. "You smell like vomit and piss."

"That's because I passed out somewhere between The Wet Rhino and here. And if I remembered the exact details, I wouldn't need you."

"You really are a bastard. You were a bastard in high school, too. You always had a girl on one arm, and one of your friends on the other. You might think you were hot shit, but that didn't give you the right to start rumors."

He could feel her breath on his right shoulder. "Hey, I've changed. Besides, your mouth hasn't changed much from what I remember. If anything, you've gotten worse. Did you get a bit jaded along the way? One of your boyfriends slap you around?"

The footsteps stopped. She sucked in a breath. "I take it back. You're an even bigger bastard than you were in high school. What the hell happened to you?"

"I don't want to talk about it." He waved his hand dismissively and looked over his right shoulder. "What about you? You still have a thing for fifty-yard lines and bleachers?"

She stiffened, her back straighter than a five-dollar bill. "I don't even know why I bother with men. You're all the same. Pieces of shit, every last one of you."

He stopped and turned back around. "Hey, there's no need for generalizations. I am a bit wasted, in case you haven't noticed."

"You think?"

His gaze softened. "Besides, I didn't mean it."

"Is that some sort of apology?"

He jammed a hand inside his pocket. "Call it what you want."

She tried another smile. "I'd like to pretend I don't need your help. But I do."

For the first time, he really saw her. The fear in her eyes, the harried expression on her face, the tension in her shoulders, the dark circles under her eyes, the rumpled clothes, the red nose, the congealed blood on her bicep, and the twigs in her hair. He slapped his cheek, but she was still there. Still staring at him with wide eyes and the hint of panic on her face.

"So are you going to help me or not?" she asked.

He shrugged. *Why the hell not?* It's not like he knew where he was headed anyway. If she really was more than an apparition, maybe she could even help him find his way home. It's not like this was the first time he'd ever been lost in the middle of the night.

CHAPTER 5

The hot spray smacked her body. Men were so easy to manipulate, and drunk men were even easier to manipulate than sober ones. In an hour, she'd helped Pete find his house—and that was only because he had temporarily forgotten where he lived, stumbled along the path that was laid out before them, fallen once, and only heard most of her questions if she repeated them more than once. His eyes remained nothing more than a clouded haze. If she hadn't needed his help, she would have abandoned him after five minutes, and possibly even sooner than that, the slaps in the face merely an added bonus.

Her mind reeled with possibilities, the most prominent of which was how she would get herself back on track. Her outfit was torn, she'd lost her shoes, and she only had her wallet from her purse, which contained a bunch of wet bills and half a dozen credit cards, a few of which might have been maxed out. She'd never learned to control her spending—her spending controlled her. But she was determined to take a more practical approach in the future, even though the future happened to start right now, in this shower that had just managed to turn cold.

After two showers, the mud and filth remained. Not on her body, but in her mind. She was numb from the waist down. Her right hand still stung from the slaps, punches, and what she hoped was an uppercut. Her vision was a bit blurry, and the bathroom had more than a hint of chill in the air. And she hadn't fully accepted the traumatic events of the past two days, the initial of which had started with her kidnapping. She had been asleep when George Bush, or possibly a close relative, had slipped a cloth under her nostrils. She'd jerked awake, punching and kicking and half blind, only to fall right back to sleep again. Her only real thought was that a masked man had invaded her home, her sanctuary, and her only real form of privacy from society, and now she was going to die. Only she didn't die. Stubbornness ran deep in her bones, all the way to her inner core. Perseverance was her only friend.

She'd spent the past two days in a dirt cellar, probably built about the time of The Great War, plotting and planning her escape. And if it hadn't been for her resourcefulness and those self-defense classes she had taken four years ago, she would probably still be among its depths. The filth seemed to seep through her pores, and the reality was that she might never be able to wash away the film. Maybe she could hope for a spiritual reawakening, even though religion was never a concept she could readily accept. It was much easier to believe, and accept, that she controlled her own destiny, not the other way around.

After she toweled off, she went in search of clothes, knowing hers were no longer a viable option. No matter how hard she tried, she couldn't wash away the stench of captivity and defeat through normal means. Riffling through the drawers, expending more energy than necessary, during a time when she had expended way too much energy already, she had little success. When it came to T-shirts, pants, and sweatshirts, she was out of luck.

The room, possibly one used by guests, was virtually empty. Minimalist was an understatement. The bed was a double, with pale blue sheets and a cream colored comforter; the dresser held six drawers, all of which were empty; and the closet held only a few outfits, none of which she'd let herself be buried in, let alone wear of her own volition. Digging through the top of the closet, she finally settled on a pair of sweatpants that she belted at the waist and a man's shirt that was two sizes too large. She buttoned it all the way up, and yet she still felt exposed, still felt as though this was one long, never-ending nightmare. She wanted to wake up, but she wasn't sure how she could accomplish the task.

Trudging down the stairs, she found him in the kitchen with a bottle in his hand and an empty one not far out of his reach. His back was turned to her, as he slumped over the table, his head not far from the chipped wood beneath him, as he stared at a spot on the far wall.

"What are you doing?" she said.

He shrugged, touched the bottle to his lips, tilted his head back, and took a long swallow. "You?"

"I could use one of those," she said.

But the thought hadn't crossed her mind to drink her problems away. In fact, her problems were only just beginning, and no amount of alcohol could numb the out of control feeling that had suddenly taken over her life. Her hands fumbled with the string around her waist. Fragments of images jarred her reality, as she tugged the string tighter.

"I don't like to drink alone," Pete said.

"It doesn't appear to have stopped you before." The smell of vomit still clung to the air. She fought the urge to turn her nose away, along with the gagging reflex that threatened to take hold of her.

He peered up at her, not really focusing. "Do you feel better?"

She shook her head. "No, I feel worse." Her mind leaped forward before she slammed on the brakes. She could nearly smell the cloth, right before she clamped her brain shut.

"Are you going to tell me what's wrong?" he said.

She sat down across from him, on a chair that was barely sturdy enough to hold her weight—the wood fragile and porous—grabbed the bottle from his outstretched hand, and took a tentative swallow before she handed it back across the table. "I'd rather not."

"Then how am I supposed to help you?"

"Who said I needed your help?" Veronica asked. She'd always felt her name suited her. Her mission in life filled with agility and purpose right before she lost her sense of movement. The confined space had caused her eyes to water.

He brought the bottle to his lips. "Then what do you need?"

"A place to crash for the evening," she said. "I'll be gone in the morning."

"You don't want to stay in a hotel?"

"It's late enough that I'd rather not, and I'd feel more comfortable if I had someone who could watch out for me." She also knew he wouldn't bother to make it up the stairs, and if he came onto her, she figured she could probably make short work of the competition. One swift kick to the balls, and he'd hug the tile like all the rest of them.

"You can't protect yourself?"

"It's not that," she said.

She didn't feel the need to tell him about the last time she had spent a night alone. Not being able to defend herself caused her the most grief. The element of surprise had worked against her, the cloth tickling her nostrils before she felt nothing at all.

He stared at her. "You don't want to be alone."

"Now you're starting to catch on," she said.

She folded one hand on top of the other. The cracks in the table resembled the cracks in her life, the refrigerator humming in the background, and the fan overhead proceeding in slow motion.

"You went through a traumatic experience?"

She looked away briefly before she met his eyes again. "You could call it that."

He reached out before he abruptly pulled his hand away. "Maybe you'll talk about it eventually."

She shook her head. "I doubt it."

He stared at the bottle before his eyes fixated in her direction. "You can sleep in the guest room."

"Does the door lock?"

"You don't trust me?" he asked.

"I don't trust anyone at this point. Nothing against you." She said good night, and then she was gone.

If he passed out at the kitchen table, it would make it easier for her to get away in the morning, to start running from a presence that she never imagined would have existed.

CHAPTER 6

He touched the open bottle to his lips, no longer worried about anything other than his next drop of alcohol, the sensation as it rushed through his body, the high followed by the subsequent low. His mind reeled with thoughts of the woman who now occupied his guest room. A woman who had come into his life—and on one of his worst days, no less. A woman with a past as long as his, a woman he hadn't truly thought about since high school, and, even then, his thoughts had been scattered intermittently, like snowflakes smacking the hood of a car.

Veronica had a reputation that preceded her; a hand that had always stood at attention; a guy on her arm, presumably a boyfriend; and a mouth that always had a swift comeback at the ready.

She wore her hair long and her attitude even longer, reading or drawing in notebooks, or raising hell on the football field, or winning some debate drama that he had managed to avoid. Leather jackets and leather skirts, and she even had a rose tattooed on her lower back. Probably hadn't thought anyone would notice, but he had.

She walked those hallowed halls with her head held high, with more than one curious look pointed in her direction. With the palest skin he had ever seen and a small freckle just below her right earlobe, she had an ephemeral beauty he hadn't truly grasped at the time. He hadn't noticed her, though. Really noticed her.

Not the way he had noticed her two hours ago with the halo above her head, the mist surrounding her lips, and the slap that was presented without an apology. Probably better he hadn't smiled at her, or even acted like he remembered her, otherwise she might have considered yanking off his head and spitting down his neck. Maybe he had imagined her sitting across the table from him and drinking from the same bottle.

He had certainly imbibed enough spirits to hallucinate the experience, and he was in need of a full discharge from the fatigue that had managed to run his otherwise beleaguered existence.

Shoving back the rest of the bottle, he dropped his head against the wood, the table swaying beneath him, and all he noticed was blackness. The coolness of night swept over him, and he gave into his surroundings, hoping that it might present him with a change of pace.

Except for the nightmares, of which there were many, night did have its advantages. It never talked back.

The refrigerator hummed, the fan sang, and his mind raced forward as his breathing turned steady and even, and his thoughts slipped away to nothing. A chance to breathe a bit easier provided a sense of comfort. As he managed to drift off, the air conditioning kicked on.

He always had the same nightmare: one in which he was falling from the top of a building. Glass and blackness surrounded him. A lone man—not familiar to him—stood on the edge staring down at him. He didn't know if the man shoved him, or if he stared from above. His heart raced against his chest, fighting for a way out. His thoughts were empty and nonexistent. A tunnel of air pushed down on him, and his breath caught at the back of his throat as he neared the bottom. He didn't scream or cry out, but he did reach out to touch the column of air. When he reached the pavement, the ground gave way, and the earth sucked him in.

The past had a sense of reckoning, a sense of darkness that he'd never quite understood. The visions of death came to him at the most inopportune moments. Cold sweats and night terror were not merely in his past.

He couldn't shake the random thoughts from his mind. Visions where he had a gun pointed at his head, a noose wrapped around his neck, an Arab in full battle garb with a subatomic machine gun at waist level, the kid no older than eight planting a landmine in a sand dune, and the woman with no legs clutching a child to her chest. He'd been in control once, but that was a long time ago, a time when he had known what he wanted, and when he'd sought it out, not even bothering to settle for less than what might have been the best. He'd seen the precipice and now he drifted to the other side, not far from the abyss. A sense of pride had washed over him, but now that pride was gone too.

Sleeping was never an option for him, not since he lost his friend. Even though there was nothing he could have done to prevent Stuart's death, he still blamed himself.

He still considered the possibilities, and he still had to live with the consequences. His best friend didn't. Another spasm shook him, reverberated throughout his body. A wave of emotion coursed through him, as his head shot up from the table. Sweat poured down his body, and a slight tremor shook his core.

Waking up in the middle of the night wasn't his choice, but it often happened, more often when he least expected it. After a long night of drinking, the peeing inevitably followed. He flipped off the kitchen fan, his feet no longer lighter than air, and the cracks no longer hidden below the surface. The wooden staircase creaked beneath him, as he dropped his hands to his sides, fighting for every breath and every step in front of him.

Rather than strip off his clothes—he still wore the same outfit from earlier today, the smell of alcohol still lingering on his lips—he dove back into bed, as the soft comfort surrounded him, a comfort that he still hadn't been able to see through all the way to the end. His heart rate slowed down, the tremors subsided, and the blackness finally set in.

CHAPTER 7

Morning didn't come easily to her. She'd locked the door to ensure the man on the other side of it wouldn't touch her. She had slept through the night, flipping and twitching and gasping for breath. Her mind was cramped, closed in. Her chest felt like someone stood on it. Sweat poured down her body. The tossing and turning had continued throughout the night and into the morning.

Thoughts from her captivity stood up for attention. The flashbacks jerked her awake, screaming, panting, reaching out to punch a face that wasn't there. The mask, the dank walls, and the dirt floor were all too familiar. These walls held her inside. The paint was bright. Too bright. The color red flashed through her mind, over and over again, the loop repeating and circling back again and again.

She blinked back tears, her breath pounding rapidly and in a staccato-like fashion. Her mind hiccupped. No, that was her breath, tears, and pain. She placed her fingers on her temple and squeezed, the sights and sounds from underground still at the forefront of her mind, the picture all too clear.

She blinked back the last remnant of her tears and noticed for the first time the walls weren't red. Instead, she stared at tan with the slightest hint of green. A neutral color. But it was too tight, the room. Or it was all in her mind. Maybe it would all go away if she wished hard enough, if she filled herself with enough hope.

She stood up, stretched, reached her hands high above her head, and grabbed onto the freedom of another day, hoping this one would turn her life around. The bathroom light flickered on when she flipped the switch. The light blinked at her, smiled, and the soft twitch shimmered, even as her mind and body held fast.

As far as she knew, the lock had held, and the house was quiet, except for a slight creaking of the stairs in the early hours of the morning. An older home that just wanted to say hello.

She'd slipped downstairs at the first sign of dawn, the light barely peeking through the blinds. She hadn't heard any stirrings, other than the stairs. So far, her plan had shown signs of perfection. Another stroke of luck that just might work out in her favor, like her jaunt through the woods with bullets and bark whirling around her. The tornado rose up out of the darkness. The creaky stair had not creaked, as her feet glided to the floor below.

She checked the kitchen. Empty. She checked the living room and the makeshift dining area. Empty. She checked the bathroom and the hall closet. Empty as well. She listened for sounds above her: the shuffling of feet, the flick of a light switch, or heavy breathing that disturbed the otherwise quiet home. Nothing. Not even the hum of the air conditioner. The refrigerator hadn't said a word either.

Returning to the kitchen, she grabbed a set of keys near the refrigerator. Looking around one more time, she stepped out into the garage, knowing full well that she couldn't turn back now. Knowing that the drunk asleep upstairs wouldn't wake for hours, and in that amount of time, she planned to put plenty of highway between her-self and him. The distant look in his eyes didn't do him any favors either.

In the two-car garage, one car said hello. She shoved the key in the door, turned it, and listened to the lock pop. At least she had the right key in her possession. At least the right car had been waiting for her. The color scheme wasn't to her liking. The car was on the downhill side of its useful life curve, the paint was chipped, the floor held crumbs and small chunks of asphalt, and the faded and sun damaged dashboard had about three layers of dirt resting on it.

Slipping behind the wheel, she pushed the button to open the electronic door and watched it rise as the rest of the house remained quiet. She turned the key in the igni-tion and cranked the engine, as it coughed and hiccupped before it sputtered to life. The stereo crackled and blasted in her ear, before she turned down the volume, backed out of the garage, and closed the door behind her. Turn-ing onto the otherwise empty street, she couldn't help but think how her luck had changed once again, and that she was in the perfect position to take control of her life.

She smiled, knowing she had given him the slip, and that when he became wise to what she had done, she would be long gone. Even though she'd never stolen a car before, she had no problem stealing his, and another one if necessary. She'd seen it in the movies. Trading cars to throw off the authorities. By the time the first car was reported stolen, she could have another one in her possession, and she could have many miles between Port City, Virginia, and whatever her final destination was. Some point west, on the other side of Richmond, where she was unknown, and where there was more land than there was people sounded just about right. The highway open and empty filled her imagination.

When it came to her life and keeping a close hold on her freedom, stealing seemed like a rather minor consequence. Giving Pete Nealey the slip was her top priority. And without even her doing, she executed her plan to perfection. She'd have to settle for imagining the look on his face, the thrill of defeat, as he realized she had taken charge of the situation. That'd teach him to look down on her and her high school days. She wasn't proud of what she had done then, or what she did now. She couldn't change the past, but she planned to have plenty to say about her future.

Punching the gas, she felt the road open up, a road that was otherwise bare, except for a line of cars on one side of the road, and a series of trees on the other. The thrill of victory went hand-in-hand with the thrill of escape. Twice now, she'd given her counterparts the slip, and she'd have no problem doing it again. But what she did deem necessary were answers. She'd searched for them for two days underground, and she hadn't managed to reach any worthwhile conclusions. But she did know that she would find the truth, or at least give it a shot, in the hope that it might help her find the reason for her present predicament. What she needed to know was why. Why was she kidnapped, for what purpose, and what would have happened to her if she had been unable to breakaway? The thought of death caused a slight tremor in her body and the first sign of a tear glistened in her eye. She turned up the heat to ensure the tremor and the tear subsided.

Less than a mile away, several feet away from the stop sign that lingered before her, winking at her, and coaxing her forward, the car just died. Her thrill of running no longer held the same appeal. She shook her head, turned the key in the ignition, and the engine didn't even bother to turn over. She pounded the steering wheel, cursed, looked all around—the roof, the dashboard, the film on the windows, the plastic wrapper on the passenger seat— and checked the fuel gauge. Empty.

How could she have been so stupid?

She pounded the faded dashboard, alternating hands, until her knuckles were swollen. And then she exited the vehicle. On an otherwise empty street, her hitchhiking options remained limited at best, and all the cars she spotted appeared to have alarms. Newer models with antitheft devices and other such nonsense that made thievery difficult. Since she didn't know the first thing about hotwiring a car, didn't like the concept of busting through a pane of glass, and damaging her knuckles further, and wanted to avoid waking the neighbors at some ungodly hour, dealing with a couple of cops that came to the scene, and then trying to explain away her troubles, when frustration was her only guide, she decided to head back to Pete Nealey's home, even though she didn't want to admit defeat. No, that wasn't right. She hated to lose.

Admitting defeat was beneath her. But if she didn't do it, then she couldn't ask for his help. Even though she didn't want to admit she needed it, it's not like she had a choice in the matter, and even though he was a bastard, both then and now, she'd take the high ground, even if she couldn't take the higher road.

The instant her time was up, she knew she would have to face reality again. Or at least the semblance of it, in the hope that it might help her control her destiny. Control, though, was the furthest thing from her mind. Reality, though, would reach out and touch her, enveloping her with a newness that she couldn't quite touch and didn't quite want to feel. Being alone had never been so difficult.

The walk back was the longest walk of her life and took her longer than she expected. Facing the truth, though, would take more out of her than she was willing to give.

CHAPTER 8

He met her at the front door, before she could even step through the threshold. Still wearing his sweatpants and large T-shirt, she felt awkward. He, on the other hand, didn't look much better than she did. The dark circles under his eyes were only the beginning. His hair stood at attention, his right eye twitched repeatedly, and his shirt was stretched at the wrong angle around his body.

She hadn't been able to call a cab. No cell phone coupled with no pay phone made it difficult to reach out and touch someone.

"Do you even bother putting gas in your vehicles?" Veronica asked.

"I suppose it's a good thing I didn't," he said. "I always meant to fill it up, but I just never got around to it. It did, however, tell me important information about you before I even bothered to get out of bed."

"That's because you slept in until noon." A slight exaggeration, but she wasn't about to back down from his hazardous gaze and accusations. To emphasize her point, she shoved past him, slammed the door, and marched in the direction of the kitchen. His feet padded behind her, but she didn't bother to turn around. She decided not to give him the satisfaction. Ceding defeat had never been her strong suit.

His voice interrupted her thoughts. "I can't trust you."

"Like I can trust you?" she said.

Opening and closing cabinets in rapid succession, she found the filters after a minute and the coffee grounds just a few seconds before. She dropped the filter into the opening at the top, dumped the coffee in without even bothering to measure the allotment, and flicked the switch only a second later. Drumming her fingers on the countertop, she lifted her head and stared out the window. The tree less than twenty feet away proved particularly interesting.

"This is liable to be an interesting relationship," he said. "You're not going to try to steal my other vehicle, are you?"

"If I could have found the keys, and if it had been parked in the garage, I just might have. But as it was, you didn't leave me a whole lot of options. Now, if you'll excuse me—" she said as she tried to shove past him. "—I'd like to call a cab company." The coffee and the countertop were long forgotten.

He placed his hands on her shoulders. She struck his forearms, but she couldn't knock his hands away. He smiled at her. She grimaced in return.

"That's why I kept them hidden. I had a feeling you might decide on a morning jaunt, and I was correct in my suspicion."

She blew out her breath and stared at a point above his head. "You're incorrigible."

He dropped his hands and watched as she stalked to the coffeemaker. "I'm full of courage," he said. "I can also read people, and you had escape written all over your face."

She harrumphed. "I suppose I'm going to have to request your help, unless you plan on letting me walk out of here again." *This time she didn't plan on coming back.*

"And just how hard was it for you to get those words out of your mouth? You're probably going to have nightmares standing up."

She gritted her teeth, bit back a curse, and plunged her cup under the empty threshold beneath the maker. "Harder than you could possibly imagine."

"You don't always have to act alone," Pete said.

"It's much easier than the alternative," she said. "I'd rather solicit the help of a few dozen elephants than deal with the likes of you."

High school hadn't been a particularly wonderful time in her life, even if she did have a man or two to help her through some of the more challenging times.

"Why don't you want to get anyone else involved?" Pete asked.

"Because I'm not even sure what my stalker is after."

He didn't ask the obvious question. "Where do you work?"

"I'm an accountant for Brogue Consulting," she said.

"That's not exactly headline material."

"And you're not exactly my favorite person at the moment." She brought the cup to her lips, sipped, and smiled in appreciation. The fog had started to clear from her mind. The clamp around her midsection held fast, though.

"What have I done to you?"

"It's what you haven't done," Veronica said. "You didn't put gas in your car. You turned my perfect plan into a poorly executed alternative. Now I have no other choice but to seek an alternate exit strategy. Dealing with the likes of you isn't exactly how I wanted to start my morning."

Pete smirked. "Still haven't gotten over high school?" When she didn't answer, he said, "I didn't realize that was a sin in Virginia."

"You've committed a slew of sins already, and I'd rather not go into specific details. I have more than enough problems of my own, without having to worry about whatever your current issues are." She paused. "At least you don't have a bottle pressed to your lips. So you do have that going for you."

She sipped more coffee. "So are you going to help me?"

He scratched his chin and his head. "You mean I actually have an option?"

She was surprised he didn't scratch between his legs. "Maybe if you stopped slamming back the alcohol, you might increase your focus. Besides, I'm not sure you have an unlimited number of brain cells."

He stalked to the coffeemaker, nearly stumbled into the table, and practically brushed up against her. "Since when do you have a right to criticize?"

She sipped more coffee. "I managed to take the initiative ahead of time. I like to stay one-step ahead of the game. You, however, manage to fall further and further behind. And it's not just my imagination."

He sipped and scratched his chin again. "What are you running from?"

"If I knew the answer to that, I wouldn't be here. I'd attack the problem head-on. When it comes to challenges, I'm not about to back down—or give in."

"But you're rather good at running," he said. "You had enough dirt in your hair to create a new form of shampoo, although you did manage to wash most of it off."

"I've managed to hone my survival instincts over the years. You'd be amazed at how far adaptability will get you. And contrary to what you might believe, dirt is not my enemy."

He sat down, leaned back in the chair, and brought the cup to his lips. She stood rigid, before she leaned back against the counter, and focused on the tree once again. Her body was still held in captivity, but her thoughts and mind were elsewhere. Drifting, pushing, and stretching the limits of what she could possibly accomplish. The car, in the middle of the road, didn't provide much of an escape.

"So now that I've managed to put a kink in your plans, how do you want to proceed?"

"Wouldn't it benefit me to know who's chasing me?" She drained the last of her cup, poured a refill, and began to consume it in the same fashion.

"And how do you propose to do that?"

"By hitting the road," she said. "The sooner we put some distance between me and whoever is chasing me, the sooner the answers might become clearer. If not, it might fill a few pages of your memoirs, shoved between the drinking chapters. It can't all be about the drinking."

"And why should I bother to help you?"

"Because the men chasing me are sophisticated enough to know that you've already helped me, and that won't bode well for your future. Unless, of course, you want the bottle to finally finish you off. In which case you can deed me the keys and location of your other vehicle, and I'll be on my way."

"How do you know I have another vehicle?"

She breathed out through her mouth. "If you're going to start asking stupid questions, then I'll be forced to give you stupid answers."

"I can take care of myself," he said.

"Yes, you've proven that already. If you didn't drink yourself into a drunken stupor last night, then I'm the tooth fairy. When my stalker friend does show up, I'm sure you'll be able to handle yourself just fine. Maybe you can dazzle him with your breath."

He placed the cup in the middle of the table and stared hard in her direction. "You have no idea what you're talking about."

"I know exactly what I'm talking about. I've seen grief before, and I'm sure I'll see it again. You can grieve all you want, and you can drink yourself right into the grave, but that's not going to change the past, and it's not going to help you in the future. Maybe you should relive your glory days in high school. That is, if you even had any."

"If this is the way you actually encourage help, I'm surprised you don't have a charity line behind you, and multiple men bowing down before you. Your throne does not await you."

Her eyes narrowed. "You really are an asshole."

"I may be an asshole," he said. "But at least I'll be alive. I'm not sure we can say the same thing for you. If I cut my losses now, maybe I'll add a few years to my life."

She set the cup aside and tossed up her hands. "Where's your sense of chivalry?"

"If you find a chivalrous individual, I'll be sure to shake his hand. I might even buy him a large popcorn, an ice-cold soda, and a bag of Twizzlers."

"I figured it might come to this," Veronica said. She pulled a gun from the waistband of her sweatpants and pointed it directly at his head. Her hand remained steady—his less so.

"Where did you get that?"

"I did some digging last night, while you managed to sleep off last night's consumption in the kitchen before you moved the party upstairs. Knowing it would come in handy, I decided to take it along for the ride."

"Do you even know how to fire a pistol?"

"Does it really matter?" she said. "The gun is less than four feet from your head. What would you say the odds are that I'll miss? Or should we even bother to calculate them?"

"What if I have a weapon on me?"

"You have no such thing," she said. "I scoured the house, but I only managed to find one loaded weapon. Based on your present attire, and the fact that you slept in those clothes, I'd say the odds are unlikely at best."

He scratched his chin as he stared at a spot just beyond her right shoulder.

"So what's it going to be?" she asked. "Do you want to do this the easy way—or the hard way? I have no reservations about pulling the trigger."

"I've always had a hard time following direct orders," he said.

"Now, I know you're lying."

"How would you know that?"

"Because I saw at least one picture of you in uniform. You were a military man, most likely army, and most likely overseas. The desert camos only further emphasize my point." She shrugged, the gun bobbing slightly with her movement. "Besides, you have a tell."

"How much reconnaissance have you done?" he asked. "Did you sift through my underwear drawer too?"

"More than enough," she said. "But there's always the possibility for more."

CHAPTER 9

Anthony Whelan's office was on the fifth floor of a six-story building, the tallest one in Port City, Virginia. Three of his four walls were covered with glass. He'd chosen this particular location because he could see much of the surrounding city, the outskirts painted off into the distance, a town on the fringes of greatness, but held back by strict building codes and development issues. Small in stature but bigger in dreams, Port City hovered between Richmond and Virginia Beach, on the Tidewater gauntlet otherwise known as I-64. Whenever there was an accident, that stretch of interstate was fucked for hours on end. But the crème de la crème was the Hampton Roads Bridge-Tunnel—or HRBT—which was often a nightmare even without an accident, and with interstate hiccups…well, you might as well just grab your balls and squeeze.

With his headset and microphone, he paced around the room, making small circles as he went, checking out the view, when the situation warranted it, and when it didn't, he managed to kick his sofa once or twice. On the outskirts of his pacing, he'd pause for three seconds, before he resumed in the opposite direction. His body rigid at attention for three seconds before he scaled back the rigidness. The back and forth motion kept him from other pointless activities, like checking his portfolio or glancing at the TV screen in the far right hand corner of his office. His secretary was in the other room, ready to do his bidding. She went all in on her subservient duties, and he was a man who didn't mind taking advantage of the situation.

"You lost her?" His voice rose in volume and pitch. "What do you mean you lost her?"

"She disappeared."

"Women don't just disappear," Anthony said. "She went somewhere. *Find her.*"

"You make it sound easy, Anthony. Life is filled with complications, and solutions aren't as easy to come by."

He cradled the top of his headset. "Of course, it's easy. She couldn't have gotten that far. Did you check the surrounding area?" He paused. "Besides, she's just one woman, and she was on foot. You let her get the better of you, and that's unacceptable." His breathing had increased in volume and pitch to match his voice.

"Sure," Thurman Busch said.

"And what did you find?" He had to do all the thinking, even when he paid for better judgment and received less than opulent results. Idiots surrounded him. Even when he managed to emphasize a thorough screening process, he still ended up with morons. If he could come up with enough locations, he should implement death by firing squad.

"It's deserted. Besides, she jumped into a small reservoir."

"And you didn't jump in after her?" Anthony demanded.

"I assumed the risk outweighed the reward."

"You thought wrong," he said. Apparently, stupidity appeared to be a rather successful profession. He should have handed out trophies. "How are you going to correct your error?"

"She can't hide forever," Thurman said. "She will surface, and when she does, I will be ready for her."

"In the meantime, I will send you someone." He probably should have had the idiot work with someone from the beginning. In Anthony's experience, the idiots tended to cancel each other out, or at least prove to be less idiotic. Although idiots squared was always a possibility.

"I don't need help, Anthony. I'm perfectly capable of taking care of a woman."

"You fooled me once, Thurman, but I'll be damned if I'll let you fool me again. I'm bringing in Elrod to help you alleviate your little situation, before it turns into a bigger situation. I have neither the time, nor the inclination, to deal with a giant problem."

"He's even crazier than the way he dresses." Thurman's voice rose about an octave. "Surely, you can think of someone else."

Elrod did have a penchant for plaid button-down shirts, fluorescent pants, goatees, and straw hats. But that only made him more interesting and easier to spot.

"Surely, you'd prefer to have your life spared," Anthony said. "If there are any further complications, I won't be so lenient the next time. Plus, his tracking skills are much better than yours. You couldn't find the radar detector on the dashboard of a maroon Cadillac without assistance."

"Mine are perfectly acceptable," Thurman said.

"Then how did she make it out of the woods? This was only two days into our operation. You had a nine-millimeter in your possession, and you are one of my smartest operatives. *Supposedly.* She was locked up underground without the slightest hint of daylight. I gave you every advantage I could think of, and still you managed to fail me." Anthony didn't bother to add how much he despised failure.

"I will make it up to you, Anthony. You can count on me."

"No, Thurman, I can no longer count on you. And that's why I'm bringing in Elrod. Should you fail me again, he won't be as lenient as I have been with you."

"What am I supposed to do until then?"

"What you do best. *Find her.* I want Mr. Jace to have options when he makes his grand appearance. She is a woman, and women are known for their subservience. If I have to remind you again, you will not like the end result."

Before Anthony lost even more of his temper, he clicked off and slammed the phone back in its cradle. With his mike flipped toward the heavens, he continued pacing for another minute or so and gave his sofa another swift kick, before he opened the lines of communication once again. The microphone dropped back into place, and he dialed a number he was all too familiar with.

"I need your assistance," he said.

"I have always been at your service," Elrod Jace said.

"I have a problem, and I need to make it go away."

"Consider it done."

Anthony informed Elrod of his problem, leaving few of the details to the operative's imagination. While the man had a limited imagination, Elrod had no problem executing whatever plan Anthony set in motion. Ruthlessness not only was required, it became his modus operandi. What Anthony needed were a few more individuals like Elrod. But the slick operative with the unique wardrobe had been a hard one to find, and he'd been even harder to control. The end result, though, was well worth the time and effort.

If Anthony decided to institute his plan of killing off operatives, he'd at least spare Elrod's life. That, he supposed, was something.

Ending the call, he walked back toward his desk. The desk was black, conveyed power, and he'd had it especially fashioned to have added room for his legs. Not because he was a particularly tall man, but because he had other intentions in mind. Urges that became extremely difficult to control, and that often increased in frequency and duration when he was under a lot of stress. And he was never far from a stressful situation.

Punching the intercom button, he called in his secretary. She referred to herself as an administrative assistant, but he'd never quite made the connection. Not that it mattered anyway. Like everyone else in his life, she served a specific purpose.

Walking as if on air, she entered the room, her bright red dress low-cut, showing off her ample breasts. Her blond hair was long, falling past her shoulders, and it swept in toward her mouth. Her pouty lips curved into the slightest hint of a smile, as she stood on the opposite side of the room, too far out of his grasp, too much space stood between them, an inquisitive look painted on her face. She'd left her notebook in the other room.

The hair just wouldn't do. He had no use for long hair. "Put your hair up."

She removed a pen tucked behind her ear, twirled her hair, and placed it on top of her head, out of the way of those precious lips. Lips that were larger and more succulent than he had anticipated.

He motioned for her to approach, her movements as fluid as those of a dancer. She'd informed him about some sort of dancing in her youth, but he hadn't been paying attention. When she talked, his mind focused on other parts of her body. Parts of her body he had yet to enjoy. He'd hired her based on the quality of her assets, not for the words that came out of her mouth, or the intelligence that she supposedly conveyed. She was from some Midwestern school in some Midwestern state—he had trouble recalling the specific details.

As he slid his chair back, he ordered her to her knees, bowing in front of him and peering up at him underneath her eyelashes, her mouth already forming a slight O. He tilted her head, as he jerked her forward, her hands only inches from his fly.

He'd never been disappointed with his choices.

CHAPTER 10

He'd contacted the cab company over an hour ago. Pete managed to pick up his car in less than five minutes and, courtesy of another phone call, he had his other car towed back to his house and dropped in his driveway.

The gas in the can on the bottom shelf would help him find the nearest gas station, a little over a mile away. Walking, he supposed, was an option, if he hadn't walked his ass off the night before.

As for his present situation, he hadn't proved as lucky. "How long are you going to continue to point my gun at me?"

She had one hand on the window, her seatbelt slung across her chest, and the other hand pointed steadily in his direction. "As long as it takes—"

"For what?" he asked.

"For you to gain sense and perspective," she said. "You have to be the most incorrigible man I've ever met, and yet no matter how hard I try, I can't seem to get rid of you. If I could have done this without you, I would have dropped you off at the nearest curb without your shoes and a sign around your shoulders."

"I'm flattered."

"You shouldn't be," Veronica said. "This isn't that kind of relationship. You're a means to an end. Nothing more."

I probably should have strived to be a better person in high school. Even now, from my current life, it probably would be an upgrade. "Then what kind of relationship is this?"

"The kind where you do exactly what I tell you to," she said.

He stared straight ahead, concentrating on white lines, asphalt, and pavement. A sigh emitted from her direction every minute or so, and the hint of body lotion wasn't far behind. He tasted yesterday's breakfast in the back of his mouth along with the hint of alcohol and breath mints. "Is that thing even loaded?"

"Do you really want to find out?"

"Not particularly," Pete said. "I thought it might benefit the two of us if I made conversation. Besides, I don't want you to develop an itch in your trigger finger."

She had on the slightest hint of perfume, or maybe it was the woods. "Why don't you work on keeping quiet?"

"Only if you promise to step up your conversational skills," he said. "You're not going to improve by sitting on the sidelines. The gun won't talk for you."

He'd been driving for almost an hour, and his present condition didn't look any more promising than the previous fifty-nine minutes. For the past hour, she'd managed to hold the gun perfectly steady, a look of collected calmness, her eyes never leaving his face, and her body wedged close enough to the door that he couldn't grab her without risking a probable accident. He liked his car too much to watch it go up in flames, even if it hadn't made it past his street on the first go round. Crashing into a tree, or sideswiping another vehicle seemed probable, but she had obeyed the law with her seatbelt buckled, despite the position of her body, and her distance from the dashboard. He'd risk injuring himself as much as her, since he had a steering wheel to contend with, and no airbags to speak of.

He'd avoided staring at her, even out of the corner of his eye, but it was hard not to notice her limber figure, and he'd always managed to be a fan of brunettes. Her eyes, though, were emotionless voids, except when she decided to open her mouth, and then her expression spoke volumes above her words. Her eyes turned to fire, her lips peeled back from her front teeth, and her mouth formed a straight line. He didn't know how she'd managed to enter his life, although he couldn't help but think it was more than a coincidence, and he wasn't quite sure how he could get rid of her without risking a shot in an enclosed space. He'd never been kidnapped before, and especially not by a beautiful woman. Not that it helped him solve his present predicament any faster.

She hadn't exactly given him a destination, even though he asked whenever he thought he might get an answer. But no answers were forthcoming. He had managed to pack a suitcase, with at least a few essentials, although she had watched him toss in all of his clothes, including his T-shirts and underwear, and even followed him into the bathroom, her back pressed up against the door, so he hadn't been quite as thorough as he should have been. The gun didn't help his thought processes either. His driving lacked a certain amount of thoroughness, although it had more to do with his impatience than the gun that constantly remained in his peripheral vision.

Every time he flipped the music on, she flipped it back off again. The gun, along with her harsh glare, had finally settled the score.

He wasn't a big fan of seatbelts, although the gun had changed his attitude on the flexible straps that locked him in one position. Despite his military training, and the fact that he'd watched his best friend enter through death's front door, he'd never had a gun pointed at him before, although some folks said the bottle offered up the same result, but the pace remained much slower, and it had always been on his timetable, instead of someone else's. He had been shot at, but he'd never seen the weapon, only heard a language that he didn't understand in a country that seemed too far away and hotter than the blazes of Hell. Women and children walking around with bombs strapped to their chests, with fear smothered on their faces. Even the nights managed more heat than he would have thought possible, pounding in through cracks and crevices until he had rolled all over his bed.

Random thoughts filled the solaces of silence. The gaps pristine in his heightened state of consciousness, the road ahead filled with gaps in the traffic. Trees lined up like soldiers up against the edge of the freeway, the drop-off several feet into a grassy and dirt filled crevice. Exit signs flew by every mile or so, the large green signs holding both promises and curses.

"Do you trust anyone?" he asked.

She stared straight ahead, her teeth clicking, or maybe it was the gun. "I didn't know that was a requirement."

"Then why did you bring me along?" Pete asked. "You could have gotten along just fine without me."

"Would you have given me the keys to your dilapidated Corolla?"

"Not likely," he said. "By the way, you still haven't told me where we're going."

"That's because I don't know myself."

He had driven north on US-60, otherwise known as Richmond Road, past Lightfoot, continuing on toward Richmond. The area was rather isolated, and thoughts of dying did begin to enter his mind. The isolation coupled with the semiautomatic spelled his doom. He wondered if this was a good place to bury a body, although he decided not to give her any bright ideas, lest she decided to finally listen to him, for the first time in her life. But she hadn't managed to find him intriguing, so he assumed the lack of interest would continue, and he might actually enjoy a few more moments of peace, even though peace had its own baggage, and it involved him staring at an open circle whenever another opportunity presented itself. The open road, however, proved much more enjoyable, offering up a form of relaxation without the full on assault to his wallet.

"Do you have any plans to bury the body?" he asked.

"What body?"

He punched the gas, hoping he might outrun his otherwise bane existence, and the demon running at the forefront of his mind. "Mine."

"Why? Do you feel like going underground?"

"Not particularly," Pete said. "I happen to like it above ground very much." He even nodded his head for emphasis.

"Are you always this wise?"

"I happen to be highly intelligent," he said.

He decided not to mention his college degree, or the fact that he had received top marks in high school, or that he had once been captain of the debate team, before the drinking started.

He had probably been a bastard as well, but he never strived for perfection. Besides, that was a long time ago, and he had proved to be a much different person with time. Life had a funny way of changing direction in an instant, much like the wind or the currents.

"You just can't be bothered to put gas in a car."

"I put gas in this one," he said. "I even managed to leave it in a prime spot at the end of the lot." Of course, had he remembered where he had left it, he might have ended up in an entirely different predicament. A night snoring in a jail cell could have headlined his past.

"You knew I'd want the other vehicle, didn't you?"

"I hadn't exactly considered that particular possibility, but sometimes you're better off when you don't have to do the thinking yourself. Things often work out a particular way for a reason." Drumming his fingers on the steering wheel helped his thoughts flow more freely. "And I'm more than happy to enjoy the ride."

"I'm sure you're enjoying the view from my side of things," Veronica said.

He stared straight ahead. "It's certainly an interesting concept."

"Do you ever take life seriously? Or do you enjoy making my life difficult?"

"When you've escaped from the jaws of death, each day happens to be a gift. As for you, I wouldn't expect anything less than difficult."

"Even though you continue to drink away, in hopes that it will help you reach the next point of impact, you must have some purpose for your life. Or maybe you're going after the next big sleep."

"You're rather cynical," he said. "Do you want to stop here? Or should we continue the back and forth banter in an otherwise haphazard manner?"

"I thought I was in control of the situation."

"Control is a rather interesting concept, and it could change at any moment."

As a gas station appeared on the horizon, he decided it was a good opportunity for escape. Even if the opportunity had more than a few holes, and even if he couldn't get his plan off the ground, he decided it was worth the effort. He didn't want to stare at the barrel of a nine-millimeter for the rest of his days, and he certainly didn't want Veronica Baird controlling his life. He had a hard enough time controlling it himself.

CHAPTER 11

The pumps lined up like warriors, three deep on both sides, and three rows of possibilities. His options, however, didn't seem as pronounced.

"You have handcuffs, too?" he asked.

He had exited the vehicle, and she had mirrored his actions, the cold glint of metal shining in her right hand, not even doing a particularly good job of concealing her weapon. His eyebrows lifted, so did her right hand.

"I've considered lots of possibilities." She slapped the cuff on his right wrist, as an obscenity or two left his lips, and slapped the other cuff on the door handle. She moved like a jaguar, and he managed to move a step or two behind her. She smiled—he didn't. He jerked his right hand. She moved in a more fluid motion.

"How long have you planned this?" Pete asked.

"When you've been sheltered from the world for two days, you have all the time in the world to consider your options. Besides, I've always been a bit of a free-thinker."

He raised his right hand as high as it would go. "Do

you honestly think I can pump gas like this?"

She nodded. "You're certainly going to try, aren't you?"

He shook his head, shifted his eyes, and reached into his back pocket with his left hand, as though this was entirely natural for him. It wasn't. "Maybe you're smarter than I gave you credit for."

"And you're certainly not smart enough," Veronica said. "You really do need to step up your game, or your ride could always take a turn for the worse."

She walked off as he slipped his credit card into the appropriate slot.

An older gentleman wearing rather prominent bifocals almost bumped into him, before he conducted an about face at the last minute. The handcuffs clanked against the rusted door handle, and Pete's mind ran through possibilities, many of which he couldn't execute with either a gun pointed at his head, or a pair of handcuffs slapped to his right wrist. He'd have to pump the gas left-handed. The fact that he still had both of his hands presented him with a few opportunities, but he wasn't as adept at outsmarting the competition as he should have been. She had always managed to stay two steps ahead of him. Her escape from an underground prison made sense. He was still a bit behind on the details. Her ability to communicate effectively lacked a certain passion and intensity. On the other hand, the quiet allowed him time to think, to plan, to outthink, and possibly to execute.

As near as he could tell, she must have had traumatizing experiences with men—probably started in high school when she'd been clamoring for attention, and proceeded on throughout her life—and maybe he was just the next one on the list. He had higher hopes for him-self—she obviously didn't. The possibilities presented him with a series of opportunities, none of which he considered likely. He could rip off the door handle, create separation between his wrist and the cuff, knock her flat on her butt, scream for help, start praying, or start running, and take the car with him.

He dragged his wrist to the right and jerked it, but the metal cuffs held. The clank proved rather prominent in the otherwise silent arena. Like the swarm from a hive before it was about to strike.

He refused to resign himself to the fate laid out before him, although there were worse situations than being kidnapped. Being a previous acquaintance long removed didn't exactly impart an optimistic atmosphere. He had trouble reaching any conclusions, the barrel of the gun still etched firmly in his mind and bigger than a baseball. But that could easily change. He considered overpowering her, but her reflexes were instinctive, quick, and resembled the fluttering of a butterfly. Just for good measure, he jerked his wrist again. The cuffs held. The clank tasted like metal in the back of his mouth.

Glancing in her direction, he saw her shake her head. She sliced her hand through the air in a horizontal fashion. The pump clicked, his thoughts vanished in a drip and a drop, and not long after so did the cuff on the door handle.

Rather than sprint away, he stood his ground. "So have you considered where we're headed?"

"Obviously we need to spend the night," she said.

Darkness wasn't his friend, and she had managed to

snag both the handcuff key as well as the car key. He was two keys short of a good time. "What for?"

"I'm being followed."

Being followed seemed like a nice cover, or ruse, for dragging him out to the middle of nowhere—preferably the western side of Richmond. Then clanking him over the head with one of the beer bottles in his backseat, burying him in an unmarked grave, or underneath an already dead body, and then executing two more showers, two hand washes, and whistling the theme for *Deliverance*. Sour milk and sulfur filled his nostrils, and he swayed slightly in the breeze.

She smacked him on the shoulder, shoved him into the front seat, and handcuffed him to the steering wheel, which brought to mind an entirely new form of unsafe driving. He had to time his movements, otherwise he'd end up on the side of the road, drifting toward the median, at passing or pursuing vehicles, or in a ditch. The road wasn't deserted, and there certainly weren't a lot of opportunities to plan his escape. Which was why she had probably chosen the road in the first place. If he hadn't been more of an interstate driver himself, he might have had a few more opportunities to veer off in other directions—none of which came to him at the moment—any of which would have taken him back to his dreary house—instead of on this insane adventure with a woman who carried his Smith & Wesson, bullets and all. Stuart had experienced his end in a similar fashion, although Smith & Wesson hadn't been involved on that particular occasion.

The end remained a projection on a monitor, a shimmering glimmer on a distant horizon, distorted from his view, and significantly out of place in his world, where Veronica had filled out in all areas from her teenage years, including an exterior harder than granite.

He wanted to keep ahead of the game, and not veer off to the side of the road, since he wasn't convinced that his driving skills were acceptable enough to navigate such a situation. Or Veronica might just fly off her handle and shoot him. For the most part, the gun remained steady, with a slight tremble here and there, possibly for effect, and she continued to remain out of his reach, her back-side firmly pressed against the window.

"Where are we headed?"

"I hadn't really thought about a specific place," she said. "In fact, I hadn't even planned to bring you along, until your car ran out of gas."

She didn't bother to smile, and her eyes didn't bother to look in his direction. The point above his head gained more attention than he did.

He jerked the steering wheel to the right. She gripped the handle overhead, her body slipping and sliding with the force of the vehicle. The breeze shifted the leaves of the trees, slightly, just enough to throw the world slightly off balance. The deer remained in place, away from the road, staring at him with lost and distant eyes: The obsta-cles proved few and far between, even the potholes were less prominent, but the intensity of the situation re-mained, as did her grip on the pistol.

Several minutes later, she rested the gun in her lap. Not that he assumed she would turn lackadaisical in the future, but if she did, it might give him an opportunity or two to make his escape. And if not, at least it would give

him some hope, something to consider besides the monotony behind the wheel without a single tune to fill the
otherwise eerie silence.

He did, however, bide his time, giving the perception
of ceding control to a half-crazed crackpot who might, or
might not, have been a crack shot. Control, however,
could come and go in an instant. If his best friend had
taught him nothing else, he had taught him that much.

CHAPTER 12

The hotel was on the outskirts of Richmond, on the eastern side, in an area called Montrose. The rooms opened to the outside, and there were three floors. It probably hadn't been redone since the 1960s. A large orange sign beckoned them, and not much else. The lobby held a tattered sofa, a smidgeon of scuffed chairs, a computer that was probably from the 1990s, and a fern that leaned a little too heavily to the right.

The desk clerk probably hadn't worked out since the 1980s, or possibly before. His belly protruded prominently underneath his shirt, stuck out at an obscene angle, and even managed to nudge the counter, despite the fact that he was nearly six inches back from the laminate countertop, a countertop with cigarette stains, stray hairs, and an unidentifiable liquid that Pete wasn't going to bother asking about.

His hands hovered over the counter, never quite finding the courage to plunge into the murky waters below, where his chances of contracting hepatitis were probably higher than usual. At least she'd freed his hands so he could make this subconscious decision, even if she did have the gun firmly jutted into his lower back.

The clerk had dark hair and his skin was the color of milk chocolate. His eyes were a deep shade of brown, and he wore a Washington Nationals baseball cap. He had his hair pulled back into a ponytail, and he wore a large ring on the third finger of his right hand. He had a gold chain around his neck, and his shirt had a large stain in the center, possibly beer. He had a chipped tooth and a crooked nose, and his skin had a smattering of acne near his left ear.

"We need two rooms," Veronica said.

The clerk pounded a series of keys on the keyboard. "We don't have two rooms."

Neither did the Hilton nor the Doubletree Inn. But at least this local motel in this local town had one room, if the sign could be believed. This was the last option at the far end of town, and Pete didn't particularly want to continue driving through the night, his hand firmly planted on the wheel, and the gun firmly planted against his side, as his mind continued to process all the ways he could meet his maker on the back of a pickup truck.

Out of spite, this place had probably made the top of his list. Even before she had exited the vehicle, she had cringed and breathed a sigh through her lips that might have contained a curse word, or it might not have. The neon orange sign lit up half the parking lot along with their vehicle. A scrum of riffraff smoked a joint outside one open room, and a transaction, possibly of a nefarious nature that might, or might not, have involved a prostitute was being conducted at the far end of the parking lot opposite the road. The bars were placed prominently on the windows to the front door. His chances of being mugged and contracting hepatitis had nearly doubled from the moment he exited the vehicle.

The street was called Gay Avenue. It intersected Masonic Lane and ended at Eanes, knifing through the center of this one-horse town. The mall, at the far end of town, hadn't even managed to enter into the equation, even if the local hoods did. All of which appeared to have bulges in their oversized pants that managed to go real well with their oversized attitudes.

He shrugged, the movement exaggerated. His mind still tentatively focused elsewhere, although Jayden's—or so his nametag said—had brought him crashing back to reality. The gun jerking against his backside hadn't hurt his focus either.

"This is a small town," Pete said.

The clerk rubbed his ample belly and nodded.

He waited for her to offer up some resistance, possibly a comment, and a hint that might have provided a solution to the situation, a credit card tossed at the countertop, or even a sigh or grunt. Nothing. His hands still hovered above the counter, his next move still being planned. The clerk stared at him. He stared at the clerk. The clerk looked away first.

"Are you going to pay for the room or not?" Pete asked.

CHAPTER 13

Y ou and I should get married," she said.
She was young, naïve, and had the best set of lips that Anthony had ever seen. She could do things with her mouth that made his toes curl. Yet, it wasn't enough. It never was. And now she wanted more. A concept that didn't sit well with him. She had an insatiable appetite, which under most circumstances proved divine. In this instance, though, she had missed the mark.

She was naked from the waist down, her skirt in peeka-boo formation, her blonde hair pulled back from her face, her mouth inches away from him, her eyes turned up in his direction, hands on either side of his upper thighs, her voice nothing more than a whisper. He leaned back in his chair, his right hand stroking the top of his head. She had a satisfied smile on her face. A smile that now threatened to turn in on itself.

"You know I don't believe in marriage."

"I thought maybe I could change your mind."

"We can do other things," Anthony said, "but marriage isn't really an option for me."

He didn't need to add that her abilities hadn't extended beyond his desk, and that if she were a lesser woman and a few years older, he would have already fired her. Youth brought out entitlement along with naïveté, and fake breasts only increased the level of the challenge. The silicon had probably caused her head to swell.

"What kind of other things would you be referring to?" Bethany Aimes said. She curled her lips into a smile, right before she licked them clean. To emphasize her point, she slapped his thigh, the sound reverberating throughout the room.

"I'm sure you could come up with a few ideas," he said.

With a flick of his hand, she was gone. Her lips vanished along with the rest of her, her thong wadded up in the palm of her hand, the sweet expression on her face having vanished the way she did.

On the other side of the door, she was safe. Less intrusive. A steel door separated him from the dark side of the world, and all the temptations that lay beyond its walls. At least that was what he hoped. But he hadn't counted on all the changes, and now they were here just the same. Accountants came and went, secretaries appeared and vanished faster than a porn star's underwear, but only one truly annoyed him. He thought he had dealt with the problem in an appropriate manner, given her futile resistance. Veronica needed to be expunged, and so he had given the order. The declaration, and now he was faced with a dereliction of duty. He'd have to make do. Or at least he'd make a valiant attempt. He'd tie up the threads, and giftwrap her death for his trouble. The trouble sim-

mering within the organization would be dealt with officially later. Effort would only take him so far—
persistence would take him a whole lot farther.

He liked Bethany. Not as much as she thought. But
there were ways to convince her that it might be enough.
That he could harness her youthful charms and grace, her
skills perfected with a bit more time and a bit more effort
inside his desk, coaching her, coaxing her toward some
greater power. Optimism, youth, and an insatiable sexual
appetite made her useful to him, but cynicism, age, and
the sun would eventually follow.

Her hands were as soft as her golden curls, her eyes
the color of the ocean, and her lips held just enough clout
to complete the task in the most efficient manner possible. She could suck a softball through a garden hose if he
asked her to, not that she needed the additional attention.
Glances from his employees had turned into longer stares
over the weeks and months, and now he was faced with
the dilemma of keeping her around or having her hit the
streets. She might have been a drug that he couldn't get
enough of, but he needed to contain his addiction before
he ended up sacrificing his authority.

She'd been down on all fours in front of him: The way
he had liked her. And her mouth had moved, done things
he'd rather not even describe. Probably couldn't even
find the words. It was comforting the way she jumped at
his every call, had a beck for his every need. His fantasies
had married up to reality, and it was a good adventure,
one with a solid core. He'd been happy with it, and he
had assumed reciprocity was in order, maybe a raise if
she were inclined to material things. Or then again, maybe all she wanted was to be seen with him. She had hint-

ed as much the last time she was at his desk, the look in her eyes filled with hope and desire.

It was enough for now, at least for him, but he wasn't convinced that it would be enough forever. He had needs. They tended to change. And he tended to enjoy the ride. He didn't always understand her point of view, but then again, he didn't have to. If she pressed him on the issue, more than just a casual office fling, he could always find another. Women needed him more than he needed them.

He dropped the microphone down over his mouth, and spoke a number into the mike. Simplicity made it all worthwhile. Maybe he'd set his expectations too high, but he didn't think so. In fact, he probably didn't set them high enough. The ladder always had another rung.

He'd discovered the space, had the office built to his specific specifications. Insisting on the panoramic view had been well worth the extra time and money, and only hiring the youngest secretaries with the most exquisite desires had truly been the right call. He had his needs, and he had his ways to fulfill them. Longing and craving permeated through the walls, inside of his masculine office space filled with hard lines and black leather, settling on the plush blue carpet before him, staring at him with eyes the color of saltwater. Control worked—control was king.

His call was picked up on the first ring.

"Why are you calling me?" Nathan Labaw asked.

"I thought we could discuss a few matters."

"I told you to never call this number."

Anthony ran a hand through his thick dark locks. "There are always exceptions."

"I'm not interested in exceptions," Nathan said. "I'm interested in eliminating the possibilities. If you do your part, then I can eradicate mine."

His nails clicked on the desk, his chair moved beneath him, an image formed in his mind. "I have a solution to our problem."

"I don't want solutions," Nathan said. The sigh was pronounced and filled with volume—the voice rising ever so slightly in pitch. "I want you to tell me the threat has been eliminated. Those are the only words I want to hear from you."

"The threat isn't as easy as I originally assumed."

"Of course, it's easy," Nathan said. "She's a woman. How much trouble could she possibly be?" He paused, the length increasing. "Should I reconsider our arrangement?"

"I've had to add another man to the equation," Anthony said. The fewer the details he needed to provide, the better.

"Sometimes your solutions become part of the problem. You have an insatiable habit that you need to control."

Anthony's hand stiffened, the papers crumpling before him on his desk, the image on his monitor scrolling across his screen. "I'm working on getting help."

"You're doing no such thing," Nathan said. "Don't lie to me again."

"How would you know?"

"I make it a habit to know my people. Besides, you're not that difficult to figure out."

Anthony controlled his needs, even if he didn't always want to. "Maybe you and I should work out a new deal."

The thought of extra bills lining his pockets formed a better image in his mind than Bethany on all fours with her lips pulled up underneath her teeth.

"You're not going to like my new terms," Nathan said.

"You're not in a position to order me around."

"Maybe I'm smarter than you think I am."

The phone clicked in his ear. Anthony didn't even have a chance to utter a single curse word.

CHAPTER 14

The cramped apartment smelled of urine, possibly the canine variety. The chipped door was burned at one time. The cement had more hairline fractures than Los Angeles after an earthquake. The studio was crammed on a side street where space was limited, and time hadn't quite managed to work itself out between the cracks. The tree in front sagged to the right, and the car just outside the front door had a flat tire. The billboard on the other side of the street was splattered with black spray paint.

Elrod heard what probably sounded like a gunshot, definitely not a car backfiring. A rusted-out clunker was parked on the curb with pride, next to the one with the flat. The kid on the street slapped the pavement with a stick and a grim expression.

The door was opened by a short man with an inferiority complex, based on his stance, the way he leaned against the doorjamb, and the smirk on his face. His attitude stood taller than he did. His feet were bare and so were his hands.

"What the hell are you doing here?"

"I'm the welcoming committee," Elrod said. He had on turquoise pants and a straw hat to match his slacks. He had a gun jammed in the waistband, and he wore a light coat to conceal the gun. He had one hand on his coat and one in his pocket.

"I didn't realize there was one in the area," the man said.

"One can always be gathered on short notice," Elrod said. He shoved past Thurman, slammed the door, and pinched his nostrils. "Your place smells like cat piss."

"I wasn't expecting visitors."

"Do you own a cat? Or did one just die?" The silence that ensued was louder than I-64 at rush hour. The stand-off stood taller than Thurman. "It doesn't appear you were expecting much of anything."

"How did you find me?"

"That's not important," Elrod said. "From what I hear, you managed to fuck up royally." He meant the mission, the girl on the run, and the underground cave. Not necessarily in that order.

"I didn't realize you and I were going to team up," Thurman said. He backed up several paces and preceded in the direction of what was probably the kitchen.

"We aren't," Elrod said. "You listen and do what I say. If you don't like it, I'll slit your throat right now. The pain might bring you your last moments of pleasure, or then again, it might not. You can worry about the cat piss."

Thurman pulled a beer from the fridge. It was eight o'clock in the morning. "There will be no throat slitting."

"I deal in usefulness," Elrod said. "Based on your cleaning skills, we have some work to do. You ever wonder about random acts of violence?"

Thurman popped the top and slugged the beer. Half of it passed through his mouth. "What do you want?"

"It's not a question of what I want," Elrod said. He flipped a chair around and jammed it at an angle away from the sink. A blue stain was to the right, a yellow one to the left. "It's a question of what Anthony wants. And what you haven't been able to deliver. I'm here to finish what you fucked up. You were a package deal with the fuckup."

Thurman slugged the rest of the beer. "Where did you learn to dress?"

"My tastes lean toward the eccentric." He smoothed out his coat. The hat proved more important than the coat or the pants. It was a one-of-a-kind, or so the redhead with the green eyes and loose lips told him. He took her up on an additional service or two outside her normal job description. It wasn't his first time in the women's bathroom. For good luck, he'd brought the hat along.

"Are you even sure what you're wearing could be considered tasteful?"

His pants did glow in the dark and might have been visible under black light. It was a theory he'd never tested. "Did I ask for your opinion?"

"You didn't." Thurman shrugged and flipped his bottle into the sink. "I've met you before, haven't I?"

"You were probably too drunk to remember," Elrod said.

Thurman placed both his hands on the back of the chair opposite Elrod and squeezed with authority. "I don't have a problem with drinking. But I do have a problem with you. You're the stupid bastard who almost got me killed."

Elrod sliced his index finger across his throat. He probably should have used said index finger to block out the pungent odor. "That's right. And you lost."

Thurman's eyes narrowed. "Is your name really Elrod?"

"Why? Does it matter?" he asked. "Do you have a problem with my name?"

Thurman pulled a toothpick out of his pocket and chomped down. "It just came to me, and I like to know who I'll be working with. But you might want to work on your casual attire."

"You're not going to be working with me," Elrod said. "You're going to be working for me. You might want to get used to the distinction."

Thurman paced in a circle. "I didn't realize you were the one calling the shots."

"My title was elevated once you screwed up." Elrod was forced to deal with a new level of idiot: one too stupid to know he wasn't in charge. The temper, however, could be controlled with the proper dose of uppercut.

"I didn't screw up: I just ran into a bigger problem than I realized."

"She's a woman," Elrod said. "Therefore, she's a small problem."

Thurman punched the chair on his way by. "But you haven't met this one."

"That doesn't mean I don't know her kind," Elrod said.

He'd dealt with his share of broads over the years, and a little masculinity went a long way. He oozed testosterone through his hat and coat and turquoise pants.

"What's your problem, dude?"

"I don't like idiots," Elrod said.

His hands rested on the table with the jagged edge. He had his left on top of his right, and he had his right ankle crossed over his left. He considered smacking the uneven table and breaking it in two. The potential outcome proved hazy at best.

"Who said I was an idiot?" Thurman asked.

"The first sign of stupidity is not being able to recognize it in yourself."

"I can recognize a lot of things," Thurman said, "and the last time I checked the law, I noticed that you'd be trespassing. You might want to tone down the 'tude."

Elrod pushed his lips out with his tongue. "Laws can be changed."

"Or you can always try to manipulate them."

"I don't have to manipulate them," Elrod said. "They just are. And you're out of your league."

If he had a female underground, she'd certainly stay that way. Hope a figment of her imagination.

"I wasn't aware that was an issue."

"It's not," Elrod said. He crossed his left ankle over his right and shrugged away from the table. The light overhead flickered in unison with his movements.

"What about an initial arrangement?"

"I'd prefer not to get into the details with you," Elrod said. Negotiating with an idiot only meant there were two instead of one, and he preferred rational over the irrational.

Thurman flicked the toothpick around in his mouth before the end poked out from his lips. "You owe Anthony, don't you?"

"Your mess is now loose in society, who knows where, doing who knows what. What kind of slipshod oversight is that?" Nonexistent certainly came to mind, and it had a prominent position at the forefront of his imagination. The thought seeped into his shoes.

"Like I said, I underestimated her."

"Next time don't underestimate your problems," Elrod said. At least on his resume he could check off the idiot box. It might even offer him a certain amount in disability benefits.

"I'll keep that in mind," Thurman said.

Elrod made another slicing motion across his throat. The refrigerator hiccupped in reply. "No, you won't."

Thurman looked out the window. His hands had long since removed themselves from the back of the chair. The sound of the fan in the next room filled the silence. "You know I could knock you to the floor easily, don't you?"

"You're more than welcome to try," Elrod said.

"I don't have to try." Thurman thrust his right hand at Elrod, who calmly caught the punch with his left hand, and twisted his grip counterclockwise.

In one smooth motion, he poked Thurman's Adam's apple. Thurman gasped for breath, and staggered back as far as his arm would allow. When his air passage freed itself, he covered his mouth and coughed. He bent his head down, coughing even more forcefully and erratically, bending over at the waist, his face near his belly button.

Elrod shoved the back of his head, and Thurman touched the ground, his head smacking the discolored linoleum near the blue stain before the rest of his body followed. Thurman rolled around on the floor for a full minute, before he sprang back to life.

"What the hell did you do that for?" he said.

"Now we're even."

"I didn't know you and I had an issue," Thurman said.

"We did before," Elrod said, "now we don't."

"What changed?"

"You kissed the floor."

"It's linoleum."

"It's stained," Elrod said, "and it's cracked." He didn't even mention the cat piss. The next time he'd bring Vaseline to block out the smell.

He whipped out the Heckler & Koch from behind his back. "Either we deal with your problem right now, or I'll just pull the trigger. Your choice. You have five seconds to decide." He slid back his coat sleeve and looked at his watch.

CHAPTER 15

Pete had managed to distract her long enough to put the handcuffs on himself, and he'd managed to keep it loose enough that he could easily break out of it. She hadn't noticed, or she hadn't cared. Based on what he had learned so far, it was the former, not the latter. He had to wait for her to nod off, and he couldn't look too overeager, otherwise she might discover his ruse, and he'd have to start all over again. Probably with a lump on his head for his trouble. Her temper flared faster than a Corvette, her skin still singed from her high school days.

She'd pointed the gun at him on multiple occasions and for random intervals—he could accept that, although he would have preferred not to. She'd handcuffed him to both the steering wheel and the door handle—these were in reverse order. She showed signs of her temper when dealing with the front desk clerk, but mostly with him and the gun jammed against his lower back—and he still couldn't figure out how to get rid of her without the gun going off somewhere near his forehead. The moral dilemma slammed home with authority, not unlike his female counterpart who had an attitude bigger than she was.

He'd probably been a masochist in his former life, but this was more entertainment than he'd had in the past two years. She was rather attractive, when the horns retracted, although at this point, he had to just imagine her without the accessory, since he'd never seen her let her guard down. For the brief instances that she did, the horns only retracted halfway. As for the key, he had no idea where she'd put it, and he had to make the leap that he could find it without arising suspicion. He had to hope, otherwise he had nothing to sustain him but handcuffs and pee breaks, the latter of which filled his bladder more often than he wanted to admit. The threat of being separated from the toilet managed to interrupt his flow.

She hadn't left him alone for five minutes. He even peed with the bathroom door open. And he had a hard enough time taking a leak when there was a guy in the stall next to him, standing tall and crowding his personal space. Luckily, he was able to turn his back to her, concentrate on the sound of the ocean, and the stream eventually came after a reasonable delay. The delayed response continued to interrupt his thoughts. He couldn't change that fact; ultimately, he'd just have to accept it, along with the consequences. Not the handcuffs, though, those were personal. She hadn't smiled once. Laughing was definitely out of the question.

She hadn't made a sound in the past fifteen minutes, most of which was spent on the bed, but that didn't mean she was asleep. Just because it was dark out—he was beginning to show the first signs of fatigue, although it had been hard to sleep since he'd been handcuffed to the air conditioning unit that continued to hum in his ear and spew cold air at the back of his skull—didn't mean he had the night all to himself. She'd turned the window unit on high before she settled in for the night, dropping like an anchor atop the full sized bed in flannel sleepwear that covered her from head to toe. He had managed to move the setting lower, but he didn't turn it off completely. The choice of hotel was his, cockroaches and mystery stains and threadbare chair, and he was forced to live with the consequences. The handcuffs hadn't been particularly necessary, but he knew she took great pride in their continued existence. She had done it on purpose—the handcuffing—just because she could. Her anger continued to reach new heights. Despite his penchant to do so, he hadn't uttered a single protest.

From the moment he'd met her, she had never managed to give up control. Not even for an instant. Maybe that was why she didn't smile, or maybe it was more along the lines of she couldn't smile. Despite his best efforts to show her otherwise, she took great pride in complicating his life by a factor of ten. She weighed in with her mouth, opinions, and superior attitude. An air of superiority she hadn't had when she walked the Port City High halls in fine leather attire and high heels.

He tried peering up at her from his position on the floor, and all he saw was her outline. The curves still managed to turn him on, even though her flannel outfit was two sizes too large. Near as he could tell, that was why she had turned the heat up. When he'd asked her what she wore underneath her clothes, she stared at him, shook her head, and turned her back on him, without even uttering a word. His imagination ran wild, and he took off at breakneck speed just to keep up. In most instances, he couldn't control it. Not that he wanted to.

He'd noticed the gun sitting next to her on the nightstand. A dilapidated piece of garbage that had probably been picked up at the local Wal-Mart and hadn't been replaced since the building was built. Maybe it had come with the floor, nailed to the concrete, with whatever nails could penetrate cement. And then they'd tossed a plaid carpet over it. That was probably original as well. The stain, however, was more recent. No padding underneath. At least that's what his butt told him. He tried his best to ignore the protests, despite their ever-increasing intensity. His butt had gone numb a half hour ago, and he'd been on the floor for almost an hour. She'd shoved him to the ground, used the same set of handcuffs she'd been using all along, the most impractical ones she could find. He might very well die with a bullet from his own gun, as he remained chained to an air conditioning unit that screamed at the top of its lungs. Even if he decided to yell, it wasn't worth the added complication. She'd probably whack him with the remote that was chained to the bureau.

Maybe that was why she was restless on the bed. It was certainly why he couldn't sleep. Or maybe it had to do with the numbness that slowly seeped its way north. If his back stiffened, then he'd have a hard night's sleep. He had enough trouble sleeping without introducing new elements like plaid carpet stapled to concrete.

Just because he could, he dragged his handcuffs against the plastic air conditioning contraption to help loosen his spirits. The sound resembled a ball and chain being dragged across asphalt. He waited. From above there wasn't even the hint of stirring. Maybe she had finally fallen asleep.

Under normal circumstances, he had trouble falling asleep, and even when he did, he had trouble remaining down for long. Probably post-traumatic stress disorder. Not that he had ever been properly diagnosed. He didn't trust military doctors, or military shrinks. And so he had avoided them, even though his doctors had recommended the therapy. Pushed hard for it. That's when he'd managed to find the bottle. He'd found it earlier, but he increased his consumption, and increased his number of visits to The Wet Rhino. Opportunities that he couldn't afford to pass up. Although most nights he managed to pass out.

When he didn't find his car, he managed to increase his chances of passing out in parking lots. The puking was often an added bonus. That was why he always had a spare around. Neither one of them was worth a darn, at least as far as cars went, but he didn't have the heart to trade up.

As his drinking increased, replacements proved harder to come by. Jack Daniels and Jim Beam devoured all of his disposable income. He even managed to keep a couple of bottles in the freezer, on a strictly probational basis. Not that he was complaining. More than anything else, he remained intrigued. Even though he craved the good stuff now, he'd do without. And his body would go through some level of withdrawal, as more sleepless nights followed.

Focusing on his needs, he'd push through the extraneous symptoms. Including the handcuffs he had currently slipped off his right wrist.

CHAPTER 16

The bed stirred, and so did Veronica. "If you touch that gun, I'll kill you."

He had tiptoed toward the bed, across the stapled carpet, his hand mere inches over the cold, hard steel. "What?"

"I've managed to take a few self-defense classes."

His eyes had adjusted to the dark, and he could just make out her shape as it slid toward him, the serpent seeking her poison. His hand stood steadfast in its position. "You're not in a position to negotiate."

She flipped on the light, and her hand plunged down toward the gun. "Neither are you."

The light assaulted his eyes, and he stepped back out of the line of fire. Covering his eyes, he stared at her, and she stared back at him. Neither blinked. She shifted first, curling her legs back behind her, the sheets rustling beneath her.

He trained his eye on the semiautomatic. The craving resembled a stiff drink placed before him, just out of his reach. Thoughts of escape flittered through his mind: diving toward the door was always an option, overpowering Veronica was another one, and biding his time until he could make a clean break entered his mind.

His breathing turned erratic and shallow, skipping forward faster than a clock with a faulty minute hand.

Footsteps shuffled along the hallway. The same set of footsteps he had heard a moment ago, pacing back and forth, before stopping just outside the door. The sound echoed louder than a giant fan in a wind tunnel.

Pete held up a hand. "Did you hear that?"

"What?"

"The scraping outside the door."

The sound resembled a dog clawing at wood, or a knife on a chalkboard. Based on the intensity of the sound, the door was thin, not as heavy as it had first appeared. He had miscalculated his surroundings, and diving was no longer an option.

"We're on the second story," she said.

"That doesn't mean anything."

"You need to work on your accommodations."

"I wanted a quick escape," he said. "Besides, you could have continued with your better-case scenarios. The string of chain hotels with no vacancies."

"You don't care about the noisy air conditioner?" Veronica asked.

"I care about whoever's on the other side of our door."

Before she could open her mouth to protest, as he was sure she was about to do, the door burst open. The flimsiness wasn't just his imagination. The door gave way beneath the heel of the large boot that smashed through the ancient wood, softened by age as well as humidity, time, and rot.

The crash pulsated throughout the room louder than a strobe light set to autopilot.

He yanked her to the other side of the bed, away from the door, as shots tore through the vast expanse separating them from freedom. She opened her mouth, and he slapped his hand over it. He could see the anger in her eyes, but he didn't care. What he cared about was getting both of them to safety, and if that meant keeping her mouth shut—as her eyes glistened with hurt, confusion, and rage—that's exactly what he'd do. She could give him hell later, as he knew she would. But at least their chances for survival significantly increased. If she happened to spew forth anger like an open wound, at least it meant they were both still alive.

He pinned her against the wall, his arm covering the tops of her shoulders, his hand reaching for the weapon. She shook her head once. He nodded and implemented his stern look, and she finally relented with a soft sigh.

The bed exploded as more shots ensued. Stuffing, padding, and dilapidated pillows filled the air. He ducked lower and pulled her down with him. Smoke and residue blocked his vision and battered his nostrils, the explosions deafening, and the taste of metal struck his mouth.

When the bullets subsided, he fired three shots and heard a grunt. He coughed, transferring his hand from Veronica's mouth to his own. Stuffing and cheap plaster disintegrated around him, confetti dropped down on his head. The nightstand, though, was virtually untouched. But it had already seen more than enough scuff marks, scrapes, and cigarette burns to warrant some sort of medal.

He fired another shot in the direction of the door. This time no reply answered him. The lull on a temporary respite. He counted to four in his head, grabbed Veronica's arm, and crab walked with her around the bed. He fired more shots as he went—he had lost count—until he heard the click, the empty sound the only sound he heard, before he dove toward the pockmarked door, dragging Veronica along for the ride. The crash was an explosion to his senses, as he surprised the two men on the other side and knocked them both to the ground. Kicking their guns away, he tightened his grip on Veronica's arm, despite her openmouthed snarl and a protest that dissipated before it reached the rest of the world.

Before she, or the hired guns, could react, he crashed through the stairwell door and shoved her down the stairs—the stairway only two doors down on the opposite side. Just as he crossed the threshold, a bullet tore into his shoulder, exiting the other side. A clean exit, before the pain registered and ratcheted down his right arm. The metallic taste burst forth and nearly swallowed him whole. He didn't bother to scream, the sound dying on his lips and dissipating from his harried existence. He bit down on his tongue instead, not hard enough to draw blood, but hard enough to keep the screaming at bay. He closed his eyes for just a moment, as he shoved her down the final two steps, her body stiffening from his grasp, or the gunfire.

He dashed for his car, as more bullets and bodies riddled the stairwell. *Veronica has a lot of explaining to do.*

"What about my credit card?" she asked.

CHAPTER 17

He started the car and slammed on the gas, peeling out of the parking lot at a high rate of speed, tires squealing as he yanked the wheel to the left before jerking the car back to the right, nearly sideswiping a Buick and then an Oldsmobile. The sound of gunshots lingered in the late evening, stirring up dust, debris, and cheap perfume. The wound in his right shoulder lingered, reminding him of what could have been.

Throughout the ordeal, Veronica had remained calm, other than the hand he had placed over her open mouth, as though she expected a confrontation and had idly waited for the aftermath, aside from the bullets and the bed. Her voice hadn't hitched or shimmied, and when he emptied his last bullet into the door before he dove through, she hadn't screamed, or cried out, or even mumbled. Her last comment focused on her rather primitive financial situation and potential cleaning bill.

"You mind telling me what the hell is going on?" Pete said.

"You're shot."

"I know. I felt the bullet enter my shoulder." He didn't bring up the exit wound, nor did he feel the need to explain that he had prevented said bullet from entering her body, pounding through the splintered wood so she didn't have to. Overstating the obvious only led to headaches and shortened conversations.

"It appears to have exited as well." Veronica paused. "Where did you learn to shoot like that? And since when do you go diving through doors and pounding down stairs? If you hadn't yanked me through, I'd still be standing there with my mouth hanging open."

Mentioning the fact that she'd depart this world for the next probably wasn't the best way to gain her trust. Not that she'd trust him anyway. Not after he'd propelled himself through the halls broadcasting her little excursion on the fifty-yard line with the offensive tackle, a jock with no more than two brain cells to his name. Since it was her word against his, he sullied her reputation in a single bound, and nearly ended up suspended for his effort.

"There are a lot of things you don't know about me." He might have only gotten drunker as the years wore on, but the army managed to turn his life around. The field of battle hardened him from the outside in, and he stomped his way through college, even if he only put forth the minimum amount of effort. He'd always excelled at school. It was the peer pressure that helped him toward a path of destruction. Or maybe it was the girls. It was easy to blame the ones in skirts and tank tops with legs longer than a flagpole.

"Maybe we should start with what you've done since high school," she said.

At least Smith & Wesson wasn't pointed in his direction. And for whatever reason, she appeared genuinely interested. In his experience, though, that could change rather quickly. Her mood stormed out quicker than the tide. "I was a soldier in Iraq."

"With the army?"

He nodded. His eyes never left the road, and his heart beat rapidly, although it wasn't from the increase in adrenaline. His breath stuttered in his chest, and the world turned a shade of gray. "Why?"

She turned her gaze away from the side of his face. "Have you ever been shot before?"

"No," Pete said. "But I've been shot at." Watching Stuart die, though, had been worse. Much worse. The wound still hurt like a mother—both the present one and the past—but the pain had started to subside, if ever so slightly. His lips curled, and his grip tightened on the steering column. *Ten and two, ten and two.*

It had been ten of two when Stuart died. The sun piled high in the sky, the men tossed in ditches and corners of the field, the sand dunes and rocks providing shelter. But not enough. Never enough. A sand dune exploded in front of him. Another man went down, his legs separated from the rest of his body, the scream echoing through Pete's consciousness and through his bones. His hands shook on either side of him, and still the men marched onward—both his and the enemy. A village had stood in the distance, rising up out of the oasis.

He blinked, blocking away the rest of the images that immediately came to mind. His mind jumped and skipped like a fractured disc, the picture a haze of solitude.

"Do you still have the gun?" she asked.

"I do." He was anything but an amateur. Not the slightest bit immature, even if it had taken him a while to get there. Multiple women over multiple years had made the process more difficult, turned a simple process into a more elaborate one. The posers, the hypocrites, and the miscreants were nothing if not sure of the trouble. He had his mother to thank for his misguided ways, most of which had seen him just short of the metal bars.

"Good," she said. "Because I'm sure we'll need it again."

"I don't think those guys are finished with you yet."

She turned her head away from him and stared out the window. Both trees and time passed, but not in equal measure. The wind howled, and his stomach rumbled.

"What if I'm finished with them?" Veronica said. Her voice lacked tone and emotion, even though it shook slightly.

"I'm not sure you get a say in the matter."

"I want an equal say," she said. "I deserve an equal say."

"I'm sure you do, or at least you think you do…" His voice trailed off, his thoughts scattered like the wind.

He had driven them in a mostly westward direction toward Richmond on US-60. The traffic remained relatively non-existent, the conversation the same but filled with pockets of consciousness. Along with the wind, the sound of the engine filled the moments of silence when those moments presented themselves.

"What is the point?" she asked.

He had stuffed the gun in the back of his pants, just in case she decided to point it at him again. Jammed against his lower back, the gun poked his spine. He shifted in his seat, from the gun not the silence. He didn't want her adrenaline overriding the situation like a Trojan horse claiming the castle. The sound of her steady breathing coincided with the roar of the engine. The two sounds competed for supremacy. "Why were those guys shooting at you?" he asked.

She lifted her shoulders. "I'm just an accountant."

"I know," he said. "You've already told me. And that doesn't really tell me much of anything. Maybe you should give me a few more details about what you do, you know since high school. If you want my help, at some point you're going to have to trust me."

She stared hard at his right cheek. "Why should I?"

"Because I was shot saving your life," Pete said.

"You were shot," she said, "because you finally showed the first signs of chivalry. If you're looking for a medal, you're not going to find it here."

He bit down on his lower lip hard enough to cause a jolt of pain. "I'm sure it was just instinct, and I'm sure it won't happen again."

"Maybe you have a few nice bones in your body, and maybe one day they'll take over, if the alcohol doesn't consume you first. Jim Beam doesn't have all the answers, Captain Obvious."

"Who said anything about the alcohol consuming me?"

"You want a drink," she said. "Don't deny it. Whatever you may think of me, I'm certainly smarter than you realize."

"I don't doubt your intelligence," he said. "But if you

have guys chasing after you, it wasn't smart to use your credit card. You might as well have painted a sign on your forehead that said: *chase me*. It would've been faster."

She ground her teeth. "I didn't think they'd find me so quickly. I planned on being gone in the morning."

Without him. That was the part left unsaid. The voice in his head said walk, or preferably run, to the nearest exit ramp and hightail it across the border. West Virginia, after all, didn't sound so bad. He'd dealt with worse. "And when did you plan to tell me this?"

"I assumed it was fairly obvious."

Flipping on his blinker, he took the exit ramp, found the nearest parking lot, and pulled in. Gravel kicked up beneath his wheels. He flipped off the engine, yanked the key from the ignition, and jerked the door open.

"Why are we stopping here?" she asked. "You're bleeding all over yourself."

She could have passed for Captain Obvious. "It's not like I have a choice in the matter."

"Maybe we should take you to a hospital."

"I'm not sure that's a good idea." He exited the vehicle and so did she. "There's a chance that your friends in high places might be able to spot us. Hospital records leave a trail."

Her teeth clicked. "Just how paranoid are you?"

He stretched and dipped his back, blood seeped through his shirt. "Maybe not paranoid enough," Pete said. "Or compared to you, I'm way over the line." He smirked. "But then again, I'm not the one who paid for our room with a credit card."

"Just how long are you going to continue to drive that one home?"

He marched toward the glass doors and freedom. "Until you start to listen to me."

"I'm not sure that's going to happen either."

CHAPTER 18

The store was a multipurpose one filled with all his basic needs from drinks to hunting supplies. Blood dribbled to the floor, splashed outward in bright red dots, and stained the off-white tile. Two security cameras winked at him from either side of the store, and an old man turned his eyes up in surprise before maneuvering away from him.

The shelves were stocked full and lined deep. The possibilities proved endless. The coffee machine had sprung a leak.

He staggered up and down aisles gathering supplies: hydrogen peroxide, rubbing alcohol, gauze, tape, a bottle of Johnnie Walker Blue, a bottle of pain pills, and Celox. The Celox proved harder to find than the other items combined, the plastic packet hidden on a bottom shelf in the middle of an aisle.

The clerk popped a wad of bubble gum and had an earring in his right ear. His long hair concealed his eyes. "You're bleeding all over my floor, man."

Pete shoved a handful of bills across the counter, saluted, grabbed his supplies, minus the plastic bag, and stumbled around the corner to the men's restroom. The redhead didn't even look up from her phone, even though he brushed her left shoulder as he powered past.

He took stock of himself in the mirror—hair disheveled, shirt torn, and shoulder exposed, eyes red rimmed and black under the bottom edges, pants crinkled, a knot on his forehead—and a breath escaped his lips, the odor from his mouth smelling like day old milk left out in the sun. The diagonal crack in the mirror distorted his view even further.

He dumped his purchases on the metal shelf above the sink, the shelf water stained and water logged. He spun the top of the bottle of Johnnie Walker, the back of his mouth suffering through a long swallow and added a second one for good measure before he set the bottle aside. He removed his shirt and stared at blood, broken skin, and shattered tissue, both front and back.

He poured rubbing alcohol over the wound and cursed, his mouth forming a large O. He gripped the metal bar and nearly yanked it from the wall. For good measure, he offered up a string of curse words at Veronica, whom he'd asked for help, before she nearly fainted in his presence. She had stuck her hand out before she pulled it back, and her mouth was a grim line. She was probably primping in the women's bathroom, or seething in the passenger seat of the Corolla. Not driving, though, since he had the keys with him. At least he'd been smart enough to keep them on his person, and she hadn't bothered to ask, once he'd headed toward freedom, or in this case, pain.

He took several shattered breaths, the shallowness surprising even him, and then he dumped the hydrogen peroxide on top of the rubbing alcohol and the wound. The curse words flowed freely again this time, but the number proved less than before. He gripped the metal bar again, but with much less authority. Convinced the wound was now clean, Pete dabbed at it with a gauze pad. To control the bleeding and aid clotting, he tore open the packet of Celox and poured it on the ripped flesh.

He shoved a handful of pain pills into his mouth, cursing himself for not swigging the pain pills and whiskey in one motion. The pain pills went down easy enough with another swig from the bottle. He'd probably read somewhere about not mixing alcohol and pills, and about it being a good way to overdose, or to speed the process along, but he couldn't recall where.

He slapped on two gauze pads—one front, one back—along with plenty of tape to hold the gauze in place. He tossed his trash in the proper receptacle, maneuvered his shirt into place, grabbed his supplies along with the booze, and headed out the door, unsure what was in store for him next. But he was fairly certain he probably wouldn't like it.

℮∽℮∽

He had finally started driving again. After the alcohol—tossed on the floor of the backseat—and the patched shoulder, the abrasion still throbbed but less so than before. With little to no traffic, he punched the gas. Silence filled the Corolla, as his eyes, and hers, stared straight ahead. Her mouth opened once but no sound escaped.

He had an empty gun with no bullets, which they would need more of soon—also tossed on the floor after one too many jabs to his spine—a pair of goons after her, and now he was caught in her web of deceit and lies. He'd acquired a new shirt, which he hadn't bothered to put on, deciding the old one worked just fine for now. Not a permanent fix, necessarily, but the temporary fix would have to do.

He continued on through the silence in a mostly west-ward direction toward Richmond, and possibly beyond, with no real plan in mind other than to keep running, to keep one chess move ahead of the competition, who might have been two nitwits, or who might have been smarter than him or her. He had no idea really, other than the growing suspicion in his gut, and the dull ache in his arm and shoulder.

"By the way," she said, "I need new handcuffs."

That didn't surprise him. Nothing she said about tying him up, or tying him down, surprised him. At least the multipurpose store didn't have handcuffs. Small favor, indeed, but still it was there. "Can't trust me?" he asked.

No reply, however, was forthcoming from her side of the arena.

"One too many crazy encounters?" When she didn't reply, he added, "Maybe you should learn to trust more often."

"Maybe you should learn to keep your mouth shut," Veronica said, "instead of opening it up for every random thought that enters your head."

He'd been the same way in high school. He didn't like silence, or first dates. He filled the void with questions,

and when the other party wasn't forthcoming with answers he filled in with a few of his own. Alcohol helped
the gaps become less prominent, and Johnnie Walker
Blue aided in the transformation process. Not so much,
though, with the rehabilitating.

"Have you managed to come up with a destination
yet?" he asked.

"I thought that was your job."

She'd been the same way in high school. Defiant. A
not-so-subtle fuck you to the world. That's why he had
wanted to put her in her place. It hadn't been her on the
fifty-yard line, but it was easy enough to imagine her
with her legs spread, her pants pulled down to her ankles,
and her head turned up to the sky. Over the years, he'd
managed to convince himself it was her, that he had seen
her, truly seen her for what she really was, and that left
tackle with the desk-sized chest had no idea what she was
truly capable of.

Being with her reminded him of all he hated about
Port City High, from arrogant teachers to arrogant students. He'd failed at football, failed at baseball, and barely made the track team. He had a gift for hurdles, bounding over the obstacles life slammed into his path, developing his style and technique with practice and precision.
When he discovered alcohol, though, the hurdles became
less important, and so did the girls.

The engine roared above the silence. In order to break
up the monotony, he flipped the radio on, more as background noise, as a way to take his mind off the fact that
he had just been shot. For an entire song and a half, rock
music filled the car from bands he had never heard of, the
guitar cutting through the bridge and the chorus.

With her, it was hard to tell where the lies ended and the truth began. Maybe it was all a pocket filled with lies, a room filled with smoke and stuffing, similar to the motel. His focus and determination faded, as a gray haze filled the horizon.

She flipped off the radio. "What the hell's the matter with you?"

"I think we should head to Charlottesville."

A string of trees flew by and might have even agreed to his proposition. A small town appeared ahead with stoplights and speed limit signs and half-improved buildings, more than one fast food joint and convenience store entered the equation.

"And why should we do that?"

"Because it's better than sticking around the Richmond area," he said.

She stared straight ahead and then flipped her head around and glared at him. "Why?"

"Because it's farther away."

She crossed her arms over her chest and huffed. "You really are a bastard."

His knuckles gripped the steering wheel hard enough to turn them white. "I believe that's already been said before. Try and keep up." Pete paused. "I seem to recall the same arrogance and high maintenance attitude in high school. If I had to guess, I'd say you walked in high heels before you lost them, based on how you lean your torso slightly forward, and the torn skirt and blouse probably came from specialty shops before the grit and grime took hold."

She clenched her teeth. "It was tailored."

"Close enough," Pete said. "And it was probably dry cleaned just before you wore it."

Her hand pushed at the dashboard. "The time before."

"Close enough."

He liked driving, enough that he didn't need a particular destination, just an open road and an open wheel, and small towns and empty woods to provide a bit of a background. Better companions helped pass the time, but nothing was ever perfect in his life. Not even close.

"What's your point?" she asked.

"You're a real piece of work," Pete said. "You're high maintenance with a capital HI, and you're only going to get worse the longer I hang around you."

His mind drifted to the army where he had enough soldiers behind him to start a battalion. The men lined up like lemmings, the same with the opposition. Men shouted orders, commands really, the alleyway provided shelter, as snipers fired overhead. Targets were acquired and locked, and all he could do was shake his head.

"We need to stop at an ATM," he said. There was no reply from her side. "We need cash and credit cards can be tracked."

Her head flipped to the right, as she stared out the window. "I don't need cash."

"You're the accountant," he said. He meant the one with the money. "Besides, I'm just going along for the ride on this crazy train."

She shuddered. "I've never had to run before. At least not for my life. And I was locked away in some dungeon built around the time of World War I." She paused. "You can track a person through ATM transactions. There's software that would pinpoint my exact location at the time of the transaction."

"Correct. But at least it provides us a layer of security that credit cards don't."

Her voice was a thin line. "My purchases are insured, except for a fifty-dollar initial fee."

Pete blew out a breath. "This isn't about keeping your accounts in balance. If you don't start thinking creatively, you and I will be dead before the next sundown."

Western music before a standoff entered his mind.

"You're a bit overdramatic."

"You should really consider all the consequences of your monetary actions, not just the ones that are most convenient for you. Besides, you're going to need some new clothes."

"You mean you don't like my flannel outfit?" She paused. "They're yours, you know."

"I happen to like them just fine," he said.

CHAPTER 19

Music had helped him reach Charlottesville. Veronica had flipped the radio on low with a flick of her wrist. He had welcomed the pop-rock music combination, the former Mouseketeers, the hard drinking and the hard living—the rock stars, not him—as he attempted to move himself to what he hoped was a safer area. She was merely along for the ride, although her mouth would have told him otherwise.

Deserted streets clamored in front of him, uneven sidewalks provided a road map or a destination. Charlottesville, the quintessential college town, had more of a small town feel with bigger town dreams. The homes were older versus more modern. Most of the town was set off I-64, with very little, if any of it visible from the interstate. The town had the feel of money, yet it resembled more old money than new. What was the downtown area had businesses and shopping and cobblestone streets and pedestrian walkways, with the residences set away from the promenade of folks that must have passed through on a daily basis.

Finding a hotel was easy, this one a bit more upscale than the last. Had it been any worse, he would have uttered his own form of protest, especially since he was relegated to the floor once again, this time minus the rats. He didn't have handcuffs around his wrists—those were left behind at the last stop and Veronica hadn't bothered to reload—and he didn't have a gun pointed at his head—since it was out of bullets and still on the floor of the backseat. Progress was alive and well. And he didn't even have to drive to reach it.

Before he settled in for the night, he found supplies at a superstore: bullets, Neosporin, and a tube of superglue. Because Veronica had still refused to help, he had checked the wound himself, after disposing of the used gauze and tape, poured more rubbing alcohol and hydrogen peroxide on the abrasion, dabbed Neosporin on the cut, and finished it off with a layer of superglue and more gauze and tape. His right hand was steady, his left less so, as pain hovered just beneath the surface. Conducting the operation in the bathroom, he avoided any strange looks from his partner. As for what the future held, he still had no idea, and he didn't plan to make any great discoveries before the sun officially came up.

Stepping past the tile and beyond the threshold, he finished off his concoction with another handful of pills and more Johnnie Walker Blue, a third of the bottle now deposited in his stomach lining.

The room held more promise than the one before it: the air conditioner hummed more than it hiccupped, the TV was less than two years old, the nightstand had only two minor scuff marks instead of an assembly that had been slathered on over a period of months and years, and the chair and ottoman actually matched. The front desk clerk hadn't swallowed a basketball, and the computer in the lobby resembled a more recent desktop.

Even with his pillow, the chair and ottoman hadn't been as comfortable as they first appeared. Maybe it was because he couldn't put the images in his head to bed, and instead of sleeping, all he did was switch positions for most of the evening.

She still had the same attitude she had in high school. Driven to succeed, to shove past all objects that stood in her way, to bulldoze her way through and over people, and he was the one currently caught in the crossfire. If he were smart, he would have left before. But he no longer had the car keys, and he had one other problem. A not so little one: He still had feelings for her.

He shook her. "It's time for breakfast."

She rubbed her eyes, rolled over, and looked at the clock and then rolled back to her original spot. "It's not even six o'clock yet."

He shook her again. She tossed a pillow at him and used the other one to cover her head. He picked the pillow up off the floor and tossed it at her head. "We need to get a head start on our competition."

"What?" the pillow said.

"They're going to come after us again. And you need a change of clothes."

She moved the pillow away from her head and glared at him. "I'd say that's pretty much a given. And this time we need to be ready for them."

"How do you suggest we do that?"

"A change of clothes and breakfast for a start."

He clenched and unclenched his right hand. The air conditioner hummed louder than a freight engine. She stood up and stretched, the shirt rising several inches, the tussling of her hair merely served as bonus material. He looked away, and when he looked back, she had a smirk plastered on her face. He heard the bathroom door close, and he heard the shower run. Twenty minutes later, she emerged.

"You're not wearing the same underwear, are you?"

She glared past him and shoved him out the door, slamming it behind her, her feet jammed against the pavement, the silence louder than the freight engine and the air conditioner. She tossed him the keys without a word, and he slid behind the wheel, as power returned to his callused hands. He had control over this situation, right now, and not much else.

Not even over her.

After he had driven for a couple of miles, he asked, "Food or clothes?"

"Isn't that a twenty-four hour diner?"

Elvis's Diner was a relic of the fifties. It was run by a man not named Elvis and who bore no resemblance to him. He was a short, blond man with a soft attitude and a little soft around the middle. He had a firm handshake and a warm smile. The menus were built with thick cardboard, and the parking lot only had three other cars, the diner more crowded than the parking lot. The waitresses were covered in pink and green and orange.

Pies were stacked in the fridge above the counter on four shelves. Thirteen in all. The booths were either neon pink, purple, green, or blue. And there was a contingent

of eight tables in the middle. Because of the hour, most of
the tables and booths were empty. In fact, except for a
contingent of college students—who had their computers
popped up, staring at their screens, with what was most
likely mugs of coffee sitting next to them and a smattering of pancakes on a plate stuffed among them that had
hardly been touched—the diner was otherwise empty.
Steam permeated from the plate, rising up toward the
rafters. A jukebox sat near the front entrance, and Elvis
sang in the background, one of his earlier hits, although
Pete couldn't recall the name. The waitresses wore long
flowing dresses with their hair pulled back in ponytails.
There were two of them, both looked about the same age
as the college students, and both were blondes. One had
blue eyes, the other green. Various records covered the
walls, which mixed well with the artwork. Caricatures of
Elvis in his prime permeated the space, with a few photos
added for good measure, and two concert shots. There
were six photos in all. Pete started to count the number of
records in the jukebox, and then he stopped. He headed
for a booth near the side entrance, on the opposite side
from the college students, the five of whom appeared en-
tranced by whatever was available to them on their
screens, as their hands danced over the keys in unison,
probably working on the latest term paper, or summer
project.

Veronica sat across from him, her eyes much heavier
than his own. She scanned a menu, peering at him with a
level of hatred that he had come to know and love. He
wouldn't have expected anything less from her. Based on
his experience, and the pie's prominent position in the
display case, it was probably better than anything else on

the menu, although he did have his eye on the lumberjack breakfast: three eggs, ham, two sausage links, hash browns, and a bottomless cup of coffee. In fact, because he knew Veronica would glare at him as he savored every morsel, he decided to make that his top priority. Then he'd worry about the pie. He'd gravitate toward one with chocolate and peanut butter and hope it had more than a smattering of caramel or butterscotch.

As he scanned the menu again, he knew exactly what she would order: a fruit and yogurt cup. It wasn't even relegated to the main part of the menu. Instead, it was listed as a possible side, and it was demoted to the bottom of the list. Right where it belonged.

The waitress—her name tag said Tammy—and the taller of the two blondes took Veronica's order and his. He received the steady glare when he placed his order, but he had been wrong on hers: She ordered the oatmeal with nuts and hot tea. Although he could have easily made some comment about the nuts, he chose to let it slide. At least for the time being.

The hot tea came, followed by the coffee and break-fast, followed by more tea and coffee. He dumped hot sauce all over his hash browns and sipped from his second cup. The blonde waitress had eyed him with a bit more than curiosity, and the caffeine started his motor running. He shoved back some hash browns, followed by some egg, sausage, and trailed that with a sliver of ham.

She dipped her spoon in the oatmeal and nuts, lifted it, blew, and took a tentative bite. "I hope you have a heart attack."

CHAPTER 20

Elrod sat on Thurman's couch. He had slept last night with neither a pillow nor a blanket, drifting off in a matter of minutes, the pain in his arm temporarily forgotten. But he did continue to think about his hat. He had molded that hat over a period of years, and it fit his head perfectly. He'd tried on more than fifty hats to get the one with just the right fit, and he had wanted a hat that would help him stand out, a calling card. A unique structure for his head. In both regards, it worked perfectly, and now it had two holes that weren't easily repaired. He had tossed it in the Dumpster after a string of expletives followed by a string of silence. Thurman, at his side, had not uttered a single syllable.

Now, Elrod stared across the small expanse in a semi-cramped space at a man with a semi-cramped attitude who had neither the time nor the inclination to perfect the job properly. If it hadn't been for the idiot sitting across from him, the whole situation could have been resolved in a rather effective and efficient manner. And then there was the matter of the cat piss smell. While it hadn't entered his subconscious or his dreams, it was at the fore-front of his every rational thought now. If he were smart-er about it, he would have decided on a hotel. But he didn't like frivolous purchases and extraneous expenses, and the bastard with the bastard apartment owed him one.

"I can't believe that reprobate shot my hat," Elrod said.

"It actually improves the look. You might want to think about putting holes in your other ones."

Elrod pulled a cigarette out of his shirt pocket, the lighter from his pants pocket, and lit up. "It's one of a kind."

"Indeed it is," Thurman said.

The idiot sitting across from him in a chair that was larger than he was had no idea what the right hat could do for a man. It held a debonair quality, the hat and him. The two were intertwined. "What do you think the boss will say?"

"About your hat?"

"No." Elrod sucked in nicotine and broken dreams and exhaled promise. "About the fact that the two of them got away." He flicked ash on the coffee table and pointed at his compatriot. "You ushered them off the stage." He paused. "What did he say the first time?"

Thurman dropped his hands on the table.

"He wasn't happy, was he? He's going to be even less happy this time. You've screwed yourself twice, me once, and I wouldn't be surprised if you screw yourself again."

"How could you let him get away?" Thurman asked. "And don't try to tell me you were focused on your hat."

"I wasn't." Another puff, another set of ashes on the table. Elrod leaned back. "I was focused on trying to nail him between the eyes. But it didn't quite work out the way I'd planned."

"I thought you were the sharpshooter."

Elrod's eyes blazed, and so did the cigarette. "I thought you were going to keep them contained."

Thurman shrugged. "I guess we both messed up."

Elrod finished off his first cigarette and decided against another. He snubbed it out on the table and laced his fingers behind his head. He waited for two beats, and he waited for two more. "That front desk clerk will probably remember our faces," he said. "Did you think about that possibility?"

"Should we go back and kill him?"

Elrod shrugged. "I'm not sure he's worth the trouble. He'll probably be too scared to remember much of anything. You tied him up, didn't you?" He paused. "Don't tell me you screwed that part up, too."

"Of course, I tied him up," Thurman said. "What kind of an idiot do you take me for?"

Elrod adjusted his hands from behind his head, shrugged, and placed his hands on either side of the couch. "The world has all kinds."

The muscle on Thurman's right cheek jumped. "You're a bigger bastard than I am."

"Only when it comes to botched jobs," Elrod said. He didn't make a habit out of losing. When he needed to, he could rectify situations in a hurry. Cleaning up was often more therapeutic than the act itself. It gave him time to reflect on any number of his successes. OxiClean and Mr. Clean were his products of choice.

"And now they've gotten away."

"At least for now," Elrod said. "But if we found them once, we'll find them again. And we're not going to be so forgiving the next time." He removed another cigarette from the pack and lit up. He decided he needed another rush of nicotine, after all.

Thurman headed in the direction of the kitchen; Elrod sucked and puffed and flicked more ash on the table and thought about a new plan. He had underestimated his adversary the first time, but he wouldn't let it happen again. He had taken a not-so-subtle approach with Thurman and his hamster-sized brain leading the charge. Maybe there was a better way to get what he needed and achieve the same result, without getting another hat shot in the process.

With glass in hand, Thurman returned and dropped back down in the oversized chair, with an attitude that was much bigger than he was. He took a swig from his glass. "One of us needs to call the boss, and I don't think it should be me."

"Fine," Elrod said. "We'll draw straws." He dropped his spent cigarette on the table and headed to the kitchen to make the arrangements. With straws in hand, he returned, and offered Thurman his choice in the matter.

Like it or not, Thurman drew the short straw. Elrod winked at his idiot companion.

CHAPTER 21

Anthony wanted some goddamn explanations. What he had was a pounding head and a racing heart. And it was only bound to get worse. He'd paced for the past half-hour, weaving concentric circles in the carpet. The plush strands tickled his bare feet, the view not as dynamic as he had hoped it would be. The tension in his left arm flowed from his fingertips to his shoulder blade. He clenched and unclenched his fist, tapping the wall on every turn, the taps coming faster and harder. The tapping increased, but his hand didn't go through the glass. At least he had spared himself that embarrassment. If Bethany were in this early, he would have gotten a blowjob. The mouth on her was definitely a force to be reckoned with. But she didn't turn up before 9:00 a.m. on a good day, and some days it was even later than that. If she didn't have a body covered in plastic surgery, and plump lips that honed every last bit of her talent, he would have shoved her out the door long before now. Probably within five minutes of meeting her, and certainly after her first day. She routed calls incorrectly, couldn't spell worth a damn, and spent all her time on her cell phone and the Internet when she wasn't blowing him or taking calls. But she had more muscles in her lips than Arnold Schwarzenegger had on his back. Even though he wouldn't have been able to get her behind out of his mind for the next three months, he would have sent her packing, if not for those lips. As it was, he'd have to live with his decisions, even when they were made based on the hardness of his cock.

He hadn't thrown a chair through his window in at least six months, and he hadn't overturned his desk in at least three. His blood pressure could only take so many jolts before it just stayed at an obscene level for hours, or so the doctor had said during his last visit. The pacing, however, he could accept.

He glanced down at his watch. A gold Rolex. The call was even more overdue than it was a few minutes ago. He'd come in early because he didn't want to take the call at home. His knuckles were red from the various taps on the various walls and, on at least two occasions, he refrained from putting his right hand through the large glass panes that covered three sides of his office. Only because it was bulletproof and reinforced, not because he hadn't tried. The view, breathtaking on a normal day, was just another pain in his ass today.

If his hemorrhoids flared up, then he'd really need Bethany in here. And he'd call her from home if he had to. For as much as he paid her, she could start making a few exceptions, maybe even answer a few more phone calls, instead of a few more text messages. If he wasn't careful, he might even need a little penetration.

He'd expected the phone call over an hour ago now. And if he hadn't been the boss, he might have put the call in himself. As it was, he wouldn't stoop to the level of his underlings. He was big enough that he could call his own shots, have his own office with his own panoramic view, and have a secretary who believed in oral sex more than Monica Lewinsky did. And based on the view he had, he had more than a few shots to call. Knowing the job was completed was only the beginning. If he wasn't careful, he might have to implement more solutions than a pickup game at Yankee Stadium. Solutions led to imminent conclusions. But so far things weren't going according to plan. They never did. He had nitwits for employees, and an idiot boss above him, a man who believed in hundred-dollar haircuts and longwinded meetings that took up more of his morning than he had to give. Either way, he was stuck in the middle, and it caused an aching pain in his side, the gift that kept on giving.

His ears still rang from what he'd had to listen to over the past months, and years, and he knew he could count on things getting even worse. He dealt with idiots, and over time, the idiots seemed to multiply, like cockroaches in the dark. Like a cancerous tumor tearing through his brain, he had to deal with the consequences of his actions. And unlike the help he had found previously, good help was hard to come by.

The room spun in a circular motion, and it wasn't based on his continued pacing. Maybe it was the view, maybe it was the cocaine he had snorted just a few minutes ago, in between the pacing and the tapping. Maybe it was the alcohol he had consumed the night before, or the bottle of scotch on his bedside table. Or maybe it was the anger, festering deep beneath the surface, and rising up, up like a whale looking for a beach.

He'd slipped between consciousness and unconsciousness before, only to have it thrown back in his face and stifle him with a bloody nose and a cold sore. If he wasn't careful, he'd have even more to worry about.

The phone on his desk rang. He pulled the microphone into place and started pacing even faster, the sea within him cascading and rising, breaking through the surface. His hands danced in front of him like a white man dribbling a basketball.

"What the hell is going on?" Anthony demanded. Pleasantries, he decided, were out of the question.

"We're still trying to determine that," Thurman said.

Anthony gritted his teeth and double tapped the glass. "I need some answers. And you'd better have some solutions."

There was a pause on the line, followed by some heavy breathing. "We're working it out."

"You're not working anything out," Anthony said. "What I gave you was help. You're supposed to tell me the problem has been eliminated."

"Have you snorted cocaine again and mixed it with alcohol?" Thurman asked.

Anthony rubbed his eyes in rapid fashion. "This isn't about me, you SOB. This is about what you're supposed to have done for me, and since you're skirting around the truth, I can only assume that the problem is still out there." His eyes flipped open and closed. The silence extended for several seconds. The pounding in his head resounded louder than a bass guitar, the chords dancing from ear to ear. "Unless the problem has been eliminated, you still have more work to do." He didn't need three idiots, but if it came to that, he'd have the third eliminate the other two. Like cockroaches devouring their young.

He rubbed his temples, his blood pressure rising with his heart rate. "I have the distinct feeling we're not getting anywhere. And it's growing inside of me like a tapeworm that was fed one too many Clark bars."

The pause on the other end of the line was shorter this time. "I didn't know they still made Clark bars."

Anthony's temple throbbed like a hard dick. He pounded his desk with both hands, loud enough to be heard on the phone and outside his office door. "What. Is. The. Plan?"

There was a sigh, and it wasn't his. "We're still in regroup mode. Elrod's mourning his hat."

Anthony paced faster, he clenched his fist tighter, and his temple throbbed harder. His white knuckles penetrated the flesh, and his headache had spread beyond the confines of his skull. He pounded the glass, and he punched through the plaster. "I don't give a shit about that."

He pulled his hand out of the wall, his knuckles bloody and swollen, the broken plaster cascading to the carpet, his bare feet covered in white dust.

Stupid was virtually impossible to educate, and he hated challenges. "What are you doing about my problem?"

Static crackled in the background. "What?" Thurman asked.

"The two idiots that you're supposed to have eliminated," Anthony screamed. "I found them for you. All you had to do was eliminate them. I even gave you Elrod, you lousy cocksucker. He's supposed to be a sharpshooting motherfucker."

His heart raced faster than a thoroughbred, slamming against his upper chest. He was having a heart attack. A goddamned heart attack, and this stupid bastard had caused it. His right hand throbbed along with his heart, and all the voices in his head screamed in unison. His head had split open, and there was a sharp pain behind his right ear.

Digging through the cabinet next to his desk, he found the bottle of scotch he kept around for emergency purposes, lifted his mug off the desk, dumped the remnants of coffee into the wastebasket, filled the cup with booze, and took a long swallow. He filled it again and took an even longer swallow, his throat muscles moving forward.

"Maybe his sharpshooting skills need polishing," Thurman said. "Along with his new hat."

"He'd better not get it on my dime. What you two cocksuckers are supposed to do is track down Veronica and Pete. That's the only item on your list, and if I hear you put anything else on there, I'm going to track you down and blow both of your fucking heads off." He tossed his empty mug at the window. It bounced back to the floor. The mug cracked, the glass, however, remained unharmed. "Have I made myself clear?"

CHAPTER 22

Do you mind telling me why we're here?" Veronica asked.

"You need some new clothes, don't you?" Pete said. "Or do you want to continue to wear flannel pants for the rest of your days?"

He didn't feel the need to point out that she said the shopping in Charlottesville severely retracted from her most basic needs. Short Pump Town Center, on the other hand, provided an outdoor plaza feel, relatively new location, and plethora of stores that offered her boundless opportunities. A double-decker location with over 100 stores and strategic gardens placed in the middle of the walkway, it was fun for everyone. Her eyes lit up faster than a halogen light bulb, even as the verbal abuse continued indefinitely.

The drive had given him more than enough time to reflect and digest, his stomach no longer feeling as though a lead weight held it in place. An accident on I-64 east had tampered down the flow of traffic to a crawl, and the fireball that had otherwise been a Camaro offered a prime viewing prospect on the side of the road for the rubber-neckers—him included. He had chosen to shower after breakfast, and before checkout, changed the dressings on his shoulder and his shirt, the wound now a jagged red line instead of an abrasion, and the pain had subsided enough to forego the pain pills, although he took a couple as a precautionary measure.

He stepped from the vehicle, and so did she, tightening the drawstring and adjusting the top. She held a certain level of attractiveness with her hair tussled and rumpled shirt. Her mouth, however, always managed to get in the way. Staying on the move was as much his idea as it was hers, the running kept his mind limber and fresh. Feeling more comfortable out in the open, as opposed to staying holed up in a motel room waiting for World War III, he walked with purpose, and she elongated her stride beside him. His hands moved with authority, hers in a more lady-like fashion, her hips swaying with every step. Not that he had noticed.

Short Pump Town Center contained a multitude of upscale stores, outdoor concerts during the summer, and enough red brick and concrete to build a series of castles in Scotland. The eye-catching scenery both inside the stores and out lightened his mood, although the greenery and flowers flared up his allergies and caused him to sneeze at multiple intervals.

The smell of cooked meat, butter, and dough sifted toward his nostrils, and he breathed in the intoxicating scent, along with a bit of pollen and ragweed. A statuesque blonde in a rather short skirt caught his eye with her long legs and even longer heels walking with more purpose than a general heading off into battle. His eyes veered off in another direction before he caused himself serious damage by staring too long at her backside.

Veronica slapped him on the shoulder. "Where are my handcuffs?"

"You don't need handcuffs."

He didn't bother to tell her he'd stuffed a pair in the trunk underneath the spare tire. If she hadn't forced him to return the keys, he might have escaped in the middle of the night, or then again, he might not. His life hadn't had this much purpose since the war and prohibitive desert conditions. And if she hadn't closed her fist tightly around them—the keys—before drifting off to sleep, he might have considered an extraction operation. He had slept lightly, and she had slept soundly, too exhausted to attempt another escape. Her snoring jerked him awake more than once, the sound resembling a jackhammer and a buzz saw.

She stopped midstride. "How would you know?"

"Because I've been on the other end." He stopped just short of crashing into her. "I've been the one tied up, and I'm tired of it." And he had done a valiant job of avoiding a repeat performance: deception, maneuver, repeat. The charade, though, would only continue for a limited time. His playbook mirrored hers. "We could always take turns."

She glared at him and continued walking. He hustled enough to catch up. She had reached the beginning of the outdoor stores, therefore so had he. She powered through the early morning crowd—the women and children and babies being pushed in carts, the older couples with coffees in one hand and shopping bags in the other—and he followed at a pace or two behind, the view as treacherous as it was scenic.

"How did you find this place?" she asked.

"I'm good at finding places," Pete said.

Losing her, though, proved to be much more of a challenge. In the end, he wasn't sure that's what he wanted either.

He waited a beat in his head then two and three. Still nothing. He tapped her on the shoulder and pointed to the bench up ahead. "We need to talk."

She took a seat on one end of the bench, he the other. "So talk."

He processed what had happened so far—the shot up hotel room, the handcuffs, the driving, the diner, the misdirection, the half-truths and any number of lies, sleeping on the floor and being chained to an air conditioner, the drinking, and his time at Port City High, a period of four years that he would just as soon forget.

He looked at her with reluctant eyes. "What the hell is going on?"

She shrugged, he sighed, she placed her hands in her lap, he shifted on the bench and waited her out, couples and people passing by in assembly line fashion.

She peered at him out of the corner of her eye and then rushed forward, spilling out the words in staccato-like fashion. "The last project I worked on was a merger that fell through, the numbers just didn't add up."

He coughed and sneezed. "Who else was working on the case?"

She drummed her fingers on her thigh and stared straight ahead. "Anthony Whelan and Nathan Labaw, the

CFO of Brogue Consulting. The two main partners on the project and with the firm."

"And then there was you?" he asked.

She nodded. "Correct."

"That's quite a big drop-off."

Her mouth formed a hard line. "Thanks."

A woman shoved a carriage past him for the second time, her cell phone plastered to her right ear. "You know that's not what I meant." He paused. "Let me guess: Anthony and Nathan were pushing the deal—"

Veronica exhaled, and so did he. "But I put a stop to it," she said. "I called them out. In the middle of a board meeting where old men in gray suits with glazed over eyes who wanted nothing more than to meet their latest tee times would have pushed the merger through—"

"I'm not the least bit surprised," he said.

Before he could say more, she hopped up from the bench and darted across the footpath in the direction of The Gap. Crossing through the open door and into the store, she turned in the direction of the women's section—after a quick turn of her head at the men's—and waved at him, her elegant fingers moving up and down like piano keys.

CHAPTER 23

She had an armful of clothes in one hand—tops in pastel colors; bottoms in tans and grays and browns; and two sweaters, possibly cashmere—and she flipped through the rack in the back with the other. And she'd acquired it all in the time it took him to catch up with her, flitting through the store with more energy than a Duracell battery.

She stopped mid-rack and turned to him. "Do you plan on following me around the whole time?"

Pete nodded, his attention focused elsewhere—on the army of helpful attendants, most of whom were helping a group of women. Two men in nearly matching outfits picked through a conglomeration of clothes on the same rack. One man held up a button-down shirt, turning in her direction, meeting her gaze, and smiling, before his continued perusal of the powder-blue shirt. The man was younger than she was, probably by at least five years, and his smile remained less than genuine. Pete continued to glance at her.

"Don't you have anything better to do?"

He shook his head. Out of the corner of his eye, he checked out the young stud with chiseled features and perfectly coiffed hair. Probably too perfect.

She marched toward the back, scooping up a handful of blouses large enough to clothe a small village into her arms, along with her other attire, and she took off in the direction of the fitting rooms. On the way, she grabbed a couple pairs of jeans, possibly the low-rider variety, the stack of clothes nearly as tall as her head.

Pete gazed after her, enjoying her backside even more than her front, the way her hips moved, along with her confident stride. He tried on several pairs of sunglasses, held up a handful of collared shirts, significantly less than the stack she had weighing her down, more than enough for her to favor her right side over her left. Two sales clerks offered to assist him: one brunette, the other blonde. He politely declined both requests.

Before much time had passed, he headed toward the back corner, the rustling of clothes and constant motion helped him identify her cubbyhole. The intermittent sighing provided another clue as well. "Are you almost done?" he asked.

"I'd be done even faster if you'd go," she replied.

"You have thirty seconds."

More rustling of clothes was his only reply. Twenty-nine seconds later the door banged open, and she marched past him toward the counter. With no one else in line, and her stack less than half as large as it once was, the clerk speedy and efficient, from what Pete could tell, the process moved forward at a pronounced pace, as he flicked his eyes among the other patrons.

He spotted a new man perusing a rack of clothes, paying more attention to him than he was the T-shirts and golf shirts that were placed strategically for his inspection. On a rack a bit farther down, he noticed jeans of the slim variety, better suited for women than men, the legs straight and narrow and never-ending. Even though the man stood next to a rack of golf shirts, with the T-shirts placed inside his reach—he was a large man with glasses and short-cropped hair, the front part of his head done in an upward spike—Pete received intermittent glances in his direction before the scrutiny resumed. Spike had a plug in his ear, which could have been a hearing aid, but based on the man's age was more than likely an earpiece, similar to those he'd seen on bodyguards or secret service agents. Spike had his hands out in front of him, instead of at his sides, as though he were ready to strike first and ask questions later.

Hiking up to Veronica, who had a bag in one hand, the other one still sitting on the counter, Pete said, "We need to go *now*." He emphasized the last word.

She pointed to the bag the salesclerk continued to stuff with equal parts precision and care. "But the clerk's not finished with this one yet."

He grabbed the bag, shoved the remaining items in the overstuffed bag, and grabbed her shoulder. "You're finished."

"Wait, sir, that one still has—"

The alarm sounded, the voice calm, respectful, and monotone broadcasted to the entire store and naïve passerby the true gravity of the current situation.

He propelled her outside, dragging her in the direction of the quad, where a throng of people, larger than before—many of whom either pushed carts, or held the hands of small children, or their significant others—tumbled along.

"What the fuck?" she said.

"We're being followed." He continued to push forward, and she continued to keep up. "There was a man in the store with an earpiece—"

"You're paranoid, and I need to change," she said.

He hadn't noticed before, but the pants were being held up by friction, and if gravity had its way, her pants would probably end up underneath the curve of her ass, and after that, the floor wouldn't be far behind. Based on a matter of simple friction and gravity. Or it could have been wishful thinking on his part.

He bumped the shoulder of a multi-tasking soccer mom, talking and texting at the same. The bag bounced at his side against his thigh. She shot him a glare that he chose to ignore. If he had been looking for it, his companion offered him one as well. He sneezed again. Out of hands, he covered the sound with his right bicep.

Ducking into a store a few doors down from The Gap, and not caring if it was men's or women's, he strode across the threshold and monitored his progress against a sea of unfamiliar faces. Veronica uttered a string of half-familiar words, most of which were lost on him, and smacked his hand from her shoulder.

She didn't look in his direction.

If he had given her the chance, she might have formed a protest, or told an outright lie to save her own behind, even if she knew Spike was nearby. When it came to women, Pete had adopted a forceful attitude, even if it was still a work in progress. Based on his experience, it

proved easier to beg forgiveness—a word probably unfamiliar to her—than to ask for permission.

The rapid pounding in his chest continued, as more
and more faces marched by. A sales clerk had offered his
help, and Pete had politely declined. He didn't bother to
remove his eyes from the glass, and his heart hadn't
bothered to slow down. When he sneezed, his whole
body shook.

He committed the faces to memory, locking each one
away. Just when he was about to give the all clear, Spike
appeared. The man's head swiveled in his direction, and
his mouth opened. Pete grabbed Veronica's bicep, flipped
her around, and thrust her in the direction of the emergency exit. She took off running, and so did he.

The man shouted a string of unintelligible words. Pete
glanced over his shoulder, as Spike shoved patrons out of
his way, before tripping over a carriage and tumbling into
a rack of underwear. Pete flipped his head around, just as
the sound of the emergency alarm blared, and he stumbled across the threshold. Veronica hung a right, and he
did the same. She came to a set of stairs and bounded up.
He matched her step-for-step. She traversed her way
through a sea of patrons better than he would have, her
small size aiding her escape. His bag ricocheted against
his thigh. He received dirty looks from a multitude of
women.

Behind him, the pounding of footsteps offered up their
own unique sound.

CHAPTER 24

Thirty minutes later, he had lost the tail, with balls-out brute force, punching through crowds and pedestrians, some fancy maneuvering, some expert weaving, two dressing rooms in two different stores, and a whole lot of dodging and zigzagging. He'd been up the stairs and down them, past stores and inside them, out front doors and past emergency exits enough times that he didn't even bother covering his ears.

Veronica had kept up, even pushing him at three different points when he had become a tad winded, sucking in breaths faster than helium balloons. His bag, and hers, had slammed against thighs and carriages, and even parted crowds with a full-on assault.

He didn't mind pushing himself, and he didn't mind putting his life on the line, even if it did mean he might meet an early demise. Just as long as it wasn't in the back of a Mercedes with a firm handshake and a stiff drink.

He had peeled out of the parking lot the same way he peeled through the crowd, as Veronica gripped the handle above her head, careening against the passenger door on a sharp turn that left the tires screeching and screaming. He'd run two red lights and three yellow, not that he was counting, and he'd come within inches of sideswiping a BMW and a minivan. The minivan proved more promising than the Beamer.

Wearing his seatbelt, a habit ingrained at birth, he still managed to do a bit of shifting in his seat, as did the merchandise in the back. Two bags of clothes made it unscathed through the mayhem, and during the advance, she had shoved him out of a dressing room and changed outfits, the top perfectly coordinated with the bottom. Not saying a word, she had stalked past him and picked up her pace when Spike had reared his ugly head.

After witnessing death firsthand, Pete had no problem if it came with its claws outstretched. He could deal with death, just as easily as he could deal with life, a fine line separating the two. Life was more about embracing the unknown, picking himself back up when he needed to, and hoping that life wouldn't emit a slap in the face or a poke in the eye. Kindness, however, was severely lacking, and there was a chance it might continue on its present course.

She had clicked her seatbelt into place and stared straight ahead throughout most of the journey, only pointing out when the tail was too close, or he was too close to the sea of cars around him. Her precise nature was uncanny in a world filled with vagueness and gray and, despite the gravity of the situation, she remained calmer than he had throughout.

Lunch and dinner proved uneventful, other than her portion size compared to his. Even as he scaled back his meals and tackled less meat during both meals than he had consumed at breakfast, she still couldn't keep up. For every glass of water she had, he had two.

When it was time to call it a night, he found a hotel in Charlottesville, Virginia, just beyond the UVA campus with a gas station just down the road. A wise abandonment of the previous establishment. It wasn't a four-star hotel, or even a three-star, but she paid cash, and even though the protests might continue, he vetoed the use of her credit and debit card.

Her harsh stare, red cheeks, and inevitable bout of silence told him everything he needed to know. She had balked at the room size, the lack of amenities, the condensed lobby, and the lack of zeal displayed by the front desk clerk, who was probably four months pregnant. Her methodic nature only further proved the point.

Even though she had objected, on health-related and monetary grounds, he found a local watering hole, with a moose plastered on the sign board, neon lights, dark tables and booths, and dark wooden doors. He found a seat at the bar—there were several empty ones available—ordered three shots of Jack, lined them up on the bar, and eyed them suspiciously. The bar had a pseudo dance floor with cracked wood, only large enough for a handful of couples.

He sniffed the air—filled with smoke, stale breath, and the hint of dead cabbage—smiled, and tapped the bar lightly with his right hand, the wood beneath his taps both chipped and cracked. The stool wobbled slightly beneath him and swiveled when he didn't want it to, but he chose to ignore its protests. The bartender was young and a redhead, her long hair cascading past her shoulders, her eyes as black as obsidian, standing out from the rest of the crowd.

Fifteen minutes later, after he had downed all three shots and considered a few additions to the family, the whiskey working its way through his system, Veronica strolled through the dark doors, her eyes searching, probing, before she found him. He had hoped the cloud of smoke would hide his existence, or the lights had been dimmed in his presence. Instead, he ended up with a bar companion on his left, and three new drinks on his right, to go along with the empty seat next to him.

"If you're going to make a habit out of drinking your problems away," she said, "you might want to find your own ride."

Calmness began to take over his life. He didn't remember driving. The drinking, however, was still at the forefront of his mind. "Are you threatening to leave me behind?"

She drummed her fingers on the bar. "I'm considering my options."

A glass of water was placed in front of her. She looked at it and looked at him.

He almost wanted to laugh. "You don't have handcuffs or the car keys."

"Handcuffs can be obtained, and I stole the keys back when you took a nap this afternoon. You shouldn't sleep in parked vehicles."

He patted all of his pockets once, and then he made a second round. Although he wasn't as quick on his feet as he had been before the three shots, and before staring at three more, he still had his faculties, and all of his parts were exactly where he'd left them. Each part just as important as the one before it. She was right. He had somehow managed to end up keyless. Sure he hadn't walked here, but unsure of how he had arrived at his present location, he was in a state of flux, the stool beneath him a bit more unsteady than it was only moments ago.

Pete stared at the whiskey, and the whiskey stared back at him. "Do you have anything better to do than harass me?"

Veronica sucked down water from her glass. "Apparently, you're this evening's entertainment," she said. "I'm just waiting to see how long it takes you to get sloshed. But if you start puking, I'm not walking you home."

"I don't puke," he said.

He had walked here after all. As he recalled—and he couldn't recall much at the moment—he was only a few blocks away from where he planned to sleep this evening, assuming he didn't end up face down in the parking lot.

She rocked back a bit in her stool, her dexterity and balance not lost on him. "Let's just hope it stays that way."

Glancing over his shoulder, and hiding a grin, he knocked the next shot back and placed the empty on the dented wood. He felt her gaze on him, but he chose to ignore it. Out of the corner of his eye, a brute of a man, who probably devoured chickens as frequently as a coyote, sized Veronica up and negotiated the distance between the dance floor and the bar, swiveling around three men as he walked. She saw the man's approach and eased out of her seat toward the women's restroom, but she didn't quite make it.

Pete shook his head. If there was one thing he didn't

have to worry about, it was her being able to take care of herself. He hoped she didn't punch the man, otherwise, the coyote might have the ride of his life. The man had a head that was twice the size of hers and was growing more confident with his every move. The coyote tried a pickup line. Pete could sense Veronica didn't like it. She gave some sort of reply, and the coyote glared at her, his eyes blood red from drink and adrenaline.

Peering over his shoulder again, Pete noticed her shove the man away and stalk the remaining steps to the bathroom. The coyote followed her, stopping just short of the restroom door. Since he'd seen it happen before, Pete waited to see if the coyote would try to enter the restroom with her, his attention no longer focused on the cute bartender with the heart-shaped ass and the two rings in her right ear. Or the two remaining drinks in front of him that smiled up at him with wide, forgiving eyes.

The bartender mixed drinks with passion and fury that he hadn't even experienced with a couple of his lovers. The thought did cross his mind that he could hand Veronica off to the coyote and be rid of his problem. For a split second, he smiled, and then the frown weighed in, once he remembered she had the car keys.

CHAPTER 25

"Maybe you should leave the lady alone," Pete said.

The space between him and the larger man could be measured in inches and centimeters.

"Who the hell are you?" the coyote asked.

"I'm her boyfriend," Pete said.

He had his back against the wall, and his hands at his sides. The hallway was narrow, confined, with posters of bikini-clad women and shirtless men.

The coyote glared at him. "Yeah, right, asshole. I saw her first. You can wait your turn."

"I'm right here, you know." Veronica had stepped out of the restroom, and stood next to him.

The hallway was barely wide enough for the three of them and the flock of pedestrians that paraded through, filling in the gaps in time and space.

With his fists clenched at his sides, Pete could strike at any moment. The military prepared him for battle, and he had gone to war. One more wouldn't add to his already present nightmares.

The coyote had a thick neck and large hands. He wore a sour expression on his face. His eyes were narrow slits, and his shoulders were wider than the rest of him. He produced the smirk on his face with a certain amount of pride. "That's what I'm counting on, babe," the coyote said. "And here in a few minutes you'll be down on your knees to please."

"I'm not sure what kind of woman you think I am," she said, "but I think you have me mistaken for someone else."

Two brunettes walked by, both with stiff shoulders, miniskirts, and high heels. The heads did nothing more than a slight shake from side to side.

The coyote smirked. "No, I know exactly who you are, and you're good enough to work for me."

She punched him in the face. The coyote growled and slapped her across the side of her head. She fell, more from being a half-second behind with her reflexes than any other reason. Her body struck the floor. She lay on the ground at an unusual angle. Her hand shot out to rub her head.

Pete jabbed a quick punch to the man's throat. The man was too quick, and he caught Pete's fist with his own much larger one. He squeezed, and Pete's eyes blazed, his heart hammering in his chest, as his adrenaline kicked into third gear.

As the coyote brought his fist toward Pete's face, Pete threw his left arm up to block the punch. He didn't completely block it, but he diverted the angle, causing a glancing blow instead of a head-on collision. Pete smiled—his opponent didn't.

Veronica was on her feet, her fists out in front of her, her left leg in front of her right balancing her weight.

"You've had a few too many," the coyote said.

"I don't fight as well sober."

"He might have," she said, "but I haven't."

"When I'm through with you," the coyote said, "you won't be able to fight at all."

The corridor proved narrower than Pete had first suspected. The coyote had a continuous smirk on his face, his lips at slightly odd angles. Since he was smaller than his opponent, Pete thought he might be able to use it to his advantage. Diverting his focus from the alcohol making its way through his system, and sidestepping his mind from doing the backstroke, he flexed his right hand, tendons popping in his wrist. The coyote danced in front of him in slow motion, his arms nearly as large as a hubcap. When the coyote inched forward, Pete took a step back, his back flush with the wall, glancing only for a split-second in Veronica's direction.

"Don't worry about your girlfriend," the coyote said. "She'll be well taken care of."

"You might want to keep your mouth shut," she said.

Pete feinted in with his left hand and, having gotten his other hand back, he clocked the coyote on the side of his head. The coyote roared in anger and swung wildly. Pete began to dodge, duck, and weave in synch with the rhythm in his head. After a combination to the stomach, throat, and side of the head, the coyote went down in a heap.

Pete grabbed Veronica, who kicked the coyote in the head when he growled and had her leg back for another blow. With her in tow, Pete left the bar, having already paid for his six drinks, and two short of a good time.

"I could have had him, you know."

He nodded and let her go. She marched ahead of him, her hands stiff at her sides, her back as stiff as her hands and mouth, a knot already forming on her temple from where she struck the broken wood.

He shuffled the four blocks to the hotel, his right hand developing its own heartbeat, or maybe it was his left. When he made it back to the hotel, a few minutes behind her, he stood in the center of the room and stared at the blank screen on the TV, before he reached for the icebox. Other than the sound of water running, silence filled the room.

While he might have gotten lucky in the fight, he did know how to defend himself, against both larger and smaller men. The military had taught him that much, his training having lasted more than just a few sessions. Hand-to-hand combat wasn't his specialty, but he had learned enough to hold his own when the situation warranted it. And he wasn't about to let the altercation stumble out of control. He had an ill-tempered man to thank for his sore hand.

It hadn't been Pete's first bar fight.

☙❧❦

Once the water had run dry, and she had paraded out in a new outfit, Pete took her place behind the bathroom door. Shedding his clothes and stepping into the shower, he turned the water on high and stood under the heated spray for twice as long as normal. His knuckles were sore, the pain shooting up his arm, the pain pills having not kicked in yet, but he did his best to ignore it. The hot spray helped, as he tried to forget his problems from less than an hour ago and the two drinks he had left behind. Although he preferred not to show signs of chivalry, occasionally he had a mental lapse, and the physical problems occurred only moments later, most having to do with a limb or his head.

Over the years, he had honed his self-defense skills, his scars worn like a badge of honor. Even when he should have just walked away, he entered the mix and tossed up his fists, striking opponents left and right, his hands quicker than a bee sting. Walking might have been easier. It was easier to say no than yes. No didn't require further commitment. He'd heard his share of no's, each one as unappealing as the one before it.

He closed his eyes.

As the spray consumed him, his mind was lost, before he was able to find it again. He didn't have a good explanation for helping Veronica, other than the simple fact that she held the car keys and possibly the very key to his existence. His mind filled with promise, hope, and desire. But she would try to leave him again. He felt it deep in his bones, the same way he felt the ache in his hand. What he needed to decide was if he would let her get away with it, or if he would fight similar to the way he had tonight. Since he wasn't good at backing down from a challenge, even one where he was clearly not wanted, he'd probably continue to help her, until she realized she needed him. If she never reached that particular conclusion…well, he would worry about that particular problem if it sprang forth.

Stepping out of the shower, he toweled himself dry, before he collapsed on the floor moments later, pillow underneath his restless head, exhaustion taking over his entire body, his hand still throbbing. Sleep, however, didn't come easily. It almost never did.

Chapter 26

She'd been running for so long maybe it was time to stop running. A glance behind her told her that he was still too close. Despite her forward plunge, the heavy footsteps closed the distance, clipping at her heels, causing her to stumble, as though there had been no distance at all. Her mind raced, searching a way out through the trees and the madness beyond. Her breathing more labored, her heart felt as though it was on the verge of exploding within her chest. The ground sank beneath her feet. She jerked her foot out of the soft earth, losing one high heel in the process, stopping, bending over, grabbing the other one, and tossing it behind her. Trees passed before her in rapid succession, some thicker than others. Bark exploded around her. A bullet whizzed by her left ear as the voice in her head grew louder. The voice called out to her, unfamiliar, and yet it still managed to hold an edge of familiarity.

She'd been told that she could stop traffic, but she hadn't taken it literally until just now. Well, not right now, but two days ago, when the end of her life drew near. She'd been on City Avenue, window shopping, passing through the crowd, stealing a glance at her phone every few minutes or so, when a Prius pulled up next to her. The gentleman held a map in his hands. She had looked down, and before she realized what had happened, he had dragged her into the passenger seat, slapped plastic ties on her wrists, and spun out into oncoming traffic.

Veronica had fought him, screaming and yelling, kicking out, jabbing a toe in his thigh, and one just outside of his balls, caught a ring on his cheek, but he had counteracted her screams—speaking in a calm, soothing voice, as he dragged her to his car—and the pedestrians around her had listened to him, instead of her. He had a nondescript face that might have been handsome, wore a business suit and tie, and dark sunglasses. Her attire by comparison was more casual, and her screams more piercing, her blows more ferocious, feral. All of it had worked against her. His entire plan had worked against her.

Less than twenty seconds later, he had pulled her inside, slapped plastic ties on her wrists in the passenger seat—that none of the pedestrians had seen—and slammed the door. His calmness infuriated her even more, and she had yelled a string of obscenities, kicking and thrashing and smacking the dashboard, until her voice grew hoarse, and she had to choke back the words. But she hadn't cried. She wouldn't shed a tear for this man, whoever he was. He hadn't even looked at her, nor had he broken any speed limits. The vehicle a white sedan with a gray interior. Not a stitch of dirt on it anywhere that she could see.

The mask had come later, and the drugs even later

than that. She couldn't say for certain that he had pumped her full of calm-inducing medication, but she slept for almost two days. Her memories blurred together, the two days blended together into one forty-eight hour wave of madness, filled with furry little creatures, rats the size of small cats, a dirt floor, and dirt walls.

Growing up, she'd been a tomboy. Playing all the sports that boys played, with baseball and soccer her two personal favorites. After all, she had three brothers: It was the only way to survive. Playing with dolls was never a viable option. And she didn't even like dolls, especially not Barbie. A couple of times, she'd ripped Barbie's head off, just for fun, just to see her mother actually bite her tongue, choke on the words that just weren't there, disappointment in her eyes, and walk away. Her dad, though, had been proud of her. Fathers wanted sons, and he often referred to her as his fourth one, the one with more promise than all the rest. And then she'd gotten breasts, discovered boys, and all bets were off. With three brothers, she knew how to manipulate men, and she was good at it. Probably a little too good. After that, everything changed. The same way her life had.

Forty-eight hours later, nothing was the same. And three days later it had changed again. A new man with a similar attitude, similar to all the other men she ever knew had entered her life and pushed her back up against the wall.

The man behind her wasn't giving up, even though she'd been running for twenty minutes. Maybe longer. Her feet slapped soft earth, a branch stumbled into her eyes—she swiped it away—a rock tripped her, and still the man behind her came for her. The full moon guided her, providing her with hope and purpose. The truth was she didn't want to know what time it was. She didn't want the clock to run her life.

Veronica pushed herself, knowing that if she were caught, she'd experience his wrath, the temper that hung just beneath the surface, the cool calm that struck her with evil precision, the mellow, monotone voice that hid the hint of something more. She had chosen complacency, fear, knowing this would appease him, as she bid her time. Without a watch on her wrist, she kept track of the time in her head, placing scratch marks on the walls with a fork.

Being underground, night blended into day and day into night. She slept. The drugs he had given her helped her with this endeavor.

She'd never thought about committing suicide. She valued her life way too much to shoot herself, or hang herself by some germ infested rope, or pop enough pills to render her comatose. She washed her hands all the time, using antibacterial soap, hand creams, and cleansers, her nails trim and polished. Germs were everywhere, and she did all that she could to avoid them. In fact, she could feel them clinging to her now, or maybe those were the bugs, the demons of the night with the whiskers and the squeaky voices. She hated bugs. She didn't like doctors or prescription medication. Even routine checkups were avoided. If she broke her arm, she'd try to figure out a way to fix it herself. If she could just get past the sight of blood.

Psychologists were even worse. That's why she'd never been to one before, although she'd had a lot of problems to deal with over the years, plenty of boyfriends who liked to slap her around. That's why she had started the self-defense classes. With men, her radar had always been a little off, and she'd chosen all the wrong men under all the wrong circumstances. She might have called it extreme dating. She pushed herself, even when it was in all the wrong directions.

Other problems filled her life. Like her mother dying on Veronica's thirteenth birthday. An aneurism before the main course. The worst birthday present imaginable. Her mother died before the ambulance had even arrived. Veronica still reeled from the effects of that traumatic experience. Her mother was a workout fiend, in the best shape of her life for a thirty-eight year old woman. The unexplainable always proved more difficult to comprehend.

Nothing in life made sense. Including right now. Mystery made things interesting, intriguing, and that was what she looked for when she dated. But it had been over a year since she'd played the field, and she wasn't looking for a date anytime soon. Of course, she never was. And with a bit of effort, she'd even managed to avoid George Bush, the mask, not the man, although he yelled her name, loud enough for her to hear, the voice slightly garbled behind the rubber. The sound of his breathing reminded her of a distant memory, of Darth Vader, or her worst nightmare.

Before the abduction, she'd lived in a little apartment—off the beaten path, but it was home to her. Her place of solace. Sometimes she forgot things like the rent and to pay her bills. Once she didn't have cable for a whole month, and she'd had to do without electricity for a week. She had more important things she needed to worry about, like why George Bush, the mask, had devoted all of his attention to her, and why he had chosen her.

She didn't think her landlord would abduct her for not paying her rent. And he certainly wouldn't have shown up on the sidewalk in a nondescript car and a business suit. Besides, he was older, lankier, less solid, and he didn't have a monotone bone in his body. She'd heard George Bush speak, behind his mask and without, and his voice didn't resemble her landlord's. Eviction. Yes. He'd even threatened it on three occasions, pounding on her door at different intervals. Being abducted and shot at, though. Not so much.

How was she going to get out of this? And how had she even gotten into this mess? Those were two questions that she definitely needed to answer, but now was not the time to stop and contemplate. She had to move on, push herself, the feet slapping a little too close to her heels, the solid man grunting and wheezing behind her. She continued to place one foot in front of the other, used her forearm to cover her face from the bark and branches. Even though her pursuer gained on her, his voice resonating in her ear, she pushed through the madness and sadness toward higher ground.

She didn't want to die.

She'd never been in this deep before. Sure, she'd been in trouble, mostly with her parents for fairly minor issues, and with various boyfriends for God only knows what reason, but this was the real deal, the gun pointed directly at her. She could tell by the footfalls behind, gradually drawing closer. Her spirit lifted before it cascaded back down to Earth, as her captor attempted to scare her, to take over her life, to hold her for God only knows what reason.

He had already fired three shots, three separate explosions that cut through the night air. Salt, sulfur, and smoke clung to the back of her throat. Even though she might have missed one or two of them as she pushed herself toward the end, she was fairly certain the trees around her had captured each one. She had dodged to her right as necessary, even stumbled at the exact moment a bullet hurtled toward her, as it struck a tree just out of her reach and where her head might have been only a moment ago, spraying her with bark, small woodchips, and debris. If he wanted her terrified, he had done his due diligence, better than any of her bastard boyfriends.

Veronica sucked in air through her mouth.

She'd never worked out this much in her life. Thanks to wonderful genes and a superfast metabolism inherited from her mother's side of the family, she entered the world thin, and she'd remained that way. But she wasn't without her faults, especially ones that hovered below the surface as well as above. One eye was slightly larger than the other, and one ear was slightly bigger than the other. She had a crooked right pinky finger, and a scar on the right side of her face. An ex-boyfriend who had a temper that was perfectly in line with his good looks was the reason she had the scar, and one day just for spite, because the bastard had a mouth, she decided to have one back. She called him Gwen, just for a grin, and that was when his fist met her face. The collision was bright, instantaneous, and filled with pain. The shock dropped her to her knees before he hit her again. It wouldn't have been so bad, if he hadn't been wearing a ring, trying to look cool, the ring gaudy and too large for his slim fingers. And it just so happened that his hand lingered on her cheek, splitting the skin open and leaving her with a nice scar to live with for the rest of her life. In one stupid instant, her life had changed forever.

But she'd gotten him back. She had kicked him in the balls repeatedly, and he'd never struck her again. Of course, she left him less than an hour later, gathering her stuff in one giant heap, taking all that she and a few plastic bags could manage, before she walked out on him, slamming the door behind her. Had the situation been reversed, he wouldn't have hesitated either. She was sure of it.

She liked to believe that she was in control of her own destiny. She liked to believe that she held power over her life, but now she wasn't so sure. Everything looked familiar to her. The trees surrounding her all looked the same. The breathing behind her hadn't changed. The ground beneath her seemed identical to when she had started her jaunt through the woods. Everywhere she ran, she saw more trees, and now she'd wished she had understood the various types like spruce, oak, and pine. But all trees looked the same to her, out in the middle of nowhere, which wasn't anywhere close to where she wanted to be. She'd always wanted to jumpstart her life, rev her destiny with the turn of a switch or the flip of the ignition, and she knew there was a good chance that wasn't going to happen now.

The footsteps were like a set of drums next to her head.

The footsteps behind her drew near, just as she saw the clearing up ahead, a separation among the trees, a new path she hadn't seen before, and she noticed the waterfall, where the liquid dashed toward the bottom, similar to her dash through the forest. Before she considered the consequences—the depth of the water, her height, the man behind her, the rocks that clung to the cliff, or her current trajectory—she jumped, kicking herself and her feet outward, before dropping straight down—and just before she hit bottom, she woke up.

Wiping her face, she looked around, unsure of her surroundings, not quite sure about the empty bed next to her or how she had ended up facedown amongst the pillows, the linen caressing her skin. A sleeping form had congregated near the window with a pillow underneath his head, not much taller than her and not much heavier. Studying her surroundings more closely, she didn't recognize the room, nor did she recognize the man on the floor. But one thought did cross her mind: She needed to make a break for it, before the hulking form woke up and attempted to take her life.

CHAPTER 27

What was she doing? She couldn't believe she'd trusted Pete—life hadn't changed him and neither had high school. Even though he had done nothing but help her so far, he was still a man, and men were shitheads. Sooner or later it all came to pass. It was only a matter of time before he hopped on board the ship and sailed off into the sunset.

If she wasn't careful, she'd get burned, scalded even, her skin peeling off in layers, along with what remained of her soul. The nightmare had started as soon as her head hit the pillow, consuming her further as the night wore on. Pete might not have hovered directly over her dream, but he was there, just the same, in the moon, the trees, and the slight breeze. The wind had cooled her skin and left her with a void, an ache.

She'd revisited the Port City woods, and it wasn't any better than her initial visit. She'd worn a similar outfit, maybe a little fancier, a little more snug around the waist. She'd experienced many of the same emotions. Each consumed her even more than the last, until she had woken up completely disoriented, her mind swimming, her face sweating, the stale air in the room stifling, the air conditioner having shut off in the middle of the night, the sheets damp around her, and the pillow hard beneath her. An infinite number of possibilities flowed through her mind like a river, all of which pointed her in exactly the wrong direction and away from her goal. The same way the man in the George Bush mask had.

Her heart felt like it might explode in her chest, the pain in her side deafening. The air around her swirled with mist and fear. While she wasn't at the precipice, the past five days had consumed her, nearly swallowed her whole, and spit her back out. That's why she finally decided she needed to escape—it wasn't the rats, or the broken promises, or the former high school bastard who still happened to be one, or the jaunt in the car, or her race through the forest. If the opportunity had presented itself, she would have done it sooner than three days ago and now, with her clammy hands and the stitch in her side.

When she woke up with a galloping heart and a hulking form on the floor, spread out like he owned the place, his pillow jammed just below the air conditioner, she had lost it, all of her senses on amber alert. It was a show, and she was the freak. She could deal with the two hired guns, who showed more balls than intelligence, busting through the door like it was a crackerjack box. If there was one thing she had learned how to do, it was to take care of herself.

She had the gun and the handcuffs—Pete had shoved them in the trunk next to the spare tire, but she had discovered them all the same—neither of which she planned on using. She wasn't about to get in a shooting match either, knowing that she might draw the short straw. She'd never fired a weapon before, not even at a gun range. She didn't know what she would have done had Pete rebelled against her.

Her skin was like sandpaper, her insides more like jelly, but she wasn't going to tell this to the man who was more outlaw than military figure. She'd discovered him the first night, a true coincidence if she'd ever seen one, after a bout of drinking, his eyes unfocused and nearly crossed, staring at her as if she were a ghost in a park out for a stroll, and she had left him this morning probably hung over, nursing a severe headache. The hugging of the toilet occurred during the night, and for all she knew would occur again this morning.

He had snored most of the night, during what had been a restless sleep for her, and resumed the engine noise this morning. She wasn't particularly good with cars, or engines for that matter. She hadn't had trouble drifting off, but she'd had trouble staying down. Probably the myriad of dreams that filled her subconscious. Ever since she ended up in that World War I dungeon belowground, sleep was hard to come by. She could thank the businessman in the George Bush mask for his trouble and for watching her every move—the rats on one side of her small prison, with beady eyes and fast moving whiskers, her on the other, and the dirt that surrounded her like a moat. If that hadn't added a new meaning to the word creepy, then she was in serious need of a cat scan.

Veronica had checked her gas tank just after she turned the key in the ignition. While she assumed there was gas in the tank, she was no longer going to take that for granted. Not after her first fiasco. She had hated crawling back to him, begging him for help, having to trust him all over again, when she didn't really have faith in him at all. If he hadn't had the keys stuffed in his pocket, the car in an unknown parking lot, far away from his place of residence, she would have walked away without him. Knowing she had needed him, if only on a temporary basis, had placed her in a precarious position, similar to her jump off the cliff into the pool of water below.

Not a situation she wanted to place herself in again soon, even if he had prevented her from dying, being recaptured, or shot in the head. Needing anyone wasn't a pleasant experience, and knowing she needed a gunslinger, who consumed booze with reckless abandon and a devil-may-care attitude toward his liver, added a new meaning to being disturbed. But she had a full tank of gas, and she had the whole road ahead of her, and a man left behind sleeping soundly next to a faulty air conditioner.

She had started on the US 29 bypass, venturing around Charlottesville, Virginia in a circular loop, finally finding her way toward I-64 east. While Charlottesville was only about two hours away, under ideal conditions, from Port City, Virginia, she hadn't ventured much beyond Port City, and she'd only been to Charlottesville once, catching a couple of the hottest tourist spots: Monticello and the downtown mall. Even though she wasn't much of a history fan, she was still enamored with the third president, considering him to be a man of great stature and nobility. His level of intelligence was remarkable, and his way with words had reached a much higher level than hers. He wrote beautifully, much more compelling than she had ever managed to do. His words had crossed generations, and even continents.

At 2:00 a.m. traffic was minimal, with traffic being at a much more reasonable level on the western side of Richmond than it was on the eastern side. With city upon city, and only four lanes of highway, cars lined up like dominoes on the eastern side, and even in the middle of the night, the road wasn't clear. In fact, the cities were lined up all the way to Virginia Beach.

Focused on the gas tank, her random thoughts, and the road ahead, she didn't give much thought to the road behind, where two sets of headlights lingered in her rearview mirror, one a bit closer, the other a bit farther behind.

CHAPTER 28

If it wasn't for the alcohol in his system, recovering from the four shots from the previous evening—two of which he had abandoned on the bar in his hasty retreat—coupled with the fact that he was always a light sleeper, he might not have seen her and her dramatic exit. Sleep affected him even more so after Stuart had passed—which made being chained to an air conditioner before even more of an issue than it might have otherwise been. After all he had been through with her—the bar fight and gun battle, the handcuffs and semiautomatic pointed at his brain, the shopping expedition and jaunt through the public—he couldn't believe she still didn't trust him.

Not that she seemed to trust many men. But still, Pete was different, or he liked to think he was, even if he did imbibe in a few more spirits than he should, whenever a bar or a local liquor store happened to present itself. If he wasn't supposed to consume any alcoholic beverages, then he shouldn't have had so many opportunities to do so.

When it came to men, she had always assumed the worst, verified her suspicions with misguided information and half-truths and compensated herself for her valiant efforts with a "fuck you" to anyone with hair on his face. When the opportunity presented itself, or even when it didn't, she chose to run as fast as possible in the opposite direction. He acknowledged her rapid speed and stealth exit into the cool night air. He even managed to give her a certain amount of leniency without even so much as a stern look, which meant Veronica chained him to various inanimate objects, including a steering wheel, a car door handle, and a window air conditioning unit that was louder than the sound of a pickup truck backfiring. Like the pickup truck, she peeled out on the gravel road ahead, leaving this world in a cloud of dust, smoke, and a noisy muffler, with wheels that fought a little too hard for purchase.

She had left the bed, changed outfits once again in the bathroom, similar to Superman in a telephone booth, after she had tossed and turned in the night, sweated profusely, with hair more than a little harried and bent out of shape, before she sank even deeper into a dream-filled sleep. He had noticed her shaking at random intervals, twitching and clawing at the night, and had she not been completely turned off by the concept of men, including him, he might have startled her earlier, held her sooner, and grinned at her longer. But thoughts of another beating or attempted handcuff maneuver had stopped him short of acting out his plans. Or she might have gone so far as to stuff him outside the motel room door, before slamming it in his face, ensuring the great divide separated his world from hers. Like the previous place, he had chosen their present setup, because it dealt in cash and asked even fewer questions. She tossed a fistful of dollars in his direction, along with a few words, that should not have been repeated in front of man or beast.

To say traveling with her these past few days had been an experience was similar to calling The Big Bang a tiny explosion. Not one he was likely to forget as long as he was among the living, or even the dead. Veronica might have been a pain, but she had filled him with pleasure as well, a sense of purpose and meaning in his otherwise bane existence where he filled his nights at bars and his days sleeping off the previous night's drinking. He had risen from a sea of ashes, if even for a brief while, where there was only fire before, and it had given him direction and some semblance of a plan. These past two years he hadn't had much of one. His life had been a bumper car ride, and he had been the one stuffed in the middle, slammed at every angle, and unable to escape his fate.

Her eyes had popped open like the top on a can of Bud, and she had sat up, the sheet dropping around her, wearing the same outfit of the previous evening, both the jeans and the blouse wrinkled from sleep. But that wasn't what had distracted him. She had entered the bathroom and come out wearing a new outfit, one he might have chosen the previous day.

Of course, Pete made it appear he was still sleeping. Even if he had been, though, he would have heard her go, with shaking walls and the sound reverberating around the small space, and he would have jumped up, ready for a fight, or the latest standoff. Even ready for what most likely awaited him on the other side.

Waiting until he heard her footsteps on the stairs, he slipped out behind her, closing the door softly behind him, and followed her down the stairs, and out into the night. When she headed for his car, he headed for the parking lot, attacking it from the opposite end, looking for a vehicle that might offer him quick transportation, a set of keys in the ignition, or in the visor above the dash. With his eyes darting left and right, he bypassed newer Accords and Civics, a Camry and Highlander, and even an Explorer, before he found a well-worn Ford pickup truck that had seen better days and slipped behind the wheel.

In another life, perfectly paired with a misspent youth, he had learned how to hotwire a vehicle, but the driver's door was unlocked, and the keys were in the visor, exactly where he hoped they would be. So he slipped out into the night a few moments behind her, trailing her at a safe distance, knowing that she'd probably need his help, even though she would say she didn't. If he had learned nothing else from her, he had learned that much. A dirty mouth mingled well with his dirty mind, and her sense of control was her only method of survival. The army had taught him about people and how to deal with them on a much different level than the average person—especially when the person on the other side of the sand dune had a crazed look in his eyes and a false sense of glory and country in his heart as he hoped for some redemption. Pete had learned to deal with rather complicated scenarios time and time again, until it was just another possibility floating through his head. Each experience had given him another flavor, another taste to add to his budding

repertoire, until he had learned to judge people on an unconscious level, making snap judgments and snap decisions. Most of it was acknowledging the world around
him, learning a standard set of personality traits, that
crossed cultures and continents, and adapting those traits
as necessary.

Veronica was more of an anomaly—possibly tainted
in her teenage years, both hers and his—than a standard
method of practice, but he had always appreciated a good
challenge, just as he enjoyed a good opportunity. All he
had needed to do was let her think she was in control.
Appearance was perception, which transformed into reality. Her reality.

◈◈◈

She tasted blood. And bile. Her own.

Veronica could feel it on her lips, and she was sure
that there was red inside of her, swirling up within her.
She wanted to cry, or lash out, kick out at the night, but
no one would hear her screams, or see her justice. She
knew the men were out there, probably waiting, probably
laughing at her, and biding their time until they struck
again, as she lay crying, or dying, or on whatever path
took her away from redemption, trying to keep her spirits
up, and stay alive. Dying might not have scared her
once—when she had a string of errant boyfriends and a
high attitude—but it scared her now. And she had the
sinking sensation that she would die, and that lightheaded
feeling took over behind the wheel.

Maybe her drink had been filled with drugs, or the last
remnants of whatever concoction the businessman had

given her in her underground prison. She had been given something. And if a toxicology report were possible, she knew she would have been off the charts, spiking and peaking at all the wrong moments.

She had tried to call out before, and she called out now, in the confines of a moving vehicle with only her actions to dissuade her thoughts. But she heard nothing. Alone. Abandoned. Maybe that hurt more than the fact that she deserved to die.

She wasn't sure anymore and tried not to focus on the inevitable. What she needed to focus on was a way out. A better plan than the one she had thus far. She was the one who was supposed to be in control. Not them. But she didn't see that happening, not with the haze still surrounding her, night and lights in front of her. The darkness swallowed her up and spit her back out, the same way these men were going to swallow her. She shuddered at the thought, flipped the heater up to alleviate the chill, and turned on the radio to help her cycle through her thoughts. The worst thing she could do was not to prepare herself for the next battle, driving to some destination where she was ready, where she could see them coming. If something happened to work in her favor, she would welcome it. But she couldn't rely on it.

The bonds seemed to tighten around her, her breathing more constricted, inside the car more contained, claustrophobic even. Or maybe that was just her imagination. She clung to the breathing motion, in and out, deeper and deeper still.

She focused on the road ahead, the white and yellow lines.

Her roadmap.
The only lines that could save her.

CHAPTER 29

A transponder and a remote control went a long way. GPS. The tracking device had been placed near the rear driver's side tire, and Elrod had used it to follow them, first to the motel, then Short Pump Town Center, and now their present location on I-64 eastbound, outside of Charlottesville. He had been clever with it, discrete enough. The transponder gave off a steady signal. A blip on a map, guiding him on his path. It might as well have been a bull's-eye with a battering ram. He had trailed far enough behind, Thurman riding shotgun and otherwise being a nuisance, without so much as a single coherent thought, sucking on Slim Jims and looking out the window. On the car ride, he'd already tossed out one toothpick. After Thurman was done with the Slim Jim, it wouldn't surprise him if he shoved another toothpick in his mouth.

Public radio played in the background. Not music. Never music. It didn't center him the way a talk show filled with national interest pieces, interviews, and facts did. He had switched cars for the job. Clean. Not a scratch or dent on her. A decent enough engine but without the true raw power and pickup of a turbocharged V-8 or V-10. Not a true muscle car, this one, but it was adequate. He made it work.

The highway was otherwise unlit, with only the moon, lights, and the little blip to guide his way, the signal strong and steady. The man who was with her was a wildcard, supposedly named Pete, with the boss's minions doing the digging. He was a sharpshooter—there was no way it was Veronica, not with the intelligence he had on her, no track record of even visiting a firing range or firing a weapon—and Elrod had underestimated Pete once, but he was determined not to let it happen again.

Thurman had on a graphic T-shirt, or some such nonsense, beneath a white button down shirt that he had left halfway open. The T-shirt, not the button down, referred to some fight Elrod had never heard of, with a woman on the front who was only half-clothed, the rest of her attire in a heap in her dressing room.

Thurman was in the passenger seat and had tried to start a conversation more than once. Each time Elrod cut him off.

He had a new hat for the occasion, not as good as the one before it, but he'd make it work all the same. Fashionable. Or maybe it was decorative.

A cigarette bobbed in his mouth, which he puffed on between his thoughts, and listened to the radio or the blip, when he wasn't thinking or puffing. He hadn't said two words, not that he was counting. When he finished the butt, he flicked it out the window and onto the road.

Pete Nealey might have been the wildcard stranger with the military background—that's what Anthony had found out about him thus far—but he was going down either way.

The transponder continued to beep. He didn't trust Thurman to hold the device, the incoherent bastard, especially based on his recent and continued ineptitude, so Elrod had propped the device on the dash, and he glanced to his right every twenty seconds or so. He hadn't trusted the bastard to drive either, but that was another story, and he preferred not to hang on all the details. He was a cat chasing after a tail, or a dog chasing after a bone, depending on which animal you loved the most.

Sure as shit, Thurman finished the Slim Jim, tossed the wrapper out the open window, the air creating a wind tunnel and disturbing Elrod's thoughts and radio—not the cigarette, it was long gone—and the man beside him popped a toothpick in his mouth, shoving it around and chomping down.

Neither he nor Thurman had gotten much sleep—the lack of a sound night's sleep seemed to affect him less than Thurman who had only managed a semi-conscious state accompanied by his continued focus on the toothpick and the open road. Maybe the lack of rest was a thing of the past, or maybe it was the new reality until the job was done and the check cleared.

This job was supposed to be easy, but it had turned out to be less so.

He had to time his next move just right—even though there were plenty of curves and wooded areas on either side to complete the task, and the road ahead was filled with few, if any, vehicles—since he had a bastard for a partner. Elrod wanted her to believe she was in the free and clear before he executed the next phase of the plan, and her trigger happy companion had no idea of the events that were about to unfold. The element of surprise did wonders for a good killing. He wanted her guard to be down, and he wanted her to concentrate on driving. The monotony.

He had tailed her for close to twenty minutes, ever since she had popped on the interstate, a bit behind just in case she decided to get suspicious. And, during that time, the transponder had beeped approximately sixty times, at least those were the ones he had counted. Thurman hadn't managed to look at him once, let alone open his mouth. The toothpick, though, had taken more than a passing glance or two. For all Elrod knew he might have been sitting next to a corpse who popped up and down with each bump in the road, uttering a curse word here or there for recreational purposes.

Entering the freeway one exit behind her, Elrod had easily caught up to her, and he now tailed her at what he considered to be an appropriate distance, approximately three seconds, keeping this space whether she sped up or slowed down, or managed to continue at a steady pace. He had plenty of gas in the tank, filling up the night before, so he could drive all night if he needed to. Not that he would need to.

He planned to dispose of her properly in the next hour or so, whether or not Thurman decided to wake up from his continued trance. She was nothing but trouble—a constant and continued distraction—and Pete was even more trouble than her, the man as fearless and trigger happy as Dirty Harry. If not for him, she'd have been dead—in some wooded enclosure on the outskirts of town for the coyotes to have a go at her—and Elrod wouldn't have two holes in his now deceased hat or Anthony bursting a knuckle and a blood vessel. The man had punched more holes in walls than a drunken carpenter and changed women as frequently as he changed hammers or clothes, and, in some cases, even sooner than that. It surprised Elrod that Bethany had lasted as long as she had. Through no fault of their own, the women didn't last, but Bethany had lasted longer than most. He did find it intriguing—nothing more, nothing less—and he'd probably continue his level of amusement for the foreseeable future.

Thurman had his hands clasped in his lap, and the toothpick still shoved in his mouth. He'd already checked his gun three times, just itching to fire it. But Elrod had warned him that they wouldn't need firepower on this particular mission, not that Thurman had listened. If the fool went against him, Elrod would dispose of three bodies instead of two. He counted on that not being a problem, but he was prepared all the same. He had enough bullets in his gun to complete the job three times over. For his companion, he'd provide a bullet through his mouth.

An errant bullet before he had time to execute his plan would only give them away, and destroy the surprise factor. An aspect he counted on and had already factored into the equation, determined not to make the same mistakes again.

He counted to ten, and then he pushed the pedal to the floor, separating the distance between the hunter and the prey in less than a second, headlights making the car in front seem larger than it was. He swerved into the other lane and cut hard to the right, smashing into the vehicle on the driver's side. An explosion of hard plastic and glass ensued, even louder than a string of fireworks on the Fourth of July. The small car—some sort of Japanese model either a Corolla or Civic—veered off to the right, coming to rest in a ditch, as he pulled in up ahead of the vehicle. Thurman popped his door open, but Elrod called him back. Instead of rushing toward a fantastic finish, Elrod waited, knowing he had plenty of time. He planned to savor every instant.

Looking in Thurman's direction, Elrod saw the right hand and the toothpick twitch, the gun in Thurman's lap where it hadn't been a moment before. Had Thurman looked in his direction, Elrod would have shaken his head in a swift, defiant manner.

This was his rodeo, and he planned to be the lead cowboy.

CHAPTER 30

Shock filled her body, and she twitched in her seat. The seatbelt jammed against her sternum and chest. Her breathing was shallow, ragged, as she hiccupped each breath, her view through the windshield hazy and blurred. The driver's side was punched inward, and her back was flush with the seat.

Had the car had airbags, they probably would have deployed. Her seatbelt had kept her in place and given her pain in her chest, but her head had jerked to the side. The side-to-side motion made her head feel like it was on top of a bowl of Jell-O. She had a slight pain running up and down her spine, forming a knot in the small of her back. Her hands hadn't left the steering wheel, her knuckles white, her grip like a pair of talons, and blackness filled her head, the landscape gray and charred.

The instant the car smacked her, even before she felt the impact or heard the glass shattering or the plastic crumpling in on itself, her mind halted. It felt as if she had taken a quick nap and had woken up in a ditch, seconds later not remembering the impact or the brief aftermath, as though the sentence in her mind missed several key words and phrases. She remembered seeing the head-lights—the swerving, erratic vehicle pounding into the left hand lane, before it pounded into her—for a brief instant before the impact.

Veronica didn't remember steering the car, not in that moment or the next. It was as though that second, or even two, had been wiped from her mind. The self-defense mechanism had kept her mind in check when her brain couldn't handle the overload.

She'd never been in an accident before, not even when she was young and filled with stupid and bad decisions, and she hadn't recognized what was about to happen until it was too late, the other vehicle already flush with her before it crushed against her. She had no warning, other than the slight erraticism and seeing the other vehicle run parallel with her own for a heartbeat. or maybe it was two, matching her tire for tire. And even though Pete's car wasn't exactly a car that he would show off, she was sure he wouldn't be thrilled with the end result: the jarred impact, broken glass, and bent plastic, although there was nothing she could have done to prevent it. Her instinct had kicked in, a small warning signal looking for a beacon, when the car had run parallel with her own on the mostly empty road.

She had been lost in her own world, focused on the driving, the flow of lines and curves and angles, and the random thoughts that she couldn't control or escape. The horrible dream she couldn't erase. Pinpricks of light entered her head, which were most likely caused by the side-to-side movement, the lines bright and many, varying in both length and width.

Veronica tried to tame the explosion in her chest, the acute pain in her lower back, and the dizzy sensation that threatened to cause her to pass out again. She focused her mind on numbers and spreadsheets and quadratic equations, the last book she had read—an Amy Tan novel—and the last song she heard, a little number by Fiona Apple.

No one had moved from the car in front of her, but at least the vehicle had stopped. Maybe the whole point was to incapacitate and disable her and strike like a praying mantis, boa constrictor, or alligator.

CHAPTER 31

Pete yanked her door open and flicked off her seatbelt. The polyester and nylon concoction managed to snag on her left arm and shoulder. She gripped the steering wheel with a ferocity normally reserved for snakes and small rodents. Her talon-like grip strangled the rubber to the point of oblivion. She stared straight ahead. He stared at her profile.

He called out to her, but she didn't seem to hear. He pried her fingers from the round wheel, and the seatbelt sprang free. Her gaze, however, remained locked in the forward position.

"I can't seem to leave you for even just a minute," he said, "without you managing to get in some sort of trouble."

She whipped her head around. "That's because trouble somehow manages to find me."

He pointed up ahead. "We need to go right now," he said, "before those two in front of us decide to come out shooting."

He helped her up. At least for the moment the wrecked

car ahead was locked in place. The night air whistled and clanged.

She stood on rickety knees. "I won't even bother to ask how you followed me."

He looked her over. "I'm a light sleeper."

"I'm fine," Veronica said. "Just a little bruised up." She paused. "I'm sure I'll look even better tomorrow."

She had a scratch above her left eye and appeared as though she might fall over at any moment, but she had no other visible damage. A pair of blood red eyes pounded into his forehead before darting dead ahead.

Pete placed her arm on his shoulder, not trusting her comments, or the state of her well-being, knowing that she would try to take on more than she could probably handle, and he'd have to sort through the ensuing tidal wave. Most likely it was in her nature, a small problem, probably a character flaw, that had only grown greater with time and independence. She was autonomous, and had stubbornness down to a science, and if she wasn't careful, obstinacy would take over her life, controlling her every move and fantasy. Possibly even lead to her ultimate demise, or a rendezvous with a large cliff.

His light sleeping and quick thinking had probably saved her life, and his instincts told him there would be trouble ahead. At the moment it was the car parked on the shoulder with the damaged front passenger side that lingered most prominently in his mind. Now maybe she would listen to him, or at least keep her objections to a minimum. But if he'd held his breath and wished on a shooting star, he would have passed out ages ago with no hope for revival.

Slipping Veronica into the passenger seat of the pickup truck before he adjusted his position behind the wheel, he cranked the ignition and pushed the pedal to the floor, at least as fast as the piece of crap would go. And it was a piece of shit, as he tried to keep up with two cars, neither of whom went much beyond the speed limit until the incident. But the pickup truck whined, took its own sweet time, and belched at semi-random intervals.

Veronica still had a look of shock painted on her face—her eyes wide, mouth opened, head unmoving—and sat as if she had a rod jammed in her spine. He could see the first signs that she was coming around and, in a little while, she might spit fire or point a gun at his forehead or handcuff him to another inanimate object. In the meantime, he'd concentrate on open freeways and winding roads.

A pop punched through the silence, and the rear windshield exploded. A taillight burst, right before a bullet slammed into the truck bed. He jerked the steering wheel hard to the right and overcorrected to the left. Zigzagging his way along the freeway, he shoved the Ford into what he hoped was another gear. Flicking his eyes to the rearview mirror, he noticed pistols out both front windows, muzzle flashes lighting up the night, and bullets whizzing by and blazing through the night. He gunned the engine through the turn ahead, tires skidding and squealing, before finding purchase, as the car behind accelerated and kept pace.

Veronica flung a string of obscenities in the confined space. He reached over with his right hand and thumped her head down. She offered another choice word or two—probably aimed at him this time, and one of which might have been motherfucker. He veered right around an SUV with tinted windows cruising along in the left-hand lane. His pickup truck might have lacked pickup, but if he could drive a tank on the field of battle, he could drive this piece of shit.

Pete slammed his foot on the gas, and the engine yelped in protest. He went up and down a series of hills, the truck bounding, whining, and grinding on the upslope before riding smoother on the down.

He could see a set of headlights closing in, and nothing but road in front of him, curving and meandering in both directions, so his opportunity to maneuver was somewhat limited, unless he veered off into the woods. Then instead of one incapacitated car, they'd have two. And several miles from civilization would make for another interesting jaunt through the woods, and once again, grandma's house wouldn't end up being the final destination. And he'd have Butch Cassidy and the Sundance Kid pumping bullets into every known form of vegetation.

Jerking the wheel hard to the left, he cut across the median, heading in the opposite direction, back toward Charlottesville, where the shots fired would set off a series of alarm bells and, hopefully, wake a sleeper from a light slumber. The twin headlights didn't have as easy a time with the median as he did, the car being smaller and having just been involved in a collision, the front end veering a little too far right. At first he thought he was home free, but persistence won the day, much to his chagrin, and the small car tore through the median, spitting up grass and flowers as it executed a somewhat lopsided turn, the back of the car fishtailing and careening before discovering more solid purchase. The distance between the two cars disappeared.

More shots were fired. The first two went wide of the passenger side, before the next one struck the rear bumper. At least one more struck the bed.

If he had been listening for it, he might have heard Veronica screaming or cursing, or possibly both, even with her head down, but he had tuned her out, focusing on keeping them alive, and jerked the car like a hooker on Las Vegas Boulevard.

The headlights drew closer, right before they slammed against the rear bumper. The Ford skidded and slipped beneath his grasp, as it fishtailed this way and that. Two sets of tires squealed, plastic buckled, and metal whined, as both his heart and the Ford galloped forward.

Without seeing the signs, he knew he was close to Charlottesville's outer limits, and before long, he'd begin seeing more pertinent exits—US 250 was his best and closest bet—any of which, though, would provide a golden opportunity for escape.

CHAPTER 32

She still had the image in her head of the errant vehicle that had smacked her at a high rate of speed and knocked her into the ditch, shoving her out of the way like a discarded pair of shoes. It wasn't a pleasant image, especially the aftermath and knowing that Pete Nealey had once again saved her skin, much to her chagrin.

He was a confident bastard, probably too confident for his own good, tracing his lineage back to high school, where the women and the men were lined up to shake his hand and buy him a round on the town.

She had her head down between her legs, staring at a bottle of beer, empty; a handful of wax wrappers; and a tube of lipstick, cherry. The floor mats, blue, and the interior, charcoal, contradicted well with the bullet holes and broken rear windshield. She had her hands on top of her head, and a grim expression on her face, as she chewed on her bottom lip.

The engine clicked, clacked, and shimmied, and Pete hummed a low, steady tone. The air conditioner blasted cold air on the top of her head and hands, her fingers already more than halfway to numb.

He had known exactly how to deal with her, probably a little too well, resurrecting a bout of silence and some crazy-assed driving. In other words, he was one giant pain in the ass: a confident, smug bastard with a chip on his shoulder. The same chip that was there when he was seventeen. Once again, he controlled the road, and she was relegated to the passenger seat. If she drove, though, it made it that much more difficult to slug him.

Her head popped up and she looked around. "What the hell happened?"

"Obviously, there was a transponder on your vehicle."

He slapped her head, then he slapped the wheel. The vehicle veered left.

"Obviously," Veronica said. "Besides, it was your vehicle. I just happened to borrow it." She sucked in a deep breath. "More importantly, though, how did it get there?"

"Our two alligators probably placed it there themselves."

"Did you give them a grand invitation?" She took in another deep breath. "Are you working for them?"

"No," Pete said. "I'm sure they took it upon themselves to track you. After what we've been through, if you honestly believe I'm working for them, you're even crazier than I am."

"You're the one with the transponder on your vehicle." *How long had it been there? Since the incident at The Montrose Inn?* She shivered, and not from the cold.

His jaw clenched, and he exhaled slowly. "Not by choice."

He told her to sit up.

Maybe the worst of it is over. Or maybe it's just beginning.

She jerked her head in his direction. "But you still had it."

He turned toward her. "And now it's gone."

Her hand was flat against the dash. One part of the cab that was bullet free. "Where did you get this truck?"

He tapped the steering wheel. "I borrowed it."

The headlights behind were getting further and further away, the wind whistled and cracked against the side of the bed.

"You might want to focus on the driving, Captain Obvious." She paused. "Are you going to return it? Or did you plan on making it your third vehicle?"

"Based on your little joyride, I'm probably down to one vehicle and a good tow. I hadn't planned on it, but then I didn't plan on having you become a permanent part of my existence."

"Trust me, it's not by choice," Veronica said. "I've done everything short of killing you to get rid of you." She counted to three. "You're just going to deposit it somewhere?"

"I figured I'd abandon it, now that they've seen it. This pickup was on the last legs of its life, anyway." His eyes flipped toward her. "Are you even listening to the engine?"

"It hiccups," she said. "There's also a whining sound." She moved her hand away from the dash. "What kind of plan is that?"

"Since when are you a critic?" Pete asked. "You're not exactly a motor vehicle expert. I'm surprised you haven't managed to cause even more vehicular damage."

Her nails tapped the dashboard, and she stared straight ahead for four beats. For good measure, she even flipped on the radio, cranked up the volume, and leaned back in her seat. "Does that even require a response?"

"Not exactly," he said. "No."

She flipped the sun visor down and flipped it back up. *No mirror*. "Do you always have to be a jerk?"

"Do you?"

"It just comes naturally," she said. "I'm sure it comes naturally for you as well."

"I have all the charm in the world."

"I'm sure you do," she said. "If you keep telling yourself that, I'm sure you'll start to believe it."

Placing her hands in her lap, she rubbed her right knee. A knot had formed there, possibly stress related, or she had banged it during one of the jarring incidents. At least she hadn't banged her head.

"Should I even bother to ask what our plan is now?" Veronica said.

"You haven't really inquired up to this point. Why start now?"

She glared at Pete. "Because I want to make it out of this alive. Whether you want to or not, well, that's your choice."

If she could have done it all over again, she certainly would have chosen a different angle altogether and a different partner with a little more sense.

"Well, if you start giving me some answers," he said, "we might make it out of this alive. You mind telling me what you were working on before you were abducted?"

She tapped the dashboard. "I already told you—"

He made a hard right turn and jerked the truck to a stop in a vacant Arby's parking lot. "That you stopped a merger. But that doesn't explain why you'd end up abducted. Even Enron made more sense."

The silence in the pickup stood at attention. "I might have worked a few shady accounts."

He jerked his head around. "What?"

She unclicked her seatbelt. "I work mainly with large corporations, banks, and the like. I balance the books for firms that skim profits off of one business and dump them into another." Her nose twitched. "It's all about corporate tax avoidance. Adding dollars to the bottom-line. I'm supposed to make that happen, or someone else becomes the new appointee."

He exhaled, his fingers gliding over the steering wheel.

"We were maximizing profits," she said. "You mind telling me where you learned to shoot and drive like a maniac? You weren't this high strung in high school."

"You and I didn't hang out."

She ran a hand through her hair, flipped an errant strand behind her ear. "True. I seem to recall that being your fault. The fifty-yard line fantasy and all." Veronica opened her door and stretched her legs. "What was it like growing up on a farm? Were you driving a tractor before you started preschool?"

"I grew up less than a mile from you." Pete clicked his teeth. "Where do you get your stereotypes?"

"Downloadable off the Internet, available at any twenty-four-hour drugstore, and passed along to you free of charge."

"There's always a hidden cost," he said. "With you, I'm not sure I can afford the price of admission, or the unspoken agenda."

She slammed the door. "With me, there's a lot you can't afford. You might as well get used to that now. It'll save us the trouble of explanations later."

He rubbed the back of his head. "You know you still haven't said thank you."

"I didn't realize it was required. You've stuck to me worse than a full-grown amoeba."

"Your handcuffs are in the trunk of my Corolla. The gun is on the backseat. As for the thank you, it's not required, but it is certainly appreciated."

Veronica paused for two beats. "For your information, I already found the handcuffs." She had dug around in the middle of the night when she couldn't sleep, slipping around in a linear fashion, knowing his simple mind had come up with a somewhat simple solution. At least he hadn't brought up the cuffs sooner, or attempted to use them.

"I'm still not sure how you manage to do the least amount of work for the maximum amount of effort," she said. "For all I know you're working for them."

A sign next door to Arby's mentioned free doughnuts: It was currently unlit. Not being hungry had its advantages.

"You add a whole other dimension to suspicion. Why would I help you then?"

"Because you're just waiting to turn me in," she said. "To you, the game is more important than the end."

"What kind of fucked-up plan is that?"

"I've heard a lot of fucked-up plans," she said. "And

this one happens to be near the top of the list. I still haven't decided if you're Butch Cassidy or the Sundance Kid."

He started the pickup and jammed on the gas. The tires squealed and the engine whined. "You're still alive, aren't you? And you're just stubborn enough to almost get yourself killed. You know, you might not want to admit it, but you need me more than you realize. Without me, you'd already be back in your hole—"

She bit her tongue, hard enough to make it go numb. "Have I already called you an asshole?"

"Indeed," he said. "Do you want to try again?"

"No. You're the cancerous growth that can't be removed, even with the aid of a laser."

Pete jerked the wheel hard to the left, cutting through a yellow light and onto a side street. "I think we should focus on the fact that you're still alive." He paused and the engine roared. "With that mouth of yours, it's no small feat."

"Do I even want to know how you got this car?"

"It's a pickup. The keys were in the visor."

She breathed in through her nose, flipped on the radio, listened to the background music, and considered punching him on his right cheek.

"Maybe we should visit your firm," he said.

She nearly smacked her head on the dash. "You're proposing we go back to the scene of the crime? I knew you were demented, but I didn't realize you were straightjacket worthy."

His eyes flicked toward her. "Have you got a better idea?"

CHAPTER 33

Thurman had a toothpick in his mouth and a cell phone in his hand. The toothpick moved around—the cell phone didn't. He paced on the side of the road near a grocery store, kicking at a rock and a cellophane wrapper. He'd dropped the cellophane wrapper, not the rock.

A stoplight blinked red in his direction.

"Did you fuck it up again?" Anthony asked.

"Yeah," Thurman said.

He'd drawn the short straw again. Fucking Elrod probably had the game rigged, and if Thurman didn't have an empty clip, he would have shot the bastard in the head to go along with a few in the roof, windshield, and possibly the dash.

Elrod had his hands between his knees in some sort of meditative state, but it looked more like he wanted to touch his own behind. He currently had his head up and his hand out the window, flipping Thurman the bird.

Static filled the silence. "And you lost the transponder, didn't you?"

"I had the perfect plan," Thurman said, "and I executed it perfectly, except there was a little snag."

Elrod couldn't shoot and drive at the same time, and he jerked the car so much Thurman had hit more trees than he had plastic. Elrod didn't hit either passenger, and neither did Thurman, which was just fucking unacceptable. He did, however, manage to shoot air, and possibly a squirrel.

"I don't want to hear about little snags, big snags, or any sort of snag. I sent you Elrod, and you still managed to fuck it up."

"You can have him back," Thurman said.

He'd even blindfold Elrod, as well as wrap a bandanna around his forehead, march him into the elevator, and kick him in the ass on his way down the shaft.

"No, you can keep him," Anthony said. "Until you get the situation taken care of, I don't want to hear from you again."

"What do you mean?"

"This isn't a hard concept," Anthony said. "If you need for me to spell out the details, you might want to gain a few more brain cells."

And then the phone slammed down in Thurman's ear, resonating inside his head for more than two seconds.

If Elrod was supposed to be an expert, then he should be able to shoot and drive with reasonable accuracy, or incapacitating precision. Instead, he jerked the car, harder than a cowboy riding a bull in the middle of a rodeo, and nearly planted the muffler in the median during his failed U-turn. His lips moved like a sea turtle, and his new hat, a gray one with a red pinstripe, didn't look any better than the previous one had. Thurman spit his toothpick on the ground and cursed at dead air, his index finger standing at attention and pointed in Elrod's direction.

Between the two guns and more than twenty rounds, a taillight died and a rear windshield exploded. Hell, he could have done that much with the steering wheel in one hand and a handgun in the other, and the same amount of bullets in the magazine. It wasn't difficult. But Elrod had stared at his gun the way he stared at women, and he'd been rather proud of his Tex-Mex shooting, as if he had just won $1000 with a scratch-off ticket.

If Thurman hadn't been forced to grip the door, unload his weapon at dead space, and poked his tongue with his toothpick when he'd cursed the moron, and Elrod hadn't blown a gasket and a tire—and gone through God only knows how many rounds, probably scaring more deer and chickens than he scared the two in front of him—then Thurman would have slapped the man, clocked him with the butt of his pistol, that he'd tossed between his feet, and duct taped and hogtied his fashionably clueless sidekick before Elrod ended up in the trunk.

It had been a good plan. That much he knew. He didn't need the boss slamming the phone in his ear, and he certainly didn't need the man's approval. Elrod had veered off the road and slammed them on the driver's side, where there was a ditch on the right and no possibility of escape. That was Thurman's plan, no one else's. If Pete Nealey had been in the passenger seat where he was damn well supposed to be, it would have been the end of the road. Both the door and the car were at an unusual angle, tilted toward the right, and jammed into the ground, the driver's side wheels hanging off the ground.

The bastard would have been pinned and forced out on the driver's side. And Elrod could have picked them off like squirrels in the snow or knocked them out, or any number of other scenarios, most of which hadn't come to Thurman beforehand. If the driving fool hadn't been staring at the weapon on his lap like he was about ready to have sex with it and pumped a few bullets through the rear window, then it was a win-win.

In twenty seconds, or maybe it was closer to thirty—Thurman wasn't counting—the pickup truck peeled away, and he was left doing all the work once again, screaming directions and gesturing with both hands, while Elrod fired away like a blind cowboy in a two-man standoff. Thurman, on the other hand, used a little more poise and precision with his gun.

Maybe the idiot would have done more damage if he had been blind. Thurman had read that the other senses were heightened, or some shit like that, and since the man obviously couldn't see worth shit, let alone fire a loaded weapon with any reasonable amount of accuracy, maybe the idiot could have hit a moving vehicle a couple of car lengths away with his eyeballs popping out of his skull.

It was a cluster fuck. There was no other way to say it, and Anthony was going to blame his ass, instead of blaming his idiot partner Elrod, the man with the loaded weapon who had the responsibility to finish the job, a job that Thurman had laid out for him on a silver platter, even spotting him the fork and knife. All he had to do was the supply the spoon. It was simple, and it would have been fine, if Elrod had known what he was doing and hadn't jerked him around more often than a shark at Sea World.

With a fully loaded weapon, instead of a half-cocked one, his arm jerking like a palsy victim, and if the man hadn't been legally blind, this all would have ended just fine. Instead, it was only just beginning.

The transponder was gone.

CHAPTER 34

The lights were dimmed in the restaurant, the tablecloths were lace, the waiters and waitresses were devoid of all piercings, the chandeliers were crystal—there was more than one—the conversation was less than elegant, but that was to be expected, and her choice of companion couldn't be avoided. The carpet sang beneath her feet, and the tables were cherry.

Veronica snapped the roll in half, staring at it for several seconds, and her mind drifted backward, spiraling through time.

Her heart had broken into a thousand pieces when Pete left her. A six-month relationship took her the entire junior year to get over. The weak moment throttled her, and the way he just walked away, fine the next day, and then when she showed up in his life again, he had no idea who she was. That was the instant when she realized there was no turning back. The instant she realized she was better on her own rather than having someone break her heart again. And he wasn't even all that great—a drinker and a joker, and not even worthy of her.

But love was crazy like that: filled with football fields and pom-poms, touchdowns and field goals, cheering from the sidelines with her hands held high, her voice projecting from the bottom of the bleachers all the way to the top. Before her life went to shit, and the leather jackets and skirts and laissez faire attitude made an appearance, and self-defense seemed like the right move to make. Rather than embrace love, she flipped it the bird from the driver's seat and controlled her life with a joystick.

Veronica just wanted her life back. And she was damn sure going to get it.

"Are you planning to skin me alive?" Pete asked.

She buttered the roll. "You don't even know who I am, do you?"

"The woman from the park."

"There's more to it than that, Captain Obvious."

He asked, so she told him the story. When she was done, she might as well have had a second head, or a third eye for all the good it did her. "Findin' a Good Man" was a Danielle Peck song, and the story of her life, with just one problem: She wasn't done yet.

The table was off to the right-hand side, sturdy and square. The room was dark with just a dim light overhead with thick wooden pillars to separate the space. The kitchen was open and expansive. The restaurant had a lower level along with an upper tier.

She refolded the napkin in her lap, took a sip from her water glass, and peered at him across the table with less than soft eyes. "So tell me about this plan of yours." Not a question.

"Well, it's not fully formed," he said.

She cut and stabbed a piece of filet mignon. "Kind of like your brain cells?"

His steak was more than twice the size of his brain, and he had made short work of it. He attacked it with the same vengeance he might reserve for a prison riot. Not even glancing once in her direction, not that she had noticed. If he had taken any more interest in his steak, shoveling in pieces at close, random intervals, and she had been the jealous type, she might have been bothered. Or then again, maybe not.

He had been a bother from the moment he met her, sophomore year in high school. There wasn't much she could have done about that either. So she had chosen to ignore it. He had a glass of wine in front of him, and it had already been refilled once. She didn't know when he'd start in on the harder stuff, and she wasn't sure how she would avoid another incident. How he would remain sober enough to execute whatever plan he had formed in his mind remained a mystery to her, but then again, she'd been good at solving mysteries.

Once the food was placed in front of him, all conversation had ceased. Not that he was good with the repartee, other than a shrug or the occasional shake of his head, or when she was really lucky, his eyes went wide, and time stood still for the briefest of moments. But with the food there, it had reached a level bordering on unconscious.

He still had a lot to process, being that he knew her and all. Pete devoured the steak the way he might devour a beautiful woman. The wine seemed to serve the sole purpose of a palate cleanser with little sips followed by larger ones.

Veronica wasn't sure how she felt about returning to her place of employment, having left out a few details. He didn't deserve to learn the whole truth, and if she could find a way to deal with it herself, she would and leave him with his thumb on the side of the road. She didn't need a man solving all her problems, especially an unreliable one with a history of being a bastard.

When she ran out of silence, she said, "What have you done with yourself since you left the military?"

He set his knife and fork in a crisscross pattern. "Why do you care?"

She stabbed a piece of filet mignon so hard she thought the fork might devour the plate. "If you want the truth, I don't. But I thought it might be nice to learn a bit more about you, since we do have history."

"I haven't exactly been employable."

She shoved the piece in her mouth and chewed. "Sobriety helps."

Pete scrunched up his right eyebrow. "Why would I need sobriety?"

She sliced a piece of asparagus in half, brought it to her lips, and chewed. Two sensations overwhelmed her mouth at once. "It's just a thought."

He downed the rest of his wine. "Are you trying to control my life?"

She hoped he wouldn't ask for a refill. "If I thought I could get away with it—"

"And if you can't?"

"Then I'll try to figure out some way around it," Veronica said.

She did have an assistant at her disposal, at least she'd had one, anyway. Like the men in her life, there was often a high rate of turnover, even when she stifled her expectations.

"But you're an accountant."

"That doesn't mean I have to think inside of the box. Liking numbers and being creative aren't entirely separate endeavors."

He dropped his napkin on the right side of his plate. "I'm sure we can arrange another game for you."

"Honestly, I'd prefer that there was no box at all," she said. "I don't need a box. The thought of being contained activates my claustrophobia." *Or at least it would have.*

He scratched his chin. "You don't have claustrophobia."

"How would you know?"

"High school," he said. "You once made out with me in a broom closet before Mr. Dewey caught us and threatened to expel us both."

"So now you remember." That wasn't a question either.

Pete tossed his napkin on his plate. "Who said I forgot?"

All she could do was shake her head. His comment bounced around in her brain like a ping-pong ball and threatened to nosedive into the net.

He smirked in her direction. "You're hiding information."

She lifted both eyebrows at once. "Like what?"

"There's more about your situation that you're not telling me," he said. "I don't need to look at profits and losses on a daily basis to know that much."

"About high school?"

He shook his head.

"Do you honestly think I would continue to hold out on you?" Veronica asked.

He nodded. "I do."

She brought the last piece of filet mignon to her lips and chewed longer than normal, the taste and flavor exploding in her mouth, the meat caressing her tongue and making her lips dance. "You're cynical."

"You haven't given me a reason not to be."

"You're not a particularly pleasant individual," she said. "You really need to learn to say no. It might help you live longer."

He picked up his napkin, wiped his mouth, and placed it back down. "Life's a lot more fun when you say yes."

CHAPTER 35

The building towered above the ones around it, punching toward the clouds in the middle of a city block. Concrete, brick, and blue glass windows reflected the light. The buildings on either side of it stood smaller, miniaturized versions, the alleyway between the buildings not wide enough for a car. Shrubs, trees, and a sign surrounded by stone flanked the front. Hairline fractures permeated the stone, puncturing cracks in the rock. A revolving door kept the heat and the cold at bay.

"Do you know what you're doing?" she asked.

Pete shoved his left hand in his pocket. "I don't break into places for a living, if that's what you're asking."

"You mean you don't have tales from a misspent youth?"

"I do," he said, "but they don't involve breaking and entering."

"You're pretty good about not talking about yourself."

"I could say the same thing about you."

He shoved through the revolving door, and she followed a few steps behind. There was an audible groan

behind him—it might have been the door, or it might
have been her—that he chose to ignore. She had been the
same way at dinner, both distant and forceful, and he was
glad they had skipped dessert, otherwise that would have
prolonged the agony and nearly guaranteed that he would
have bolted for the door without her. It wasn't exactly a
plan built on sound judgment. He'd always preferred his
instincts, wits, and knowledge of the streets. Of course,
there were times when his instincts didn't work right—
wires might have been crossed, signals might have been
manipulated—but those times were few and far between.
He'd made a lot of headway in the meantime, since those
days two years ago, or maybe he hadn't. Either way, it
was progress of some sort, and progress meant that he
was still on the field of battle, heaving a sword, rifle, or
machine gun at the enemy flanks.

Maybe he would never discover the truth. That was
okay. He could deal with it. But most of the time Pete
chose not to.

She had a keycard, and his first option was to swipe
the badge to ensure it hadn't been deactivated. In compa-
nies filled with layers and layers of bureaucracy—the
government was notorious for such things—there was
often a time lag for badge deactivation, simply because it
required more than one person and more than one step in
the process. Possibly more than one piece of paper and
multiple signatures to complete the transaction. It was all
bullshit, but he had learned to expect it, and in times like
this, it meant a series of green lights for the road ahead.

She entered her pin, and the door to the area beyond
the entryway opened up. The lobby was marble, granite,
and tree-filled, not small shrubs either, but fully formed

young saplings that would grow big and strong with time and with the proper sunlight, provided courtesy of a glass roof and windows. A lone security guard checked four monitors in front of him, and eight more on either side of him, the chair beside him empty and turned to the side. Pete walked stride for stride with Veronica to the front desk, where she flashed her badge, another bureaucratic formality, and he signed in, signing Sam Snead in the appropriate block.

"Hey, are you related to the golfer?" the guard asked.

"I'm his grandson."

"Hey, that's awesome. What was he like in real life?"

"Similar to the way he acted on the golf course," Pete said. "He was a hard person to know. But he had his moments of brilliance."

The guard leaned forward. "Do you follow the tour?"

"Not as much as I used to," Pete said.

"Do you play?"

"Not very well. The golfing gene was never passed on to me. But I'll hack it around a few times a year to better understand the madness and complexity of the sport. White balls and white flags are the bane of my existence."

"But if it had been," the guard said, "you would have had a foot in the door."

Even sitting down, the guard was tall, with a long torso, close-cropped hair, dark eyeglasses, and a day's worth of stubble on his chin. His mouth moved in exaggerated fashion, and his hands were the size of two chickens.

"Or one foot out of it," Pete said.

The guard just shook his head, his eyes flicking among

the monitors. Meanwhile, Veronica had already sauntered off toward the twin elevators, tapping her foot in time with the Muzak. Pete jogged to catch up with her.

"What was that about?" she asked.

"You mean you don't know Sam Snead?"

She punched the up button twice: It was already lit up. "Should I?"

"He's only one of the greatest golfers of all time," Pete said. "He's not exactly one of the friendliest men, but he had a mean golf game, and the temperament to match his low scores."

"So in his old age," she said, "he probably has your level of personality. I can see why you chose him."

"Did you honestly think I would sign my real name?"

"Great, so I'm being tracked, logged, and monitored, and you're getting away scot-free."

"I'm hanging out with you," he said. "I wouldn't exactly call it a clean escape."

The slap to his face resembled a small firecracker. His head jerked to the left. As for the guard, he whipped his head around.

"If you keep it up," she said, "there's more where that came from, and I might not be so nice the next go round."

The elevator dinged. She stepped on. Pete followed closely behind, his cheek still stinging, ears ringing.

"Let's just get this over with," she said.

"That's what she said."

This time the slap landed on the other cheek. His head, however, remained in a stationary position. Her slap wasn't completely unexpected. The doors closed, and one upbeat instrumental was exchanged for another.

"I'm just going to alternate cheeks until you actually

say something without being a bastard," Veronica said. "If you keep it up, your face will hurt worse than my hand."

With the button pushed for the fourth floor, the elevator moved at a steady pace, local news and weather portrayed on a small monitor. Rather than watch the screen, he watched the floor, which was covered in plush maroon carpet that was probably less than a year old.

"I feel like I'm walking the plank," Pete said, "and you're the one holding a gun to my head. If your finger starts to itch—"

"Maybe I am," she said.

The elevator opened. She made a hard left. He followed. She scanned her badge and entered her pass code once more at two glass doors—his bureaucratic dollars hard at work. A second later, the doors opened automatically.

On the other side of the doors, darkness had taken over, and a cubicle farm was doing rather well for itself, spreading and populating throughout the available space. Its growth was only limited by the size of the room. Wealth and ambitious executives, however, could fix the problem with a contractor and a building permit.

"Where are you located?" he asked.

She pointed to the left. "All the way in the back."

"Why am I not surprised?" If he had a choice, he probably would have chosen a similar location, out of the way of idle office chitchat.

He navigated the maze behind her, resembling a dog seeking out peanut butter, only his nose had deceived him before. Light background music played overhead, possibly either Mozart or Beethoven, similar to what had been playing on the elevator.

Overhead lights flickered on automatically lighting the way, spotlighting his moves from above him. The space between the cubes was narrow, not much more room than single file.

Coming up behind her, Pete watched as she rifled through papers, systematically dismantling the three piles on her desk in succinct fashion. Each pile was overturned and placed on her keyboard.

Three minutes later, her head popped up from behind her monitor. "It's not here."

"What do you mean 'it's not here'?"

"Gone."

His head jerked. "What?"

"I have no idea. It was at the bottom of that stack—" She pointed to the middle one. "—and now it's not. I checked the last one just in case it had been moved—"

"Maybe someone came by and borrowed it."

Her look put that possibility somewhere between zero and subzero. The chill in the air deepened and elongated, her hand slicing through the air. "Do you honestly believe I would let that happen?"

He was willing to believe she could control the time of day.

CHAPTER 36

Veronica woke to the sound of the phone ringing. Her hand shot out, scooped the phone that Pete had set next to the bed and placed it against her ear. She might have mumbled hello.

"You're a hard one to track down," a male voice said.

She paused for a beat, trying to shake off the remnants of sleep. "Who is this?"

"Deputy Sheldon Michael."

"And why are you calling me?" she asked.

Her eyes were still filled with sleep. The room was a hazy blur, and her mind moved rapidly to fill in the blanks.

A hotel. Somewhere between Richmond and Port City. That much she knew. The room was dark, the curtains drawn. She flipped on the light. A shape on the floor grunted and flipped over, a hand popping out from beneath the comforter. How much had she had to drink? Not even a glass of wine at dinner. She peered beneath the covers—fully clothed, pajamas rayon, not silk. Good sign, on the fully clothed part.

"Several shots were fired at The Montrose Inn outside of Richmond. I'm one of the deputies in the county, and I was the unfortunate recipient of your case."

She rolled over and stretched. "What case?"

"So you were just having target practice in your hotel room at two a.m. and things got a little out of hand? I don't buy it. Six slugs were found inside the hotel room, most concentrated on the opposite wall, with one found outside the door, right before the two of you dove through and bounded down the stairwell. Or have I been misinformed?"

She rubbed her temple and turned on her side. "Well, if you have all the details, why do you need me?"

"When can I see you?" he asked.

"I don't do dates based on a phone conversation. As for the Internet, that's completely out of the question." She shuddered at the thought. Half a dozen horror stories were more than enough to convince her to find her companionship elsewhere.

"I need for you and Pete Nealey to come to the station and make a statement," the deputy said. "I have a fairly good idea about what happened, but I want to hear your version of events." He paused. "For the record, I don't do phone dates either," he continued. "Once you wake up your partner, you need to pay me a visit, otherwise you might see the end of my southern hospitality."

The deputy hung up before she could come up with an appropriate reply.

With her head swimming upstream, Veronica rubbed her temple again. She'd been disappointed that she hadn't found the file, and she'd been even more disappointed by the phone call from a cop who had his head so far up his butt that daylight was no longer an option. She hadn't expected an investigation, and she hadn't expected the idiot sleeping on the floor—the one who followed her around and acted like a pompous ass, the way he had ever since high school. He hadn't even bothered to wake up for the phone call but managed to wake up for everything else, a man who ruined the better half of her week and was hell bent on working toward a full one.

This whole ordeal had been one long nightmare, the end nowhere in sight, if it ever was on the horizon. If it hadn't been for some serious handiwork on her part, the two of them might have spent a night in jail, as the guard had suspected foul play, and he had pulled a gun on Pete, forced his hands in the air, and frisked him. But she had talked her way out of it before the guard had gotten around to touching her, although it required more from her fancy mouth than she cared to admit.

She slammed her hand against Pete's head, and he shot awake, punching her in the shoulder and nearly knocking her over. He could have taken out her eye. She had dodged to the left, and he'd swung right. She'd always had quick reflexes, and she was glad she could put them to good use.

While it might have been foggy before, the path in her head was suddenly clear.

"We need to make a trip to Montrose."

Pete rubbed his eyes. "Are you arresting me?"

"No," she said, "but we're wanted for questioning."

"With regard to what?"

"You shelling The Montrose Inn like it was the local shooting range."

He stood up and tossed his arms over his head. "I saved your ass."

"Just keep telling yourself that," she said.

The room was neat but sparse. A few of her things were next to the door in an overnight bag. A TV stood atop an entertainment center, and there was a mirror just to the right of the entertainment center and the TV. Had she developed a bit more courage, she might have peered at herself. Instead, she focused her attention on the man with the large hands. At one time, he had put them to good use.

"We need to visit Deputy Sheldon Michael," she said.

"I don't trust a man named Sheldon, and since you don't trust anyone, you probably shouldn't either."

"Maybe I don't," Veronica said. "But that doesn't mean we can avoid talking to him altogether. Whether it fits into your plan or not, it's now a part of the agenda."

CHAPTER 37

Anthony zipped up his fly and grabbed Bethany by the hair, pulling her out from underneath his desk, where her panties were currently around her ankles. Her lips were swollen, and her chin glistened. She used her tongue to wipe the remnants of him off, staring deep into his eyes the whole time, before she pulled up her panties, without even bothering to turn her back. If she was anything, she was the boldest lover he had ever known. Brazen. And he was proud to have her around, even if she couldn't answer a phone to save her life, locate the filing cabinet—let alone spell the word correctly—or the coffeemaker, and her temperament and work ethic left much to be desired. As for her organizational skills, she couldn't have organized a pep rally or an office Christmas party. But when push came to shove, she would do whatever she could to please him. And sometimes that was enough.

Her lips were pouty, her tongue protruding from the edge of her mouth. He had to breathe deeply to calm himself. Her skirt shimmied into place, and she rubbed him one last time between the legs, the motion both firm and bold. He made a spinning motion with his hand. Obediently, she turned away from him. He slapped her on the ass, as she left his office, sashaying the whole time, not missing a beat, or an opportunity to show off for him. Her butt was toned, firm, and round from yoga, Pilates, or some other shit.

He'd been working late, and by extension so had she. He'd gone through four secretaries in four years, each one servicing him in a different manner, some more competent than others.

The women often tired of him. During one exit interview in particular, the brunette—he couldn't recall her name—bared her breasts and walked out of the interview topless, causing more than one male to make a run for the men's bathroom. Another one—a brunette as well—tossed a phone in his direction, before she picked up her things and marched down the stairs. The redhead, though, remained calmest of all, even if she did call him a bastard, before she turned in her key and marched out of the office, without taking her personal items along for the ride.

Never engaged or married, he preferred the wild, unstable ones, about twenty years his junior, small in stature with big hearts. The irony, however, wasn't lost on him.

With one last look out his window trifecta, he dropped his microphone home and placed the call. The man on other end answered, skipping right over the pleasantries.

"Is it done?" Nathan Labaw asked.

Anthony's right hand ached, the knuckles still swollen. "No."

"I can't afford more fuckups," Nathan said. "I've already given you plenty of leniency, and you've thrown my kindness back in my face."

"I know," Anthony said. "I thought by bringing Elrod onto the team it would be taken care of. The transponder tracked our problem, and the solution should have been close at hand. I don't know why—"

"But it's only gotten worse, hasn't it? One problem has led to another, and the solution appears to have gotten away from us. This should have been solved below ground. It never should have resurfaced." Nathan paused. "How much does she know?"

"Enough to bring us down," Anthony said. "That was why I got rid of the file. The contents, however, still remain in her mind."

"And you think that will solve all of our problems?"

"No, but at least it's a start," Anthony said. "If she talks, there will be nothing to back up her claims. It's not an answer, but it's a start."

"I'm not sure I like your starts, and you need to improve your follow through. I expected more out of you, and I've been disappointed. Once again, you might find yourself at the end of my leniency."

Anthony rubbed the back of his neck, before he tripled-tapped the window. "Maybe you should learn to trust me."

The last time Nathan reached the end of the swimming pool, Anthony found himself with a bullet in his thigh, bleeding out on the concrete deck. The wound healed, but the scar remained.

He wasn't worried about being shot again, only about the aim of his adversary, a little higher and to the right, and he would have a whole new set of issues. "I only trust the dead."

"Why?" Anthony asked.

"Because they don't reveal secrets."

Anthony had an innate ability to pick locks, which managed to help him in his misspent youth, discovering a slew of secrets from teachers, principals, architects, lawyers, and pool cleaners. Youth didn't last; neither did the lock picking. The secrets, however, remained firmly in his possession. He'd killed people before over less, the bodies buried in the woods, the locations strategically placed throughout the Hampton Roads area. He'd lost count of the number of bodies years ago. "She won't talk."

The pause was longer this time. "She received a call from the police."

Anthony ramped up his pacing; the tapping followed suit. "How do you know?"

"Are you questioning me?"

"Merely curious about your information," Anthony said. "I trust your sources."

"You don't need to concern yourself just yet," Nathan said. "Just control the situation. If I hear from you again, without our little problem being solved, I'll aim higher next time."

Anthony didn't need the details, the image from a year ago still as clear in his mind as if it happened yesterday. "It is under control."

"You call a car wreck, a shot up hotel room, and talking to the police controlling a situation? Control is an illusion—"

Anthony slammed his hand against the window, his

knuckles splitting open, blood dripping onto the pristine carpet. "She's not going to say anything."

"I'm not sure I'd make guarantees if I were you..." Static filled in a few gaps. "...what are you going to do?"

"I can bring in another expert."

"You don't need another expert," Nathan said. "What you need is to utilize the resources you have at your disposal. What you need is a better course of action."

Anthony grabbed a tissue from his desk and used it to staunch the bleeding. "What are you talking about?"

"Maybe it's time to use Bethany."

"She's good at what she does," Anthony said, "but her uses are rather limited."

"The situation between Veronica and Pete is on shaky ground. Maybe she could help diffuse it. I hear she's rather talented in that particular area."

"Are you suggesting I put her life in danger?"

"Would you prefer I put yours in danger instead?" Nathan asked.

Anthony slammed the tissue harder against his right hand. "What do you want her to do?"

"I hear her penetration skills are excellent. Maybe we should start at the heart of her talent base and let the situation ride itself out."

Anthony had never had her on top before. "You don't need to be so crude."

"How would you put it?" Nathan asked.

"Do you think she can handle the job?"

"I'm not really concerned about what she can or can't handle at this point. I just need someone involved with more than two brain cells. Your supposed hit men have severely lacked in the hit department. At least we know what she's good at and, if what you mentioned is even half true, she's a goddamn expert."

Bethany had more than her share of potential. However, he hadn't quite figured out a way to tap into her talent beyond the greed of his own pleasure. "And if something happens to her?"

"Since when have you worried about that?" Nathan paused. "You just don't want to lose a woman who can suck a softball through a garden hose. Maybe you should be concerned about more than just the tip of your penis."

The phone slammed down in his ear.

CHAPTER 38

The cramped interrogation room oozed masculinity, proving harder than Veronica expected it to be. The metal table sat at a slight angle, her chair scraped across the cement floor, the one-way mirror took up most of one wall, the door was cold, hard steel, and a slight chill filled the air—the air conditioning pumped harder than a jackhammer. She had been dropped there with Pete, even though Pete was currently sitting on the other side of the table with his hands on the metal and his eyes on his hands. She didn't bother to look at him.

Even though she had told him this was out of her control, he didn't believe her. In fact, he had questioned her for the past hour—when he wasn't looking at his hands—which consisted of the drive to the station, and the sitting. The sitting was the worst of it, waiting in limbo with the fan whining and the air blowing, and the small space even more confining. She'd been staring at the door, scratch marks dragged across the metal, waiting for it to open, summoning forth the demons on the other side, while Pete had stared at his hands and subsequently the table. There was nothing she could do about his staring. He was as stubborn as she was. Well, maybe not quite as stubborn, but close enough.

The wall was gray. There were paint chips on the floor, congregated in two out of the four corners. The metal table rocked with the movement of Pete's hands, and the silence could have filled the Sears Tower. The table was at a slight angle to the rest of the room, and thick, dark glass covered the mirror.

Looking up at her for the first time in over eight minutes, he asked, "Are you enjoying yourself?"

"I'm not enjoying this any more than you are."

He crossed his wrists and drummed his fingers. "Well, maybe you could wipe the smug look off your face."

"It's not a smug look," she said. "I have no idea what awaits us on the other side of the door, or if they're even watching us now. Maybe the lines have already been drawn, and we're pawns in some larger game."

"You're still holding out on me."

"And this concerns you now?" she asked.

He looked at his hands again. "I'm concerned you don't trust me."

"Trust is an operative word," Veronica said. "I thought you'd respect me enough to let me have my space."

"You might want to work on our freedom—"

"I can get us out of this." A slight nod of her head followed before she looked once more at the door, hoping the chess match would begin.

Ten minutes later, the cop entered, with a look of contempt plastered on his face, his mouth a firm hard line. He said he was a deputy. He didn't have on a uniform, but that didn't make her position any more comfortable.

It was all she could do to keep her voice level and even, keep her gaze away from his face, and not stare at Pete, who was just waiting for the next round, and who could probably go for as long as she could, with equal parts silence and stubbornness.

Deputy Sheldon Michael was tall, rail thin, with curly brown hair, and an off-putting stare. He had his right thumb hooked inside his pocket. In his left hand, he carried a manila folder. It looked empty. He dropped himself into a chair and dropped the folder on the table. It struck the metal with a thud.

"I'm not sure whether I should have you two arrested, fingerprinted, and thrown in jail, as you spend the night thinking about your many sins, or if I should use your vast array of resources to really do some damage."

"You could always let me go," she said, "and you could leave Pete in jail. I'm not his biggest fan anyway. Besides, he's the one with an itch to scratch."

"Is there any explanation for what you've done?" the deputy asked.

"I'm not sure you want to hear the real version." She pointed across the table. "As for him, he's a terrible influence."

The table rocked beneath Pete's hands, the metal screeching in the small space.

"You have information that you shouldn't have."

"A deal fell through," she said, "and now all the pieces are slowly disappearing. I worked the deal with two other individuals, both of whom bring new meaning to the word ruthless. I was caught in the water without a raft. If I hadn't learned how to swim, I'd be caught at the bottom of the river, the current swallowing me whole."

"And what does that make you?"

"I'm just a woman with too much knowledge." Veronica smirked. Neither of the men returned the favor. She tried a more neutral expression: It didn't work either. "You're worse than a Saturday night hangover."

The deputy shifted the folder on the table. "You're on thin ice as it is," he said. "Maybe you should start talking."

"And what if you don't believe me?"

"We'll cross that bridge when we get there."

She leaned back in her chair, scraping it against the cement floor. The scraping metal sent a chill through the air, but her voice was hard and firm, as though it had been ready all along. When she talked, her eyes narrowed, as she concentrated on every word.

"I'm an accountant with Brogue Consulting. A deal was supposed to take place, but the other side backed out. I'd been working on the deal for three months, probably the longest three months of my life. The new firm was supposed to serve as a slush fund. Anthony Whelan and Nathan Labaw had been skimming money from the firm for years, and no one was the wiser, especially with Nathan as the CFO. The millions he made each year weren't nearly enough to sustain him. He had big plans, and even bigger ambitions.

"In the process of working the deal, I uncovered records I shouldn't have, files that could no longer remain hidden, so the deal was canceled, and I was deemed expendable. But their plan backfired. George Bush—not our former president—kidnapped me, but I escaped from the underground dungeon where he held me for two days, and now my life is in the hands of the man you see sitting across from me. At least for the time being, or until I come up with a more suitable method to end this little charade. I'm sure I can figure out a way to survive, or at least remain alive and a thorn in their side, which is more than I can say for George."

The deputy rubbed his chin. "George Bush?"

"I saw his face on the street, not that I remember what he looked like. I didn't recognize his face. Handsome. Short, dark hair. Tailored business suit. He was some hired gun to keep me contained. His plan backfired. Mine didn't."

"If even half of what you're telling me is true," the deputy said, "you need protection."

"That's the problem," Veronica said. "I can't prove any of this, not without the files, and they've vanished. Like I'm supposed to."

CHAPTER 39

Revenge could make or break her. Fear could drive her or eat her from the inside out. Her voice was steady and even as she relayed her situation. The deputy jotted notes on a pad, looking up on occasion, passing along encouraging sounds with his mouth. The information dump had taken over an hour. Most of what she conveyed he already knew. When she was done, she didn't even look in his direction, just stood up from the table, brushed off the front of her pants, and made a beeline for the metal door.

She was reckless, out of control, and that's why Pete decided to get away from her. She had his number, and it wasn't just the one inked on the back of his jacket.

The deputy had been more than cordial, or at least as cordial as he could be, the room filled with tension and suspense. Pete had learned more about Veronica than he wanted to know, the pieces snapping into place like Legos. He had jerked more than once, not that either of them had noticed, or cared.

The table had screeched twice, both times his doing,

before she truly took over, commanding the room like a colonel.

It was all he could do to keep the game going, to keep the hammer from falling to the pavement, his back and chair straight, his mind blank and at ease. He had seen the look of pure anger on her face, a feeling of deception, and there was nothing he could do to change it. All he could do was hope for the best—and hope she didn't get caught like all the rest. She was on a mission, and it didn't matter where that mission took her, as long as she was able to get the results she wanted, no matter the cost. After she had marched out of the room, Pete had followed close behind, avoiding the deputy's outstretched hand. Pete's mind was filled with pain and sorrow.

Questions flowed through his head, but the answers were out of his hands. His hands had been tied by outside influences, influences that remained unreal to him. Unforeseen. And what he didn't know strangled him with even more passion than what he did know. The distance between the two was growing, the gap increasing. Unsettled. The slight shifting of his body, the drink in his hand that he brought toward his lips, the honk of a horn cutting through the air, the rev of an engine. Other noises from outside—a dog barking off in the distance, a siren coursing through the air, and a car starting approximately a block over—jerked his mind and body.

What was left of his imagination couldn't be left to chance. He closed off the possibilities, realizing they hadn't filled his mind. But he did have a sense of control, not that it would have bothered to stick around.

Drifting back to happier moments, Pete knew the bar

had been his savior. Drinking was the only random possibility in his life he could control, the only sense of security he had left. It was a staple, the one true lifeline in a series of unremorseful possibilities. The only need that remained day after day. And it was all he could do to let the thought of control slip through his fingertips.

"What do you want?" he asked.

He waited for an answer. There was none. But he called to it again anyway, asking for guidance. It didn't provide any more answers than it did the first time. The bed had been hard and firm beneath him, the bottle on the nightstand beside him, the curtains drawn, the window closed.

When the bullet had torn through Stuart, the sense of agony on his face was more than enough to turn the dreams into nightmares, the pain into a constant companion. The nightmares had turned even more horrid, and the past had done what it could to catch up with Pete. Each day was just as horrible as the one before it, and the one after it. Sleep was often a foregone conclusion, but all the same, he tried to salvage it when he could, savoring the moments when the darkness took over his life.

He wrapped his arms around himself, hugging his chest, before his hands returned to the bottle, and the darkness it offered him in return. It was his only way through the madness, the only clear-cut and narrow path.

Pete stared at a spot on the other side of the room, an empty space between his dresser and a small bureau—both gifts from his parents, from a former life. He continued to stare, not knowing how much or how little time had passed. Before he even realized it, night had taken over his room and his world, and he was all alone.

The Wet Rhino beckoned him, and he listened to its seductive call. It was all he could do to keep it going, to keep the liquor flowing through his system. Maybe if he stuck his head inside the bottle, he would get the results he wanted. He'd slammed back three shots, and he had a glass in front of him filled with another. The drink didn't matter, the dark liquid all the same. He didn't know how it had gotten there, but he wasn't going to let it go to waste. The bartender looked at him as if he'd be passed out in less than five minutes, but that was fifteen minutes ago.

It was a dive, filled with smoke, and loud music pumped through speakers in the ceiling, the stools wooden and uneven, the bar itself was one long wooden monstrosity off to the left hand side inside the door, the floor sticky.

"You look like you could use a friend," a woman said. She shifted her position on the seat next to him.

Pete knocked back the shot. "And you're in the business of offering friendships?"

"I happen to hold you in high regard," she said.

The skirt was black, her hair blonde, and her eyes blue-green. Her lips, slightly larger than normal, formed a little pout, and her tongue was bright pink. Her breasts pulled away from her thin white blouse.

He picked up the empty glass in front of him, stared at it for a minute, and put it back down. "All you've managed to do is watch me drink."

She sat on the stool next to him, but she'd only recently arrived at her present location. "How did you know I was sitting at the other end of the bar?"

"I might be on my way to drunk," Pete said, "but I haven't lost my observational skills. Besides, that skirt of yours could blow away in the wind."

Her legs, however, weren't long enough to get anywhere near the floor.

Her eyes flicked to the bar before focusing on him once again. "Would you like to test your theory?"

"Just how drunk am I?"

"Probably not drunk enough yet," she said. "But we could always help you get there." She slid a glass in his direction.

"Are you offering?"

Her hair hung loosely around her shoulders, full and straight. "I thought you might accept my proposal." She tilted her head at a slight angle, before inching the glass a bit closer.

The slight hint of bare skin peered up at him, her neck thin and long. "And just what is your proposal exactly?"

"You should probably have a few more first." She pointed at the shot. "And we should probably find the back of the bar, so I can help you find a few other things." The look in her eyes was mischievous, similar to a kid who had just discovered how to lie.

He whipped his head around. "Do I need a flashlight?"

"Probably not," she said. "But we could always arrange for one."

Pete smiled. "And who are you?"

She said her name was Bethany. No last name. "I'm going to be your new best friend."

"Did I lose the other one?" he asked.

He told her his name and stuck out his hand. She shook it, more firmly than he had anticipated. Her fingers held his an instant longer than necessary, nails digging into the soft flesh when she pulled her hand away.

She shoved her chair closer to his. "Tragic accident. You might want to look the other way next time."

The uneasy aroma of cigar smoke drifted toward him, the cloud hovering just above his head. Music blared from the speakers, either heavy metal or alternative rock. She had to lean in his direction every time she opened her mouth, her voice soft and airy. He tapped his fingers on the bar to the rhythm of the music. A pulsating beat worked through his subconscious. "What do you work?"

She winked at him. "I can work wonders when it comes to zippers." She stuck her tongue out and slid it back in.

Pete smiled again. "We really haven't met before, have we?"

He would have remembered her. She would have stuck out at a Sarah McLachlan concert.

Her fingers slid across the bar, touched his hand. "Probably not. Otherwise, I would have remembered."

"Shouldn't that be my line?"

"Aren't you out of lines?" She hopped off her stool and held out her hand.

"I thought that was just excuses."

She pulled him to the back of the room, propelling him around tables and people, using her body as leverage, and he followed, probably a little too obediently, caught in a whimsical fantasy, where she controlled his fate, as though he had finally found a new home. She didn't seem to mind, the control factor held firmly in place, and she hadn't slapped him yet.

Even heading toward the near side of drunk, he still had control of his mental faculties, along with his muscular ones. Keeping his hand in hers, he felt like a child who had just gotten propelled off the playground. He kept it there in neutral territory. To place it elsewhere would have given rise to a riot.

The table in the back had a gash in the center and rocked back and forth whenever his glass moved. He didn't remember how it had gotten there either, but he decided to help it along. He brought the glass to his lips, his tongue licking around the rim, savoring every morsel of pure alcoholic bliss, before he swallowed.

"We could use your tongue in other ways," Bethany said.

"You know, my place isn't that far." As long as he followed a straight line, instead of the detour through the park in the imaginative dark.

"I thought you'd never ask," she said.

He never did learn if Bethany was her real name.

CHAPTER 40

Bethany had her hand in his lap, while he tried to return the favor. The sofa was long and straight and had more than a few threads missing. One minute she was next to him, the next she was at the opposite end with her arms crossed over her chest, complaining of a chill in the air. The TV was in the off position, and his mind was in second gear. It would have been in third if he hadn't had a beer after the liquor: a stupid, amateur move. But she had brought the bottle to his lips in seductive fashion, right around the time she had decided it might be a good idea to disrobe, dropping her clothes faster than he could down the bottle.

"You need to watch where you're putting those paws, mister."

She had been hot one minute, cold the next. Pete thought it was a new game of playing hard to get, but now he wasn't so sure. She had stripped down in less than five minutes, offered him the bottle in the first four, and he had stripped down soon afterward, setting the bottle on the kitchen table. His pants and her skirt comingled together. And then she'd walked away. To the living room where the TV snapped on before he trailed behind her and flipped it off, staring at a black screen and not much else, peering at her out of the corner of his eye.

She tucked her right leg underneath her, patted the cushion next to her, and winked in his direction. He shook his head, getting rid of the cobwebs that had gradually taken over his mind, along with a bit of the alcohol. The leg on his makeshift coffee table might as well have come out of a magazine. Her panties were red lace, her stockings black, and she had on a black lace bra. Her mouth was turned in the form of a pout, and she had one hand on her hip, jutting out to the side, the other resting on his sofa near the back, which just happened to have some of its stuffing missing along with the threads. He hadn't bothered to replace it. She didn't appear to notice.

Without giving it much thought, Pete hopped down beside her, scooting toward her, and she'd shoved him away, not hard, but not all that gentle either. The cobwebs returned. And then his hands started roaming, and his mouth might have opened, as the sofa shifted, and the fog lifted.

Right around the time he grabbed her upper thigh, she'd become violent, striking out at him on more than one occasion, with one of her nails catching part of his earlobe, and her ring catching the top of his head. As he jumped away from her, she settled back into the sofa, her eyes darting back and forth between the blank TV and him, but more often than not, the TV, or at least the space around it, was her main focus. The pout managed to reach a deeper meaning.

Her breasts filled out her bra, and she moved like a

snake ready to strike. With fluid movements and soft hands, she was as graceful as a dancer. These worked in sharp contrast to the hardest nails he had ever seen with daisies painted on every other one. Her skin was the color of white chocolate, probably the palest skin he had ever seen, and he wondered if she had bright red nipples. His hands darted out again, and she slapped them away, nearly slugging him in the process. The sound reverberated in the small room, the stinging dissipated more quickly.

"Would you like me to get nasty?" Bethany asked.

He had a feeling it wasn't the nasty he would have preferred. "If that's what you want."

"Do you *only* think about sex?"

"When I'm sitting next to a half-naked woman, my options tend to narrow." His actions followed his words. His eyes narrowed, and he imagined nipples as big as flying saucers.

She glared at him, hands covering her chest. "I should have kept my clothes on if I had known you were going to be this much trouble."

"In my experience," Pete said, "women know exactly what they're doing. It's the men who seem to get caught up in the game, losing sight of the prize." Trying not to stare proved difficult. He pictured a rabid dog with teeth bared barking inches away from his face. He added a foaming mouth to keep the image fully formed. It helped.

Her right leg shifted out from underneath her. "Do you still see the prize?"

"It hasn't strayed far from my mind," he said.

Convinced about her nipples, he hoped he could test his theory. Otherwise, he might have to discover the inside of the bottle again. Preferably not one filled with beer.

Her right leg snapped out, striking the table and over-turning it. "I'm not just some prize you can win. I'm much more than that."

At a loss for words, he wasn't used to this particular game. Or women in black lace bras. "I never doubted it for a second. But I didn't expect the game to take such a sharp turn." It had started spinning in circles like a drunken cyclist. He was headed down the mountain.

"I'm rather new at this."

"I find that hard to believe," Pete said.

She certainly hadn't wasted any time with her clothes, dropping them faster than a stripper on the second song of her act. As for her other accessories, those could easily be discarded as well.

"Are you good at reading people?"

He nodded. This one, though, was all over the place.

"What do you see?"

"I see a woman out of her element, unsure how I'm going to react, probably thinking she should have left fifteen minutes ago. Even though you want to, you're not going to walk away. You've gotten this far, and you want to see what happens next. You have a playbook in your head, but you started improvising more than ten minutes ago."

"You're not as drunk as you first appeared to be," Bethany said.

"I'm good at a few games myself."

"Well, you're not going to win this one."

She pulled a gun from her cleavage, and he stared hard at her, before he dove away from her and her weapon.

Where he was just a moment ago, the sofa exploded in a puff of cotton. She fired at where he dove, but he was already rolling, on the move, scrambling toward purchase on the other side of the room.

"You're faster than I expected," she said.

Pete said nothing. Running in his boxer shorts, he skidded around the corner, the carpet being the only thing that stopped him from slamming against a wall or a door, his unsure legs suddenly sure of themselves. A bullet flew over his head, and one just missed his right side, embedding itself in the wall.

"But you can't run forever."

He heard her feet on the carpet, his senses tuned to the sounds surrounding him. That's why the gunshot had sounded like an explosion in his right ear, worse than the sound of flesh meeting the back of his hand. It was a nine-millimeter—compact, but it was more than strong enough to do damage.

He noticed her inexperience with the weapon, the faintest hint of hesitation, the half-second delay on the trigger. This dance was not her own, but she was willing to hit the hardwood floor with all her assets firmly locked into place.

He had a weapon in his house, other than the one that Veronica had taken from him. Loaded. But it was in the master bedroom. Somehow, he had to navigate the stairs, without getting shot in the ass for his trouble, dig it out from its hiding place—in the bottom of the closet—and be ready to stand his ground like Wyatt Earp. The stairs were narrow, with a slight bend, and there were seventeen of them between the first floor and the second, and no matter how fast he ran, he wouldn't make it up in time. Not with her so close behind.

Drinking had never led to small pistols and breasts, both of which he considered major weapons. One or the other, but definitely not both at the same time. And not with a woman this beautiful before. In the back of his mind, he knew it was all too good to be true, but he had fallen for the oldest trick in the book: seduction. Even when he'd been behind the wheel of a car, navigating the interstate, or what passed for a freeway these days, he hadn't discovered this alternate universe. His options were limited, and his hope rested in all the wrong places.

"You're going to be my first—" Bethany said.

Even though she'd stopped, he didn't need her to finish the statement. But he noticed that she was still in the living room, biding her time, waiting to strike. Gun in her hand.

He grabbed a shoe, poked his head around the corner as plaster exploded inches away from his face, and tossed the shoe at her. The shoe knocked her backward. She struck the edge of the sofa, as he darted up the stairs, sailing over the last three with his body in a prone position. He turned his head and struck the wall with his shoulder, as a bullet impaled the plaster just inches above him.

Her feet pounded up the stairs, as he darted over to the closet and his safe, unlocked it, and removed his gun. He turned and fired, just as she stepped through the threshold with her gun raised in the firing position and her feet spread shoulder width apart. Red and black lace, covering a rather lush body—and all the sins within—fell to the floor. The bullet had entered her brain through what remained of her forehead.

CHAPTER 41

He paced in the small space, counting every other step, his boxer shorts hanging low at his waist. Time moved with him. The sound of a ceiling fan whirred in the distance, cutting through his otherwise silent domain. Adrenaline rushed through his body and his brain, similar to oncoming traffic pointed in his direction at rush hour, the force felt against his Corolla.

Pete dropped the gun on the bed and continued his pacing, his mind racing forward faster than his strides could take him. The world was blurred and uneven around him, the floor at a slight angle. The pacing was measured, his strides jagged and uneven. He marched in a straight line forward and backward.

After he had calmed down, he picked up the phone.

"I need to speak to Deputy Sheldon Michael," he said.

"He's off-duty," a male voice replied.

"You might want to bring him on duty for this one."

"What happened, sir?"

Pete's hand wouldn't stop shaking. "A woman is dead in my home."

Her blood had already seeped into his carpet the way alcohol had seeped into his brain.

"What's your address?"

He gave it.

"This isn't in our jurisdiction," the man replied.

"Trust me," Pete said, "he'll want to be here for this one. I can guarantee it."

"Someone will be there shortly."

He hung up the phone and waited. The pacing continued, but it decreased in intensity, along with his heart rate. The rocking in his chest reached more of a resounding whimper, the stitch in his side divided through time. Minutes might have passed, or seconds, he wasn't sure which. While he waited, he made another phone call.

He didn't identify himself, and she didn't ask him to. "Do you know what time it is?"

"I have a vague idea," he said.

"Then why are you calling me?" Veronica asked.

"Because there's a dead woman in my home." *And she was alive when she walked through the door.* He didn't mention the half-naked part, since it would only confuse matters.

"Why didn't you call the police?"

"I already have."

"Then why involve me?" she asked.

"Because I'm pretty sure she's somehow related to the two men who were chasing us." He didn't add that he'd been held against his will on more than one occasion and experienced more than one sleepless night based on the day's activities.

"Did she tell you this? How did you get my number?"

"No," he said, "but I can read people pretty well." He

never bothered to answer her second question.

"You say that an awful lot."

"If I say it long enough, you may start to believe it."

Her ability to trust hovered somewhere near the rat-infested basement of a condemned building where shackles hung from the dank and dreary walls. "Highly doubtful."

"Are you going to help me?"

There was a pause on the other end of the line, which coincided with several deep breathing exercises. Static might have been involved as well. "What do you want?"

"Deputy Sheldon Michael's home number."

"And what makes you think he gave it to me?" Veronica asked.

"Because I know you can be charming when you want to be, and I saw you in action. He admired you." He paused. "Probably more than that."

"And if I do have it?" There was suspicion in her voice.

"I'd be forever in your debt."

"You're already in my debt," she said.

His ledger remained different from hers, and it was much more than an issue of semantics. "Actually, if you want to get a little technical about it—"

"Which I'm sure you do—"

"You owe me," he said. But he'd never see an actual payment on his end, and even if he did, the transaction wouldn't go through.

"I knew—"

"I did save your life," Pete said. "Actually more than once, as I recall." And he'd put up with her shenanigans like being hog-tied to a window air conditioning unit that grunted and burped in the night.

After a long pause that might have coincided with some paper shuffling, she gave him the number. "I'm coming over. Give me your address."

"You've already been here," he said.

The hint of rose petals still lingered on both floors and probably would for the foreseeable future. He never was a big fan of roses.

Despite the urge to duck and run for cover, he gave her his address. And then he started pacing again. Every thirty seconds or so, he peered at the gun taking up space at the left edge of his bed, staring up at him, coaxing him away from his thoughts and memories.

It had been self-defense. Bethany had pulled the gun from her cleavage, and he saw the look in her eyes. If he hadn't taken her out, she would have helped him reach the end of the queue with a hole in the ground and a rose on his grave. Not a particularly pleasant thought.

Veronica showed up at the same time the police did. He didn't see Deputy Sheldon Michael—he had a long drive ahead of him—yet, one of the few men he could trust. Sure, it was a long shot, and not a simple task to cut through the bureaucracy and jurisdiction, but he believed in strong will over strong won't.

She had on a baggy outfit. The four cops were in uniform, each one walking with a slightly different swagger that could be spotted from two blocks away—the walk of a cop, a walk filled with confidence and jelly doughnuts. Even though none of them had viewed the crime scene, Pete could already feel their judgments against him. He was at the top of the hit list.

Inside his house, Veronica stood next to him just outside his bedroom door, staring straight ahead with a slight shake of her head.

"What have you gotten yourself into now?" she asked.

He held up his hands. "She attacked me."

"While she was naked?"

"It was meant as a distraction."

The distraction had proved only temporary. Reality, however, proved much more permanent, bordering on the psychotic.

Silence filled the air with even more silence. "But you still managed to shoot her in the forehead?"

"It wasn't an easy shot," he said. "I had to shoot her without really looking at her."

"Do you have eyes in the back of your head?"

"I sensed her."

Her perfume, more than anything else, had led to her demise. The scent proved earthier than rose petals and even more distinct, lingering in the air like a sentry.

He placed his right hand on the wall, stretching out the muscles that had tensed up with the increase in stress. The stitch in his side was on full amber alert, pounding away at his kidney.

He felt a hand on his shoulder, digging into the bone.

"We need to talk with you, sir."

He hadn't even heard the door.

"I knew it was merely a matter of when, not if," he said.

"Maybe we should go into the other room." The cop motioned to a room across the hall. The spare bedroom with an emphasis on spare.

Pete nodded.

Upon close examination, simple matters never turned out to be so simple.

CHAPTER 42

Pete told his story four different times to two different cops, in the same room on the same bed with the same poster staring at him—an iconic Marilyn Monroe shot—each one probably focused on the possibility of a new tale, each cop with a slightly different expression painted on his face. It was a simple story, and Pete was good with details. His facts didn't change, his voice didn't waver, and his eyes didn't flicker.

And then Deputy Sheldon Michael showed up. Pete hadn't had the time to call him personally, so he assumed Veronica had. She had obviously gotten further than he would have. But it wouldn't have been for a lack of effort.

Pete repeated his story again to the tall man with broad shoulders and the only one in a tan uniform, only this time it finally managed to sink in. The light changed, the clouds parted, and the skies opened up. Pete knew he had to stay in control, but adrenaline still coursed through his body, his thoughts elsewhere, and the alcohol still worked its magic in his system. It had been a long night, and it had somehow managed to turn out even longer. "What should I do now, Deputy?" he asked.

"Well, forensics is already working the scene. That's an interesting position of the body, and she is missing all of her clothes."

Pete ran a hand through his unkempt hair, his voice strained. "I told you: She pulled the gun out of her cleavage."

"Have you touched anything?" the deputy asked.

"If you mean have I touched the body, no. But this is my home, and I did touch the safe, doorknob, and I'm sure you'll find my fingerprints all over the bedroom. That's where I sleep."

"And it's also where you keep your gun," the deputy said. "That must have been a difficult shot."

"I'm trained not to fail," Pete said.

He had managed to fail in life, over and over again, in fact, but not in combat.

The deputy raised an eyebrow. "You're prior military?"

"Key word being prior," Pete said.

Deputy Michael pulled out a notepad and used it to tap his thigh. "You lost someone close to you?"

Pete looked down at his hands. "My best friend."

"I'm sorry," the deputy said.

"It was two years ago." Pete continued to stare at his cuticles. "I've adjusted back to normal life."

Or so he had thought. But now he wasn't so sure.

"It appears that's still an ongoing process," Veronica said.

"I need closure."

She leaned on her right hip, her eyes steady. "You're getting it now."

"It's the adrenaline." Pete lifted his head. "I'm sure it'll die down soon."

"If it doesn't, you may want to focus on relaxing," the deputy said. "Deep breathing helps. If you slow your heart rate, the adrenaline will follow suit."

Pete nodded. He had expected the pessimism. "How long will forensics remain?"

"It's a straightforward crime scene," the deputy said, "and it appears you haven't held anything back. Still it could take a couple of hours. Do you have somewhere you can go?"

Pete shook his head. "This is all I know."

"Then you might want to stay with Veronica. I'll let you know if I have more questions."

Deputy Michael handed him one of his cards, and then he vanished, almost as if he had been nothing more than a fleeting encounter.

Chatter filled the air, more bodies showed up, all of them living, trudging up the stairs to the second floor, before Pete decided even the living room had become too cramped. He stepped outside and found Veronica on the porch, the top step, as far right as she could go with her hands on either side of her.

"You stuck around?"

"You need me." There wasn't a hint of malice in her voice.

He stared straight ahead. "I can take care of myself."

"You've proven this point on more than one occasion," she said, "but Deputy Michael isn't one of your biggest fans. I, however, happen to have a little more charm than you do." She closed her hands into tight fists, her body as taut as razor wire.

"I don't need charm."

She turned her head in his direction. "In this case, you do. There's a dead body in your bedroom, and that's not going to be easy to explain." She unclenched her right fist, and her left. "But I might have a few details that you don't have."

"Like what?"

"Like I can confirm your suspicions." A slight nod of her head followed.

"How would you know about my suspicions?"

"You think she's somehow involved in this whole mess, and you're right. You've gotten yourself in the middle of the ring, against the bull, and now you're going to have to fight your way out without the aid of the rodeo clown."

"Who is she?"

"Bethany Aimes," she said. "She *worked* for Anthony Whelan."

He noticed the extra emphasis on the word work. "And this is the same Anthony Whelan who wants you dead?"

"Exactly."

"Why would she come after me?" he asked.

"She has ample assets and feminine wiles. For the average male, that's a deadly combination. But you managed to overlook her charms."

He didn't know whether it was a compliment or an insult. With Veronica, it could have gone either way.

"That's because I wanted to stay alive. When she pulled the gun out of her cleavage, I knew my chances were slim. So I reacted based on my instincts. What I had been trained to do in the past took over—similar to riding a bike."

"The average American male wouldn't have gotten past her ample assets," she said. "She could have pulled a king cobra out of her bra, and the average male wouldn't have been the wiser. It could have hissed and struck with accurate precision. So how did you do it?"

"Because I recognized she was a bit off," Pete said. "It all seemed too easy. She was coming onto me a lot harder than most women, and for her level of attractiveness, it seemed too good to be true. And when she stripped to a bra and panties in less than five minutes, I knew our situation had stretched beyond reality."

She stared hard at him. "You're not completely distasteful."

He smirked and shrugged. "But, again, she's out of my league. As you would say, the numbers just don't add up."

A light rain splattered his face. He brushed a drop off the tip of his nose.

She caught a drop of rain in her palm. "I use numbers for other purposes."

"So why me?"

"Because Anthony thought he could get to you through her," Veronica said, "and then that would leave me as the last woman standing."

"And if it didn't work?"

"Anthony Whelan doesn't count on failure," she said.

"Being a former military member, I figured you'd understand the simplicity of it."

"You think more firepower is on its way?"

Her head bobbed. A few drops splashed out of her hair onto the concrete. "I'd say almost definitely. Since Plan B backfired, he'll return to Plan A, and he'll hope for the best. Or he might throw another plan into the mix. We'll call it Plan C."

"And if we manage to stop them?"

"At least now we have a contact in the police department," she said. "He gave you his card, didn't he?"

CHAPTER 43

The room was large. Expansive. A brief stop on the highway. Filled with tables and chairs and broken cabinets. Abandoned. With cement walls and a cement ceiling, it might have been a former warehouse. The walls and ceiling were covered with chips and cracks. One crack in particular—a long, jagged one—Thurman couldn't get out of his mind.

"You've done nothing but underestimate me since the moment I met you." He had both hands in his pockets searching for a toothpick. He was out.

"That's easy to do. Your plan failed."

Thurman pointed a finger at the man less than two feet away from him. "Actually, you were the one who was supposed to finish the job. You slacked off on your duties, not the other way around."

"You're just now getting around to telling me that?" Elrod asked. "Maybe you should focus on your failures, not mine."

I should have stopped at the convenience store less than three blocks away. "I haven't exactly enjoyed the pleasure of your company. You're worse than a bee sting."

"I'd say the same," Elrod said, "but that might be overshooting the obvious."

"You failed to pull the trigger. You're not exactly the expert marksman I was led to believe. Either you overstated your qualifications, or the boss needs a new pair of bifocals."

Elrod jabbed a finger at Thurman's chest. "You failed in your duty. You should have anticipated that he would be in a separate car. You didn't count on a set of unforeseen circumstances, and now you're the one that should face the consequences. If we're playing the blame game, you're well ahead of me, and your pace is increasing."

Thurman laughed. "Now you want me to read minds? Do you have a set of tarot cards I can borrow, or maybe an unused crystal ball?"

"It certainly wouldn't hurt," Elrod said. "You're not exactly one of the most accomplished men I've ever worked with. I'd be better off with a half-blind sidekick who's missing his right arm."

"Is that why you're carrying a gun that hasn't been fired? You're even better at confrontations than I am."

Elrod pulled his .38 caliber revolver up until it was level with Thurman's face. The motion was slow, rehearsed, and filled with resentment. He hated the man with the George Bush mask, and the simple way he approached more complicated matters. The car ride here had been one toothpick chewing frenzy with scattered wood all over the passenger floor. Bouts of chewing silence were measured in minutes, not seconds. Elrod hadn't been able to punch the volume on the radio high enough to get the smattering of toothpicks out of his brain.

The warehouse was musty and dank with more than one window busted, sunlight and heavy air seeping through the gaps. The gun in his hand was steady, sure.

Thurman could have stared down a polar bear on a melting ice cap. "Now you're going to kill me?"

Elrod took a step forward. A small step but a step forward nonetheless. The tiny space getting even tinier. The air thick and hefty.

"The boss wants the job finished, and I'm going to see that it is. We'll chalk up your death to a casualty of war, you stupid son of a bitch."

He pulled the trigger. Nothing happened. He pulled it again. The hammer pulled back and clicked a second time. Smacking against dead air. "What's going on?"

"Did you actually think I'd let you walk into this meeting with a loaded weapon? Stupid doesn't even begin to describe you."

Elrod narrowed his eyes. "How?"

Thurman smiled, the evil stretching its way to the surface. He balled his right hand into a fist. "It's not all that hard. You're easily distracted."

"I could say the same for you," Elrod said.

Thurman whipped out his pistol, the one he had stashed in his jacket, and pulled the trigger. His gun clicked, but nothing else happened. He pulled the trigger again. The same result followed. He cursed until he was red, white, and blue. He tossed his gun: It bounced off a table and struck a chair before hitting the cement.

"Now we're even," Elrod said.

"No, actually, the fun is just beginning."

Thurman struck Elrod with his shoulder. Elrod managed to dart forward at the same time. They connected in the middle of the open space. Momentum knocked them into a scarred wooden table and a chair, before all three were knocked to the floor. The chair broke, the two of them didn't. Thurman managed to pull away from Elrod long enough to land a hard right and then another, one to the forehead and one to the chin. He shoved his left fist into Elrod's stomach. Elrod coughed, roared, and surged his head forward, slamming his forehead into Thurman's skull. With Thurman dazed and confused, Elrod kneed him in the balls, and Thurman toppled over onto his side, striking the concrete before he rolled onto his back.

Elrod climbed on top of the table, balancing his weight on the unstable wood, and jumped from the additional height, his elbow extended, aimed at Thurman's forehead, where a gash had opened, and blood had seeped onto the gray floor, creating a small pool the size of a nickel. Thurman rolled out of the way, as Elrod's elbow connected with the cement, the crack and splintering of bone echoing in the large room, his right arm dangling uselessly at his side. He bellowed, assaulting the room and the wooden audience with the sound of his voice.

Thurman hopped to his feet, his stance resembling a boxer's, even though he'd never entered a ring. Except for a few street brawls, which had ended well before they had ever really started, he had little fighting experience, unless he could count two broken noses. But he was more than ready for this challenge, the man opposite him down an arm. Thurman smirked, wiped his forehead, and charged at Elrod, who was picking himself up off the floor with his left arm, his right arm hanging in an awkward position, the right elbow already swollen. Broken. This was the chance Thurman needed, especially if he was going to be the last man standing, the one who would finish the job and win the boss's favor. Anthony had sent a rookie to do the job that was rightfully Thurman's, without even consulting the senior associate.

Elrod was merely an imposter, a man called in at the last minute, a hired gun who hadn't even managed to do his job right in the first place, and he was the one who wanted all the glory, the one who wanted a song and a dance and a free peep show. Fuck that. It wasn't going to happen. He would meet the same end as his awful hat.

Thurman's elbow connected with the left side of Elrod's face, throwing the man's head in a side-to-side motion, as Thurman added a few jabs for emphasis. Elrod struck out with a vicious uppercut and brought a knee into Thurman's crotch. Thurman nearly fell and doubled over, and Elrod attacked his head with a knee to the face. Thurman hit the concrete, motionless, blacking out in the middle of the cement, with an overturned table and a busted chair not far out of his reach.

Elrod rubbed his face with one hand, his other arm dangling helplessly at his side, and headed toward the large steel door, next to one of the many windows. His right elbow throbbed like a mother, and he had the beginnings of one massive headache. His eyes felt like they wanted to escape his head, and sweat dribbled down his chin and off his skin, leaving splotches all over the concrete. His walk was unsteady, his movements slow and delayed, but at least he was alive.

Thurman, however, jarred awake with a start, his momentary blackness merely a distant memory. He saw Elrod march toward the steel door, his right side shuffling a little more slowly than his left, with a trail of red behind him, and more than halfway toward his ultimate goal.

Hurting Elrod was Thurman's first priority, and it appeared he had succeeded. The fool still thought he could win. Impossible. The game wasn't over until Thurman said it was over. The last man standing wasn't always the first one up.

The bastard had left him, not the other way around. Thurman put his hands on either side of himself and lifted himself up, the world spinning and circling around him. He almost fell over, but he was able to move one foot and then the other. With each step, he was more surefooted than the one before it, closing the gap in seconds.

The fool turned around, but it was already too late. Thurman swung his arm in an arc, connecting with Elrod's jaw and sending the man sailing through the window, out onto the asphalt, and down for the count—a count from which Thurman knew Elrod wouldn't get back up.

CHAPTER 44

To the victor went the spoils. Thurman dug out his phone, after he'd driven home, and called a pair of hookers. Probably one of the better investments he had managed, if he did say so himself. He'd have his fun, and he'd have a bit more: twice the amount of fun for twice the amount of work. The break would come his way and, when it did, he'd be prepared for it. He'd redeem himself in his boss's eyes. He'd show Anthony he was more than capable of being a leader.

While he waited for the party to start, he'd showered, shaved, and bandaged himself up. Both his clothes and brain were stained. His whole body ached enough for four Advil. He stayed under the water much longer than usual, the spray hard and hot against his skin. He stumbled out of the bathroom and into a pair of boxers before he completed the rest of his attire: jeans, golf shirt, and no hat.

A half hour later, the two women showed up on his doorstep. One was blonde, the other a redhead. He'd managed to dispose of his bloody clothes and wash away the remnants of the encounter from his body and his mind.

The hookers were dressed as cops—slutty cops in half-uniforms, bras partially exposed, skirts slit up toward the promised land—and had even offered to show him their badges. He had declined with a slight shake of his head. But he did want to see their handcuffs. They had laughed, tossed their long hair back, and exposed the soft formidable skin of their throats, before cuffing him to a chair, next to an end table, stripping off his clothes, all the way down to his boxers, before they themselves stripped. He received two lap dances, first the redhead and then the blonde, and then they brought out the multi-colored condoms, the blonde held the wrapper between her teeth, while the redhead yanked down his boxers. The handcuffs, however, remained in place, scuffing up a chair that had already seen its best days.

In two and a half hours, they went through four of them, condoms, before they told him they needed to leave. He had only paid for three hours, after all.

The women were attractive, not as attractive as he had hoped, not the women he had fantasized about, but they had done the job, and they had done it well, serving his needs and expelling his adrenaline.

Neither of them was the wiser as to what had happened several hours ago. Neither of them had bothered to remove the handcuffs, until they were nearly finished. The fourth time had been without the handcuffs. He had been angry enough to handcuff both of them, their eyes wide. The game had been fun in the beginning, but he had grown tired of it. Control changed as often as the wind blew. Apparently, they didn't trust him. Fucking amateurs. So after the fourth time, after their guard was down, he had handcuffed them to each other, before dragging them back to his bedroom and handcuffing them to the bed. Then it was his turn to have his way. The fifth time had been more than he could have ever hoped for. The fifth time he hadn't bothered to use a condom. He felt the raw surge of energy between his toes. He made sure he received every bit of his three thousand dollars. Both of them had screamed, long, hard, and good, thrashing about on the bed as he nearly ripped each of them in two. First, the blonde from the front, and then the redhead from the back. The ache in their mouths fueled him. Their screams caused energy to course through his veins. He had threatened to make their lives even more miserable than they already were. They believed him. The wide eyes, the fear, the choked back sobs, the runny noses, the beads of sweat that clung to their bodies. Sweat and semen pooled on the sheets, the air nearly stifling in its raw power.

And then the fix was over, the anger was gone, and he was all alone again.

His dick ached. He showered, dressed his wounds with gauze and hydrogen peroxide, and looked at himself in the mirror. He was even stronger than he had been before. He flexed one bicep and then the other, the smile on his face as wide as a Virginia highway. He had a good feeling about the hookers. He knew they wouldn't talk, not if they wanted to live. The fear in their eyes, their looks of pure horror had fueled him. That was all he had needed. Killing Elrod hadn't given him as much power as their fear.

Their tattered uniforms gave him the last bit of control he had desired.

He ran a comb through his hair, after staring at his nude body in the mirror, smirking back at what he had become, the need and desire that had replaced the feeling of emptiness. He had arrived at a new power, a new threshold that he couldn't turn away from, and as soon as he rid his life of Pete and Veronica, his transformation would be complete.

The chasing had been fun for a while, until the miles that separated him from his ultimate goal had built up, and he had lost the transponder. It was Elrod's fault. If he had just been quick enough, the job would have been completed by now. As it was, Thurman would have to finish the job himself. The car had a torn front bumper, so he'd had to ditch it and find another one. He had found a Mercedes, about eight years old, without a car alarm. It was an easy swipe, and he had taken it without a second thought.

Wiping Elrod's body clean, he'd stuffed it in the trunk of the abandoned vehicle.

CHAPTER 45

Pete had a plate of scrambled eggs and bacon in front of him. He'd cooked the eggs on the stove, the bacon in the microwave. He'd slept on her sofa, a black leather monstrosity that took up half a wall, with reclining seats and cup holders on either end, rolling around from dusk 'til dawn, because he'd insisted on not leaving her alone, and she'd insisted on staying at her place for the first time in nearly a week.

The apartment reminded him of a dystopian society with nothing touching the floor other than sofas, tables, and chairs. The floors and walls were neutral, and the furniture was either black or gray. With a massive living room, small dining room, and even smaller kitchen, it was a bachelor's wet dream. It even had a huge flat screen. Access to the second floor had been forbidden— he did have a half bath to work with—not that he had any plans to step foot onto the next level. It was more about the principles, her demand for control. For all he knew, she did it because she thought it might upset him, tweaking the rules and giving herself every advantage possible.

Being too tired to argue with her, he saluted smartly and made the domain his own. Not bothering with a shower, he washed his face in the sink, and nearly fell asleep standing up.

When Veronica came down later for the kitchen, not him, her near nakedness hadn't affected him as much as it should have. Maybe he saw the half-lies lingering below the surface. The way she forced herself upon a situation as if she might attack an angry, drunk midget who had become belligerent in the middle of a crowded bar, the way her eyes always managed to convey more than the rest of her body.

Throughout his tossing and turning, his dreams had run off in a million different directions, never quite coming back toward home. The comforter flipped, and so did he, the voices inside his head reached the level of an opera singer had she sung off key. The combination of alcohol and adrenaline were lethal, at least for sleeping purposes. The Wet Rhino was a lighthouse for him as he navigated the rough, violent waters toward the shore, never quite reaching the sand.

If she had a single book in the house, he might have opened his eyes long enough to read it, at least the first several pages or so. But he just lay there, staring up at the ceiling, counting the blobs of spattered paint, the rough texture peering back at him, even going so far as to stare at it through half-closed lids.

The result was exactly the same: nothing.

The cops hadn't managed to shake him up. The thought of heading downtown again offered him nothing but acceptance and a look of serenity. The bare walls were devoid of all feeling, and the random officers devoid of all emotion, as the soldiers in his head marched in unison. The intense bouts of silence caught him completely off guard, a stillness where he would have appreciated a rugged hostility. A simple, steady clacking from possibly an air vent had nearly shoved him toward compliance.

Veronica hadn't said two words to him, even after the cops were gone and night turned into day. But she'd stuck around, even if her attitude didn't match up with reality, and he had no idea why. Just a few days ago, she would have done everything in her power to rid herself of him, diving out of a car, or thrusting herself uphill in the middle of a hard rain. Trusting people wasn't natural for her, and it was a battle filled with rocks, sharp drop-offs, and creatures that slithered across the earth.

She made no attempt to remove herself from the sink, where she leaned against it, back stiff. She leaned and stared at him, eyeing his plate of mostly eaten eggs as though it was the only food in the house, as the fridge kept him upright. Her fridge had a nearly full gallon of expired milk, a bottle of orange juice, not expired, five eggs—before he made short work of those—and a half-stick of butter. Her cupboards held a box of quick oats, nearly full, and a jar of peanut butter, mostly full. She had enough food in the house to feed a hamster and two of its friends.

She drank from the glass in her hand and refilled it from the tap when it was empty. He finished his plate standing up, reached around her to drop it in the sink, and resumed his position against the fridge. Now that the eggs and bacon were gone, he reevaluated his options.

"Why didn't you tell me all of this sooner?" Pete asked. He waited…and waited some more. He nudged the floor with his heel, shoved open the refrigerator door, poked his head around—still the same inventory as before—closed it, and leaned his elbow against metal.

"Are you continuing your vow of silence that started last night?" he asked.

She just shook her head. Her hair tossed about in a mostly uneven manner, the glass in her hand half-empty.

"What's going on?" His elbow dug in deeper. "Are you holding some grudge against me that I'm not aware of?"

"You were almost killed, and it was nearly my fault." Her voice was clipped, efficient.

Nearly might not have been a strong enough word. He stared at his hands, collecting the parts of her that he still couldn't figure out. "Is that what this is about?"

She nodded, the action strong and attentive.

"Bethany had it in for me, and it wouldn't have mattered if I was in your life or not. She wasn't exactly assassin material, but she certainly gave it her best effort. Her assets exceeded her experience."

Veronica turned on the tap and refilled her glass. "You know that's not true."

"You and I have been through a lot lately," he said, "and it hasn't bothered you before. Death seems to follow me around. It might even know my address."

"This was more personal," she said. "If you had been distracted, you'd have ended up dead." The glass in her hand took a tentative shake.

Knowing she cared didn't ease his mind the way he thought it would have. If anything, it made the situation more problematic, not less so. "I didn't know you had feelings." He winked. "You never told me."

She glared at him. "I never wanted to see anyone hurt."

He peered at a point just above her head. "I signed on for this."

She shoved away from the sink. "You should go."

He looked down at his right hand. "Why?"

"Before something really does happen to you," she said. "I'm bad luck."

"That's not why you want me to go."

CHAPTER 46

Veronica didn't really care. Not that much. Mixed up in the head, and she hadn't even had a near death experience today. Yesterday was the most recent attempt. He cared, on some level that she hadn't been able to process thoroughly. And it was her fault. But he didn't blame her. If he had, it would have been easier to lash out, to handcuff him to an inanimate object, and walk away. Restlessness caused her to shift in her seat, the hard wood beneath poking at her skin in all the wrong places.

Feeling was in the past. But now it had caught up with the present, struck her on the forehead with the force of a small mallet, and left a mark. A bruise. With the mallet removed, the impression remained. She shook her head, but the shock persisted. She didn't care, not at first, and then she did. That was the worst of it. She had failed, when only success would do. She grabbed a glass from the cabinet, ran the tap, placed her glass under it, and filled it to the brim. In one smooth motion, she downed the whole glass, knowing that the liquid would help ease her head, and hopefully her mind. The force of the mallet, however, lingered.

Pete's mind had been mucked up, and so had hers. The confusion compounded, and temptation produced a foul aftertaste. Her smile could have been beautiful, wonderful, envious even in its severity, but it remained hidden in plain sight. The water helped the numbing sensation in her throat, but it didn't help her forget.

Neediness was an unfamiliar concept to her. When he returned, she planned on heading out the door and not looking back, marching out of her own house and into the garage. She could finish this herself. She had to. If she needed assistance, the police were close at hand. Only a phone call away. They were paid to protect and serve, not that she needed much protecting, just a bit of serving. Her life back. That's all she really wanted. This past week, where she'd been drugged, abducted, forced on the run, shot at more than once, and driven to the edge and back. Fuck, she hadn't had a vacation in years, and this was what the universe handed her? Returning it for a refund and demanding her money back—that would have been too kind.

The thought of having Pete around wasn't worth all the trouble. He was just as stubborn as she was, maybe even more so. Especially when he thought it served a much larger purpose. Hope took hold of her, gave her a little something extra when she needed it. A little bit, in fact, went a long way. She looked out her window at the life beyond the glass, a life with beautiful sunrises and sunsets, a life with IKEA trips and picture frames.

She set her glass in the sink, rubbed her eyes, and

stared out at another day slowly breaking through the surface. She hadn't slept well last night, her brain going full speed ahead, through every red light in front of her. She couldn't slow down. She'd even started doing long division in her head. But it didn't work. An hour later, she was still as wired as ever, her thoughts still as scattered as the previous sixty minutes. She thought about trudging to the living room, checking on Pete as he slept on the sofa, hoping his shallow breathing would somehow put her mind to rest, but she quickly shoved that thought aside: He was already gone. Weakness was for the uninitiated.

He'd only left twenty minutes ago, but it felt more like an hour. A day even. Her house could have passed for a mausoleum or an art gallery. Her sink dripped, the water dropping faster and faster, cascading around her, the splish splash striking the metal surface. A pool formed as the ping lingered in the small space, resounding around her. Like the water, her mind wandered, and she could feel her feet moving, even though she stood her ground.

Her mind drifted, and she felt lost, seeing her future unfold before her as if in a dream. There was nothing. Not a single sound or smell that she could identify. So she ran even faster, her feet striking with the same speed and precision as the water, the pounding reverberated in her joints. Her arms pumped at her sides, and she looked behind her, turning her head for just an instant. Nothing. A sense of calm swept her up off the ground. Just when she thought she had disappeared from him, her escape a firmly etched plan, another one appeared in the opposite direction, coming toward her, and calling her by name. Her voice rose above his, as she called out, hoping someone would hear her, rescue her. But no one came, and she didn't have time to wait. Not wanting to accept her fate, she pressed onward, the soles of her feet digging into the soft earth. With each step, her feet lingered for an instant before she was able to move, pressing herself between the trees.

She feinted, her whole body jerking, but the man behind her clamped ahold of her shoulder as she did, and he caught her, his fingers digging into her like talons. She tried to kick behind her, aiming for his balls, but his other hand slapped her foot away. She tried an elbow, lashing back with all her strength, but he blocked it, too. A series of combinations involving hands, feet, and elbows soon followed. Each was blocked or struck only air.

And now the other guy was upon her. She had fallen right into the trap, the cheese in her jaws as the metal broke her neck. Simple really. She was disgusted with herself for succumbing to it. When the gun was pointed at her head, her mind leapt forward. To an alleyway. The sky dark. Pitch black. She couldn't see two feet in front of her, and she heard all kinds of strange noises: a cat meowing, a car backfiring, a string of curse words from a psychotic individual, a hard slap, and a much softer one, a car engine, a siren blaring, and a TV playing. Time passed more slowly now. She wasn't sure what it meant. Maybe it meant nothing.

The worst seemed to wait for her, calling her name, and pounding into her brain. It clung there, held in place by the wind or a string. To what she wasn't sure. But it was there all the same. A need. A desire. That was how she had always lived her life, even as the past threatened to catch up to her.

She shuddered as various thoughts ratcheted through her brain, crawling all over and on top of each other. Getting more intense by the minute. Nothing was as it seemed, or how it should have been. The man in the dark hat and sunglasses took one step toward her—and then another—and another. His steps echoed in the small space, his heel striking like drops of rain. The sound of his voice was calm and steady, reedy, with a nasal intonation. His mouth was a black hole, and his head turned away from her, even as his steps continued in her direction.

She backed up, her feet moving steadily underneath her, her steps more forced. More hurried. The click of her heels echoed against the pavement, her steps short and filled with purpose, her legs moving steadily, assuredly, her arms pumping at her sides, her thoughts flowing freely and openly, nearly as quick as her legs. Her voice caught in her throat, unable to call out.

She turned on her heels, all out sprinting, her steps quicker and quicker, as her arms moved faster and faster.

The presence, though, drew ever nearer.

She leaned away and felt cold water on her face. And she blinked. Once. Twice. Three times, as the water stained her face, dripping down into her mouth. Two men had nearly killed her, and she had no idea who they were. It might have been a daydream, but it felt too real to ignore, her heart nearly coming up through her throat, her feet pounding nearly as fast as her head. Without even realizing it, she had begun to pace, walking the length of her kitchen, which wasn't long at all. Not by kitchen standards. Modern sure.

But she didn't have an island in the center. Small and

sturdy with stainless steel appliances and sharp, defined angles.

Now that she was home, over a half hour since Pete left, and from where this had all started, with her front door fixed, and the spirit of the man in the mask long gone, Veronica felt safe and secure. Her sanity had returned, and she had an entire wardrobe from which to choose, her clothes lined up like iPods on a shelf, a multitude of outfits at her disposal, and yet she didn't want to choose.

What she wanted to do was stop running. Only she wasn't going to end up back underground, find herself in another car accident, or have her hotel room, a room that she had paid for herself, shot to hell. That had been a difficult thing to explain to the cops. The deputy, or maybe he was a detective, hadn't considered her tale a lie. He had believed her: She could see it in his eyes, twin beacons into an otherwise existential universe. And it wasn't because she was a beautiful woman. Not that she considered herself beautiful, but she'd been told this, all the same, throughout most of her life.

Her looks had given her an advantage or two. But they weren't advantages she actively pursued. They were merely there, like the coffee and doughnuts that showed up at work every third Friday, and she hadn't turned away from her looks, not like she did the doughnuts and coffee. So what did that make her? On second thought, she didn't want to know.

Her escapes were convenient, maybe a little bit too convenient, and she wasn't sure luck would stick with her. The gods might have blessed her once, twice, or three times, but she wasn't sure about a fourth or fifth, just like she wasn't sure where Pete would go, or what she should do now. She'd concentrated all of her efforts on staying alive, and staying ahead of the two idiots with the itchy trigger fingers, and now she had no idea what her next move should be.

She'd seen one man killed, his body dumped from the fifth floor of her office building on a Thursday evening, and she didn't want to see another one. Her world had changed that day, and not for the better.

A car door opened and closed. She wasn't ready to deal with Pete yet, but she'd somehow manage just the same, and then she'd disappear out of his life, vanishing in the same manner that the man in the mask had. After that, she'd deal with the overzealous men herself, who were hired by an overzealous boss, Anthony Whelan, and possibly even Nathan Labaw, a bastard of an entirely different nature. Anthony was crazy enough to turn his secretary, a woman he pimped out for his own pleasure, onto the man who had tried to help Veronica, and it was time to set this fucked-up equation right. She'd make his actions known to the world, bring him down with the force of Athena, but she'd do it using the proper authorities.

Coasting toward her front door, her mind and body on autopilot, her thoughts scattered, battered, and shattered, Veronica saw the man before he saw her. It didn't appear to be Pete. Not at first glance through her peephole anyway.

In fact, she wasn't sure she had ever seen the man before. With short hair, gaze turned in the opposite direction, rigid posture, and hands behind his back, something was off. Like the universe had been tossed aside in a

massive tidal wave, and she was the only one left clinging to a tree. Not right.

She couldn't place her finger on her level of discon-
tent, the slight jagged edge of her resistance. And then he
turned around. Definitely not Pete. The strange man had a
sinister look in his eyes, as if he had just killed some-
body, and he probably wouldn't mind doing it again. It
wasn't a look she knew well, but she noticed it just the
same. Her heart quickened, her breathing stiffened, and
her mind went blank. When he placed his hands in front
of him, he had a magazine in his left hand—maybe *Rolling Stone*—and nothing in his right with his palm at waist
level. He stared hard at the peephole, his head turned
slightly to the side, not saying a word, and a million
thoughts entered her mind, none of them pleasant, or particularly comforting.

Before she could engage the deadbolt, or even lock the
door—fucking Pete and his dramatic exit—the strange
man turned the knob and opened the door. Surprised and
pleased with his discovery, he stepped inside, his head
held high. She backed up a step. And then another. Her
right arm felt around behind her for some sort of weapon
to magically appear and save the day, too shocked to
even open her mouth, her thoughts too scattered to form
one coherent picture.

The grin grew wider, and he opened his mouth. Words
came out of it, but she didn't hear them, couldn't, because she was backing away, feeling around, and tuning
out the world all at the same time. Once again, her home,
her sanctuary, had been invaded, and she was too petri-
fied to fight back.

And then Veronica did the only thing she could think to do: She screamed.

He reached his hand out to her, slapping her across the jaw, then he dropped the magazine on the stand by the door. He took several steps toward her, each one faster than the one before it, and he was on her before her mind had finished computing her options. Screaming was her only mode of defense.

His hands reached for her neck, both hands this time, and she screamed louder, ducking back, dipping just out of the way of his outstretched fingers. He grasped only air. She jabbed her fist at him, but he was much taller than she was, and her hand struck empty air. He smiled at her again then, the grin more sinister than the devil himself. He wanted to fight, to strike, and lash out until she was either exhausted or dead.

She calculated the odds in her head. Not good. The evil remained like a thick haze between them, the darkness clouding around her and growing more powerful with each passing second. Time jammed together, the seconds fumbling on top of one another, as her thoughts fought with each other.

He charged her. She turned and ran. She screamed at the top of her lungs, as the strange man chased her, a man with dead eyes and a vicious hand, a man who managed to look vaguely familiar, even though she couldn't quite place where she'd seen him before. Was he one of Anthony's hired goons? Had to be. She wondered what happened to the other one. And suddenly killing didn't seem so farfetched, that he might have done it already, and that he might very well try again.

Sonofabitch, she didn't want her life to end like this.

Whatever limited powers she had, that stupid series of self-defense classes that she'd taken many years ago, too long ago to remember anything other than just the salient points, Veronica would use what she could against him, even if he was bigger, stronger, and moved with a grace and ease that was reserved for a ballet dancer performing *The Nutcracker*. Fate would step in. Fate would take control of her life. Fate would save her, or she'd do it her damn self.

She screamed again, but her lungs were filled with this black mist, and fog enveloped her. She didn't know where the fog came from. But it was there all the same, the mist darker and heavier than anything she had ever experienced before. She staggered backward, bumped into a wall, and her back slid down, the floor much closer than she had originally thought.

Before she passed out in his arms, she had one final thought: Maybe she had been doomed right from the start.

CHAPTER 47

Thurman didn't have any trouble finding her. Women were so predictable. And stupid. She went back to her house, on the quiet street, in the quiet neighborhood, where nothing bad ever happened, where she was as safe and secure as she was once before, with the idiot Pete Nealey watching over her, until he wasn't, as he marched out her front door, and left this moment for the next, starting the pickup and driving away.

Thurman had discovered her in the hotel and confounded her world with more holes than a maze, as well as a clean getaway in a slow-moving truck, the car wheezing and gasping and somehow surviving. Not that he could blame the man for creating a scene filled with green, and fighting back with whatever he had. But what Thurman didn't like was that Pete had eluded him for this long, the man as slippery as a snake in the grass, and Thurman would have preferred to have both of them here together, lives intertwined at the end of a rope.

That would have made it easier.

But he would take the morsels presented before him, the scraps and scrapes left at the table, and he wouldn't leave a trace behind. Not as long as he was still the last one standing.

Anthony wanted Veronica, and that's what he'd get, tied and bound and delivered to his doorstep in a silver bow, hold the wrapping paper. Veronica was for the boss—the slimy, malignant bastard with the outstanding view and the eager to please blonde sitting behind her desk, all prim and proper—but Pete would have been for Thurman. He didn't like the fact that the fool had bested him and managed to elude him for as long as he had. It was too convenient, like destiny had smiled down on him and offered its right hand, and Thurman shuddered at the pure audacity of it. There was only so much luck to go around, and Pete Nealey had just reached the end of the plank, and he was staring at a drop of approximately ten feet.

The boss had given Thurman the address, and he had plugged it in his GPS. He'd arrived just a few minutes before Pete left, after Thurman had finished things off with Elrod, and waited for broad daylight, figuring both of them would be around with their guard down.

He'd walk through the front door and back out again with a prize for either hand, and all the glory the world could possibly offer. It might have been easy, but that didn't mean he couldn't enjoy it.

He picked Veronica up—she was lighter than he figured, especially for someone who had as much spunk as she did—in a fireman's carry, her body slung over his right shoulder, and marched out the front door with her.

He would have preferred more of a struggle, a climactic conclusion instead of a whimper, and he could have strung her out, given her a bit more hope, fought with her until her nose was black and purple, her eyes nearly popping out of their sockets, her body battered and bruised. But after a few thrusts at dead air, he knew there was a chance she might get lucky, the way she tossed punches around like ice cubes, and he didn't want to ruin one of his favorite shirts, with either her blood or his, staining the occasion and leaving him sweaty and bothered, and possibly ruining a perfectly fine button-down.

The look she gave him, before she'd thrust her fist at him, could have melted steel, the eyes cold, dead, and hard. And if his reflexes hadn't been as quick as they were, she might have touched more than dead air, and she might have leapt on him like a jaguar. When she struck, her eyes were like little slits, similar to a king cobra, her small hands dancing and prancing in front of him with self-assured fists and an evil glance.

She might have been pretty if he hadn't seen the bitch within. The bitch that tried to punch out his esophagus with one particularly well-placed strike. Even as he backed her into a corner, her body going taut and rigid, ready to spring at the first sign of weakness—even as she knew that he was the stronger of the two—still she fought with a primal scream and a carnal rage. Luck might have helped guide her, but he still would have been the one on the floor passed out cold from one too many blows to the head.

Quick reflexes saved him. Reflexes he'd developed from his high school football days. Being one of the scrawniest guys on the team, and in the league, Thurman had to learn how to maneuver out of the way of the bigger men. And it had worked. He had been a star, until he got into the women chasing business. After that, it went straight to hell faster than he could strike the match. Everything suffered, including his grades. Women were the heart attack, clogging his arteries and his mind. And they were also the ache that he tried to avoid. Even though he saw Veronica for what she was, the devil within her soul fighting for a way out, he couldn't help but wonder what she might have been without the hard times and hard lines. Thus, the hookers filled an ever-prominent need.

His growth spurt came late, but he was glad to have it nonetheless. It helped with the women, and chicks really did dig scars, his body a riddled mess of torn flesh. Through a series of fights, that had developed from a series of tempers, he'd developed a few rather prominent scars, most of which were hidden beneath his clothing, the three on his left bicep and two on his stomach were the worst. Constant reminders of how his life had played out.

He wanted to find a cabin, but the boss had a better idea. They were going to kill her out in the open, leave her body on the street at dusk, and send a message that Anthony Whelan wasn't one to double cross. It had been Anthony's idea from the start. Thurman wasn't quite sure about it, especially with the cops now weaved into the mix, and Pete Nealey still at-large, the one joker in a hand full of aces. But Thurman could deal with Pete. The cops, however, were another matter entirely. He hated the slimy bastards.

He tossed her in the passenger seat, reached for the

duct tape he'd stuffed in the back, bound her hands and ankles, and slapped a couple extra strips over her mouth, just in case the screaming reached a new crescendo. He didn't want to hear her scream again, the sound had nearly torn him in two.

He started the car, shifted to drive, and peeled away from the curb, tires squealing along the quiet street. Thurman saw the idiot before he'd gotten more than a block, sitting on the sidewalk next to the pickup, staring at nothing. And he couldn't resist the urge to take him out as well. He veered toward Pete, jumped the curb, just as the idiot dove out of the way and found a bed of green. And then the fool whipped out a knife—it wasn't there one minute but it was the next—and threw it at the front passenger tire. The tire popped, deflated, two wheels on the sidewalk—one deflated, one not—and he was caught. He wrenched open the door, hopped out of the car, and took off after Pete Nealey for all he was worth, charging faster than a linebacker hell bent on sacking the quarterback.

Thurman pulled the knife out of his tire—spit flying from his lips, a death grip on the deadly weapon—whirled it around in his hand, twirling it with a flick of his wrist, and watching with delight as it whistled through the air, before nicking Pete's left ear, drops of blood mixing with the green below. The idiot, though, charged him with the same ferocity. Pete threw his forearm into Thurman's, knocking the fist away, as he tried to come across his body again for another blow.

His knee thrust out, but it failed to hit home, striking only the dead air between them.

Pete sent a couple of jabs in his direction, neither of

which managed to strike bone. Thurman struck out with his right leg, aiming for Pete's ankle, but Pete easily maneuvered out of the way, spinning away from his errant leg. Thurman lunged at the man, his elbow ready to strike the idiot's skull, sending the fool into an unconscious state. But the elbow missed, glanced off a shoulder, and Thurman was clipped from behind, his legs buckling beneath him.

He went down, striking the pavement, first his knees and then his torso, as sirens pierced the air. Too stunned to move, his legs and torso flat against concrete, knees slathered in pain, Thurman waited as the sirens closed in on them. Maybe he shouldn't have struck in broad daylight, after all. He hadn't considered the possibility that some meddlesome neighbor would call the cops, probably some nosy old bat with too much time on her hands, and too many episodes of Oprah under her belt, feeling all high and mighty behind her velvet curtain.

He placed his palms on the concrete to pick himself up, but he was knocked on top of the head, and his forehead struck the pavement, as the lights went out over Richmond, and he plunged into pure blackness.

CHAPTER 48

Pete yanked the duct tape off her mouth, and she yelped. In the same manner also, he removed the duct tape from her ankles and wrists, which were bound in front, instead of from behind. Pete assumed that was based on a lack of time. Nothing more. Or the man surrounded by a sea of blue uniforms really was an idiot. The car was still in gear, but with two tires on the sidewalk—one of which was flat—and two on the asphalt, it wasn't going anywhere. Neither was the crazy man who had attacked him, wielding the knife as if he was a half-drugged soldier fighting on the field of battle. Pete had seen him before, at the motel, and for all he knew, he was the one driving, or riding shotgun when the errant car had veered in Veronica's direction.

Her eyes watered, but no tears were shed. She might not cry, but he wanted proof that she was still human, and that all of this was filled with more than just circumstance and second chances. After everything they had been through together, he thought he at least deserved a thank you. He had walked away from her, and a half-crazed lunatic on a power trip had nearly kidnapped her. Once again, he had saved her, and once again, Veronica thought she didn't need his help. Or at least that was what she had said before.

She was even more stubborn than he was.

She peered up at him, eyelids blinking, nose running away from her. A sneeze bigger than her appeared. After she cleared the air, and probably half the block, he thought he heard a thank you, although that could have been his imagination again, running off in the opposite direction. Maybe he'd start seeing monsters in the closet, or beautiful women accosting him as he walked down the street, shoving their hands in his back pocket. He smiled, nodded, and heard voices behind him. Near as he could tell, they must have been coming from every direction, and they must have sent every available man on the force, which wouldn't have been an abundant number. But it would have been enough to cause a slight stirring in this sleepy town with tree-lined streets and paved sidewalks.

Cruisers barricaded the street, dividing it in two, as the voices around him increased in intensity, cutting through the air and lingering in his ears. With Veronica beside him, he stared off into the distance. Few words were spoken between them, even fewer words needed to be said.

The hitman with the crazy eyes was loaded into the nearest cruiser, but not before he had screamed and shouted, said more than a few four-letter words, and slugged one cop on the side of the head. With his face shoved to the ground, he had kissed the grass, as his hands were shoved behind his back and handcuffed, and he was jerked to his feet. His head had bobbed in Pete's direction, and his face had scrunched in on itself. Pete had offered a finger wave in return.

The call had already been placed to the loyal county deputy with two first names. Whether he decided to show or not, though, was another matter entirely.

Two cops came by and took their statements, but the details were clear-cut without a lot of margin for error. At some point, the engine had been turned off, and a few cruisers departed, while two remained.

"Two incidents in less than twenty-four hours," Deputy Sheldon Michael said. "That must be some kind of record." He left out the part about being an accountant. Maybe it was on purpose, or maybe it wasn't.

"At least he's still alive," Pete said. He couldn't say the same for the blonde with the watermelon breasts and stiff upper lip.

"Well, that's a good start. So it wasn't kill or be killed this time?"

Pete stood up and brushed off his pants. "Not exactly."

Veronica told Deputy Michael what happened with rather animated details.

The deputy kicked a pebble on the sidewalk. A few neighbors stood on porches, as the scene unfolded, while others had already wandered back inside. "Whose thugs?"

"Anthony Whelan," she said. "My boss."

Another pebble shot down the sidewalk. "The one you mentioned before?"

Veronica nodded. "One and the same." Her wrists were raw and chaffed, the skin red.

"You must have a lot of information on him."

"I'm not sure how Anthony would survive in a contained facility," she said. "He wouldn't be able to use the intimidation factor with fellow prisoners more than twice his size."

"You're willing to testify against him?" the deputy asked.

"He's already made four attempts on my life, and one attempt on Pete's." She offered the faintest hint of a smile. "It would be my pleasure."

"Are you sure you don't want to think about it first?" The deputy had his notepad out, and his hand darted across the page.

"There's nothing he can't do to me that he hasn't already tried," she said.

Pete looked down at his hands, fingers that had killed a woman. Hands that had killed soldiers before he'd killed Bethany, eyes that had seen the most despicable parts of the human existence, images that always managed to float across his mind at the wrong time. Nothing he could do about it, though, other than to continue to see it through and hope his mind somehow improved. The shrink—or at least the quack the army had offered up—wasn't worth a damn, but then again neither was Pete's mind.

Veronica had more trust issues than an abandoned dog left in the woods for six months. But at least she had stuck by him. That's more than he could say for the others. But he could hear the finality in her voice, like she had already moved on with her life.

At some point, the deputy had wandered away. She stared at Pete with narrow eyes and a focused gaze.

He shrugged. "If I hadn't come back when I did, he would have gotten away."

"And I would have escaped again." She pumped her left fist into her right palm. "I did it once, I could do it again."

"I thought I heard a thank you earlier."

The stare remained focused in his direction. "I'm sure that was your imagination playing tricks on you."

He shrugged again. "Must have been."

The hard look softened just a tad. "You might want to keep it in check next time."

"I'll be sure to do that."

He told her his plan, and she was none too happy about it. But she didn't have a choice in the matter. Because, if anything, he was more determined now than he ever had been.

CHAPTER 49

"Who the hell are you?" Anthony said. "And how did you manage to get in here?"

The microphone was pushed upward, and the pacing proceeded in a back and forth fashion. He tapped the walls and windows every few seconds with a stern expression and not much else.

The air conditioner pumped harder than a washing machine, pounding away at Pete's skin. His eyes were cold, dark, and observant. The room had an excellent view, the chill in the air reminding him of a refrigerator. Masculine. With three glass panels, black leather furniture, and a desk the size of a Christmas tree, the office was bigger than Pete's first apartment and, possibly, even his second. The doors were large and oak, the panels hand carved. An echo filled the small space, or maybe that was his head and heart doing battle.

Like every other drone, he'd walked through the front door, past security, to the elevators, rode it all the way to the top, and sweet-talked the secretary outside of Anthony's office. The secretary was slim and proper with graying hair and dark frames covering her eyes. She held a smile for a split second before she offered up the standard greeting, her eyes locked firmly on his. He gave back more than a hint of charm and dropped a few names. She pointed to a sofa—microfiber and neutral of color—where Pete had a stack of magazines from which to choose. Instead of picking one up, he placed his hands on his knees and leaned back, glancing at odd moments in the secretary's direction, and offering a few extra smiles.

The doors alone probably cost more than his military pay for an entire year, and that included duty pay of the hazardous variety. He had on a standard shirt and a pair of slacks, with his hair slicked back, and his face shaved. He had clipped his nails short and shined his shoes. To anyone else, he was about to be interviewed for the present opening in the accounting department, where he could complete a few books in his spare time.

The secretary was skeptical at first, as was the guard, but Pete had used his mouth when it counted most, spinning a tale he and Veronica had crafted, and he did have the element of surprise working in his favor. An element that would render itself nonexistent when he answered Anthony's question.

So he stood his ground on the far side of the room, just inside the double doors with the intricate panels, that had closed swiftly behind him. He'd waited for over an hour, with plenty of time to study the secretary and his surroundings. Her movements were jerky, and she fumbled the receiver on more than one occasion. Background music of the instrumental variety pumped through the ceiling, and the lights that surrounded him responded to movement. The carpet underneath his feet was probably less than a year old. Photos and stock certificates covered the walls, and the office space outside the double glass doors of the executive suite reminded him of a cube farm on steroids.

With three windows to choose from, he was easily distracted. Although Port City, Virginia, wasn't large by any measure, it did have its pleasant elements, filled with tourists in the summer and devoid of snow most of the winter, and the dude on the other side of the room had found as many of them as he could in one location. The buildings surrounding this one weren't tall, but they were old, brick, and kept up with historic, as well as modern, standards. A rather appealing combination.

The sound of a ticking grandfather clock filled the cavernous space.

"How did you get in here?" Anthony asked.

"Your secretary was nice enough to grant me a favor." Pete didn't need to offer up the details of said favor.

Her smile had proved whiter than most. Her dark hair, painted with gray, and her soft features gave her a rather charming beauty element. Middle age had been kind to her, and it had probably been even kinder in her youth. She was just a bit over average in height and weight.

Anthony gritted his teeth. "She's just temporary. She hasn't learned all of our policies yet."

"You probably haven't had time to teach her," Pete said. "That's understandable. You're a busy man."

"Indeed, I am. And I think you should leave—" Anthony pointed toward the door. "—before I call the police." The mike dropped into position.

"You'll do no such thing," Pete said. "If you call the

police, you'll be the one walking out of here in handcuffs, not me. And I wouldn't want you to leave your plush blue carpet behind."

Anthony's eyes went wide. "Who are you?"

"I'm a friend of Veronica's."

Anthony's face displayed no sign of guilt. "And how is she doing?"

"Perfectly fine, thanks to a bit of help from me," Pete said. "Although she's still too stubborn to admit she needs me. But I'm sure that'll change with time. You, on the other hand, are at the other end of my services spectrum."

"Not likely. So you're Pete Nealey?" Anthony nodded. "You've caused me more problems than I care to admit. Well, just because you made it here, doesn't mean you'll make it back out again." The mike flipped up once again, and he took two steps around his desk.

"Are you threatening me?"

"No, that's a promise," Anthony said. "You should have never dipped your toes into the ocean, unless you're perfectly willing to wade all the way in."

"Why do you think I'm here?"

"Because you have a problem with rationality," Anthony said. "You somehow think that you might be able to get the better of me. Well, just because you got lucky initially doesn't mean your lucky streak will continue."

"I'm part Irish."

"I don't care if you're part American Indian," Anthony said. "You've seen your last days." He flew across his desk like Superman.

He didn't know where this Pete bastard came from, nor did he know why the hell his good-for-nothing secretary had let him in. Either way, it didn't matter, because Anthony would offer up his head on a platter. No one had ever walked into his office, talked to him in this particular manner, and walked out the door standing on both legs.

Pete's mind might have wandered a bit too freely, or maybe the pause in the beginning was merely his way of testing the situation. Maybe this was all a game to him. Well, Anthony hadn't killed a snitch and stashed away plenty of hard-earned company profits to have some accountant from the fourth floor deliver him from evil. He had his arm extended out in front of him as he dove toward the man wearing the smug expression.

Standing his ground, Pete thrust his arm upward, striking the crazy bastard on the chin. Anthony hit the plush carpet, offered up a twitch of his leg, and that was the extent of his movement. His head, however, had avoided all the major furniture, as his face tapped into luxury.

Peering down at his unconscious adversary, Pete just shook his head.

Anthony's actions were those of a desperate man. A man with his own share of psychotic episodes, possibly even of the monumental variety. A man who was used to getting what he wanted, and, when he didn't, he resembled a spoiled child, with screaming tantrums and flying furniture, and one set of knuckles more swollen than the other.

Pete had seen the same thing in the military with colonels and generals, both of whom could resemble angry stepchildren in the right situation.

He heard the door open, and he looked up in time to

see the secretary scream. And that meant his ten minutes were over. Or it might have been only five.

The cops streamed in, five or six, for just one man, with holsters open and guns drawn. Maybe they didn't trust him after all.

CHAPTER 50

Pete met her at a bar, his favorite spot. A drink in front of him, a glass of water in front of her. The drink was either Johnnie Walker Blue, or bourbon. He couldn't remember. It wasn't his first drink—she still had the remnants from her first glass of water—and this wasn't his first visit with her. She came of her own volition, but the expression on her face told him she wasn't happy about it. She might have been propositioned once, or maybe it was twice—he did have two bathroom trips in the past two hours—shoving one guy and nearly coming to blows with another. More than a little surprised she had actually shown up, after what had happened the last time—her face hugging the hardwood after a blow to the head—he did admire her tenacity.

Veronica had on a simple outfit—skirt, blouse, and heels—while he had on his uniform from the office visit earlier. There was no tie in sight. It wasn't that kind of bar, and he wasn't that kind of man. She had her stool scooted an extra half foot away from him, her back straight, her purse on the bar in front of her. He didn't look at the purse, or the stool. He looked at her. She had dark brown eyes with dark circles under them that she tried to hide with makeup. It didn't have the desired effect.

"You know you stole my thunder," she said.

Her hands were pressed tight enough together to show the whites of her knuckles. She had them crammed in her lap and only lifted them to the bar to take sips from her glass.

"I know."

"But I forgive you," she said. "You were only trying to keep me out of trouble. My emotions sometimes speak louder than my words."

Her emotions were louder than a church bell being struck with a wrecking ball. "You mean you have emotions?"

She slugged him, the punch had force behind it. "So what are you going to do now?"

"I have no idea."

He needed another drink on the one hand, but on the other, he had temporarily decided against such an irrational response. Maybe she had messed with whatever brain cells he had left, that weren't drowned in a sea of alcohol.

She took a tentative sip from her glass and tapped it on the bar. "There's probably some other damsel in distress you can save."

"Possibly."

The music blaring out from the speakers hid his thoughts. Instead of alternative or heavy metal, this one was more entrenched in the hard rock genre.

"Even though you don't really look for them," she said.

She swung her legs forward, striking the underbelly of the bar with a light tap.

He tried not to look at her legs, with the firm calves and thighs. Or the way the flickering light caught her brown hair just right and gave it an added depth. "At least with you that was the case—"

"You still didn't tell me why you offered."

"You looked like you could use the help," he said, "and I happened to have a bit of time on my hands." His shoulders sagged a bit.

Her eyes flicked to the mirror above her. "That's gotta be some sort of understatement. You have nothing but time."

He smirked. "But I spend it wisely."

She shook her head and brought the water glass to her lips and took another sip. "No, you don't."

"But I have fun doing it."

Her eyes flicked in his direction. "Wrong again," Veronica said. "You're the worst liar I've ever met."

"Okay," he said, "I probably have one or two issues to work through."

And he didn't think the whisky would enlighten him. At least not at the moment. But Pete signaled the bartender anyway, hoping he might dull the pain.

"At least," she said. "But you're making progress."

"Progress is a slow road," he said.

And he had more than enough time to get there. For once in his life, he planned to enjoy the scenery. He couldn't do it with a mug or glass stapled to his lips. He'd start right after the next round, or the round after that.

She placed a hand on the bar, her nails digging into the wood. "So how did you leave him?"

"Well, I figured it wouldn't be fair to leave him conscious, and I only had ten minutes—"

"Before the cavalry came to rescue you."

"Exactly," he said. "So when he dove across the desk at me, I hit him with everything I had. The uppercut had force behind it—"

She showed the faintest hint of a grin. "I'm sure."

"He struck the ground in between his two closest desk chairs. And, fortunately for him, he decided not to get back up. Otherwise, I might have stapled his head to the silk carpet, and danced out of the room."

"You never did tell me where you learned to fight."

His voice was clipped, even. "The military does a great job of training its folks for hand-to-hand combat. I happened to be one of the beneficiaries of said training."

It was often less formal than that, but it achieved the same end result. Even boxers, wearing gloves and diapers on their heads, managed to end up with a certain amount of brain damage later in life. The head wasn't meant to sustain repeated blows. For that matter, neither was the heart.

"I bet that was one of your favorite parts."

"I don't like backing down from a good fight." Pete paused. "So are you going to find a new employer right away, or head back to your old job?" He didn't particularly care, but he felt it was the right question to ask given the circumstances.

"Even the police, with their limited number of resources at their disposal, might not be able to tie Nathan

Labaw to the crime, and since I know he's behind it, I'm not sure I should stick around with Brogue Consulting. As for another firm, I'm probably better off taking a break." She wanted that damn vacation she'd been promised for the past four years...or five.

"You mean you might actually relax?" he asked. "Will you send me photos of you on the beach in a string bikini sipping a margarita?"

"You have some rather interesting fantasies."

Maybe he wasn't the vile individual she had originally made him out to be, maybe he had changed since high school, or maybe there was a defect in her armor. *A defect sounded about right.*

"It sure beats reality, at least some of the time anyway. And if I didn't actually leave reality, I might not be here right now."

He kicked his feet out in front of him, tapping the bar.

She needed to find more stable individuals. "Is it really that bad?"

"Some days are worse than others," Pete said.

"Well, you should at least take care of yourself." She paused. "If you don't, I might have to check on you."

"So you have half a heart?"

Veronica slugged him again. This time in the stomach. Not hard enough to leave a mark, just hard enough to let him know she was there. "I'm not half as bad as you think I am."

"I'm not all that bad either."

"Yes, you are," she said. "And as soon as you stop looking at the bottom of a shot glass, cut back your visits to The Wet Rhino, and stop feeling sorry for yourself, you might actually hold some appeal with the ladies." Even to her. *Fucking men.*

"Did Veronica Baird actually pay me a compliment?"

"I did," she said. "And you better not let it go to your head."

The memory of making out with him in a closet came rushing back to her, and her face warmed. Feelings and thoughts she had repressed crashed back to the surface, and her unstable stool nearly tipped over.

He clasped one hand on top of the other and placed them both on top of his chest. "Oh, I plan on treasuring it for the rest of my life."

"I had a feeling you might say that. But all the same, you can keep it. You need it more than I do."

Before he could say another word, she stood up, shook his hand, offered a salute of sorts, and disappeared without so much as a goodbye.

When he left The Wet Rhino later, a light rain splashed his face, mixing with the tears that had congregated on his cheek.

About the Author

Robert Downs aspired to be a writer before he realized how difficult the writing process was. Fortunately, he'd already fallen in love with the craft, otherwise his tales might never have seen print. Originally from West Virginia, he has lived in Virginia, Massachusetts, New Mexico, and now resides in California. When he's not writing, Downs can be found reading, reviewing, blogging, or smiling. To find out more about his latest projects, or to reach out to him on the Internet, visit his website: www.RobertDowns.net.